PRAISE FOR CLAY MCLEOD CHAPMAN

THE REMAKING

A 2019 Goodreads Choice Awards Semifinalist, Horror

"An ambitious mosaic novel exploring the power of urban myth and superstition."—*Guardian*

"Horror in fiction is a little trickier, but occasionally you get something special like Mark Z. Danielewski's puzzle box, *House of Leaves* (2000), John Ajvide Lindqvist's *Let the Right One In* (2007), or, more recently, Josh Malerman's runaway hit *Bird Box* (2014). Chapman's (*Nothing Untoward*, 2017, etc.) spooky story solidly fits the mold of nothing you've ever read before...something like Stephen King's imperfect masterpiece *The Shining*."—*Kirkus Reviews*

"This disorienting and immersive story anchors itself in history but stretches its terrifying tentacles into the present, producing intense chills."—*Library Journal*

"Jumps out the gate and takes the reader on [a] wild and unnerving ride."—*Horror DNA*, 4 out of 5 stars

"A streamlined page-turner of clearly cut supernatural encounters that moonlights as a frighteningly lucid story of injustice. Be it a specter or a painful recollection, Chapman teaches an absolutely chilling lesson on just how long the past will wait to bite you."—*Fangoria*

"A ripping good yarn. *The Remaking* first takes you into its confidence and then makes you wonder if you are also cursed with and by this story. Because, incidentally, you are."—*Richmond* magazine

"Chapman tells a well-paced, spare story with original twists and some definite shocks."—*Star News*

"If there's any justice, *The Remaking* will introduce Chapman to a wider audience of readers anxious for the kind of horror tale that claims a little piece of your brain as its own."—*BookTrib*

"Chapman has crafted a fascinating horror novel that is both excellent within itself and a sharp commentary on an element of the genre."
—*SFFWorld*

"As both a novel of psychological terror and a traditional ghost story, this short, chilling read is recommended for all collections."—*Booklist*

"An obvious valentine to the horror genre."—*The Big Thrill*

"Chapman has expertly crafted an ouroboros of a horror story. *The Remaking* is a fast-paced and haunting examination of how misogyny poisons our culture, generation after generation. It's absolutely chilling. You won't be able to put it down or stop thinking about it after the lights go out."—Mallory O'Meara, author of *The Lady from the Black Lagoon*

MISS CORPUS

"Buckle your seatbelt and lock the car doors; Clay Chapman's about to take you for a hair-raising ride."—*New Yorker*

"In a slow, simmering style that melds Southern folklore with a gothic sensibility, Chapman concocts a powerful tale that is suspenseful and moving. . . . Chapman's knack for storytelling and his vigorous prose establish a dramatic momentum, moving the tale to a violent, tragic crescendo. Suffused with a compassion, the novel transcends its bizarre premise and suggests that the magic of literature can make sense of life."—*Publishers Weekly*

"Chapman's powerful, intense gifts are not for the faint of heart or weak of stomach."—*Booklist*

WHISPER DOWN the LANE

WHISPER DOWN the LANE

CLAY McLEOD CHAPMAN

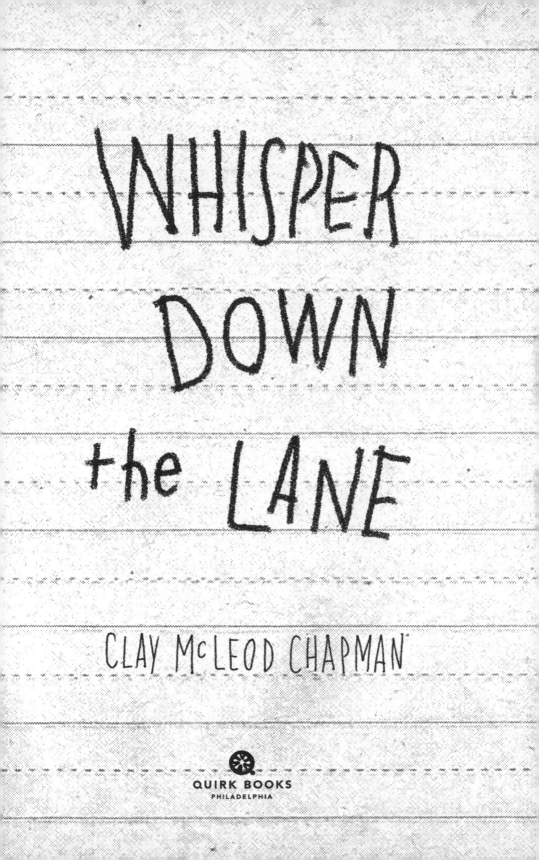

QUIRK BOOKS
PHILADELPHIA

Library of Congress Cataloging in Publication Data

Chapman, Clay McLeod, 1977- author.

Whisper down the lane / Clay McLeod Chapman.

Summary: "Two narratives—Richard in present day, settling into a quiet but pleasant life as a newly married
art teacher; Sean in 1980s Virginia, when cult leaders,
serial killers, and stranger danger are on the rise—
converge around a few small lies that spiraled into a
terrible tragedy. Thirty years later, it seems someone is
out for revenge."—Provided by publisher.
LCC PS3603.H36 W55 2021
DDC 813/.6—dc23   2020047601

ISBN: 978-1-68369-215-7

Printed in the United States of America

Typeset in Chronicle + Albertus

Designed by Ryan Hayes
Cover photo by Oksana Shufrych/Shutterstock
Production management by John J. McGurk

Quirk Books
215 Church Street
Philadelphia, PA 19106
quirkbooks.com

10 9 8 7 6 5 4 3 2 1

FOR MOM

"Estimates are that there are over one million Satanists in this country. The majority of them are linked in a highly organized, very secretive network. From small towns to large cities, they have attracted police and FBI attention to their Satanic ritual child abuse, child pornography, and grizzly Satanic murders. The odds are that this is happening in your town."

—Geraldo Rivera in *Devil Worship: Exposing Satan's Underground*

"The stubborn fact remains," one read, "that whether or not *we* believe, *they* most assuredly do."

—*Rosemary's Baby*

DAMNED IF YOU DON'T
RICHARD: 2013

They found Professor Howdy spread across the soccer field. What was left of him, anyway.

His chest cavity had been carefully cracked open, his rib cage fanning back as if it were the glistening crimson trigger hairs on a Venus flytrap, patiently waiting for its prey to wander inside its gaping maw. The entirety of his intestines, large and small, had been gingerly unspooled to the end of their connective tissues across the lawn in some sort of luminous pattern.

I say *luminous* because his guts looked like beams of wet sunlight radiating out from the rest of his hollow self.

Pattern because there seemed to be a particular—I don't know—*methodology* to the placement of his organs. Someone arranged them to look this way. On purpose. To see.

For who, though?

It felt like he was meant to be revered. I say *revered* because, even to my eye, there was something beatific to the way his body was presented. Holy, almost. And trust me—this is coming from a completely nonreligious person. I've never even set foot inside a church.

That's not entirely true. There were a few visits to Sunday school that I can barely recall at this point. Distant memories by now. I vaguely remember taking communion as a kid. Once.

Take and eat, the pastor said as he pressed a stale cracker past my lips, *for this is my body.* That dry sacramental wafer adhered itself to the roof of my mouth. I couldn't wash out the pasty undertaste for the rest of the day, stuck with this phantom flavor on my tongue.

But that was years ago. A whole other lifetime ago.

All I'm trying to say is, even I could sense the awe of this grisly exhibition. *Feel it,* somehow. The downright ardor of it.

Professor Howdy's lungs fanned out like angel wings flapping against the grass. The liver, the stomach, the spleen—*that is the spleen, isn't it?*—placed with exacting precision. Each organ was its own celestial body orbiting the corpse it had erupted from.

His heart now rested in the patch of grass directly above his head.

A bleeding crown.

Dawn broke an hour or so before our school's groundskeeper—Diego, I think his name is—discovered the poor professor. The morning sun found his body first, pelt glistening in dew. His blood had a crystalline sheen against the green, like red stained glass. Something you might see in Sunday services. *Saint Howdy.* Our school's tragic rabbit, angelic white fur and glazed-over pink eyes, captured among all the other apostles.

Professor Howdy was always kept in Miss Castevet's classroom. He belonged to the school, its students, but Miss Castevet was ultimately responsible for his upkeep. That meant cleaning out his cage. Feeding him. Picking up the poo pellets. The nitty-gritty stuff nobody else, particularly the kids, ever wanted to get their hands dirty doing.

Students were always welcome to stop by Miss Castevet's room and pay Professor Howdy a visit. She set up designated feeding hours for anyone to swing by and offer up a handful of rabbit chow for him to nibble directly from their palm. And sometimes, on the *specialest of occasions*, as Miss Castevet liked to say, she would even pull Professor Howdy out from his cage and let him hop around the room. Door closed, of course. There had been one particular incident at the very beginning of the school year, when someone—I'm not naming any names here (*cough, cough,* Benjamin Pendleton, *cough cough*)—left the classroom door open and the professor broke free, hopping down the hall. The ensuing manhunt—*bunny*hunt?—was a school-wide event. All the students got involved in the search party.

Eventually, he popped up in my classroom. I spotted him tucked behind the tempera paints, struggling to squirm further in. I was hailed as a hero for returning the professor to his cage unharmed, alive, and in one piece. *The new art teacher saves the day!* the students sang out. *Yay, Mr. Bellamy!*

Everybody loved Professor Howdy. He was, without a doubt, the Danvers School's unofficial mascot. Who would think about doing something as awful as this? To a rabbit?

Our rabbit?

Teachers always arrive early to school to kick-start their day. Get those lesson plans prepped. Get their classrooms in order. Get ready for the oncoming onslaught of students.

Miss Castevet is always one of the very first teachers to arrive. You'll find her Nova parked in one of the nearest spots to the main entrance. When she enters her classroom first thing in the morning, she's greeted by the gentle sounds of Professor Howdy leaping about in his cage, his fur brushing up against the thin metal bars. The pads of his feet strum the spokes.

Not this morning. Miss Castevet sensed the silence coming from his corner of the room as soon as she called out to him. *Good morning, Professor Howdy.*

He wasn't in his cage. The gate had been left wide open.

Once students started shuffling into class, they noticed his absence as well. *Where's Professor Howdy, Miss Castevet?* they all asked. *What happened to Professor Howdy?*

Professor Howdy's just feeling a little sick, she lied. She had no clue where he was. Not yet. Only the groundskeeper and our principal, Mrs. Condrey, were aware of the kindergarten crime scene on the soccer field. They were keeping this bit of grisly information to themselves for now.

Rumors quickly began working their way through the faculty. Condrey called Miss Castevet into her office to break the news about her beloved bunny. I wasn't there to hear it myself, but several teachers whispered to one another in the lounge that they'd heard an audible sob escape from behind Condrey's closed door. A moan. You would've thought a member of her family had passed away. In a sense, one had. Miss Castevet needed to take a moment before the bell for second period rang to collect herself. Even then, she broke down during class. Simply glancing at his empty cage, gate open, was enough to summon her tears.

Summon. I can't stop myself. What other words were there to describe what happened?

Where'd you go? Tamara always asks me in moments like these, whenever she catches me drifting off into my thoughts. *Lost you there for a second . . .*

Sorry, I'd probably say, most likely smiling back. *Just remembered something.*

The students are still in the dark. No press release from the main office just yet. Kids can't understand why Miss Castevet is so upset. It won't be long before some second-grade sleuth puts two and two together. The whispers are already drifting through the faculty now, a brushfire passing from class to class. The teachers' lounge is festering with speculation and it's not even fourth period yet. We've all become embroiled in detective work, a bunch of amateur Sherlock Holmeses.

Elementary school, my dear Watson . . .

A yummy morsel of gossip like this is too good to pass up. *Did you hear?* each teacher whispers. *Professor Howdy's been gutted. Torn open along his underbelly, groin to gullet . . .*

It wasn't until lunch period that word finally reached me.

I pulled cafeteria detail today. That meant surveying the students as they munched their nuggets, like I'm some police guard standing watch over gen pop. Miss Castevet usually takes this shift, but she'd called out, and as the alternate turnkey, I'm on deck to replace her. I honestly thought I'd never get called. Miss Castevet never misses her lunch shift. Never misses anything. She constantly volunteers to chaperone after-school events. This school is her life.

And somebody just gutted it.

"Have you heard?" Mr. Dunstan, our music teacher, murmurs over the lunchtime din. The two of us stand at the back of the cafeteria by the trash cans. Kids dump what is left of their lunch, creating a congealing mound of breaded chicken cutlets and chocolate milk.

"Hear what?"

"Professor Howdy," he whispers, rather mock conspiratorially, as if the students might be eavesdropping on our conversation. Not that these kids care what us adults natter on about.

Except her.

That girl. Over there. All the way across the cafeteria. Corn-silk blonde hair. She's looking right at me. I spot her as Mr. Dunstan murmurs into my ear. She's sitting by herself. The contents of her bagged lunch spread out evenly before her, both hands gripping her sandwich. Just staring back. Not blinking. At least, I think she's staring. Maybe I am imagining it. Her eyes don't drift. Perhaps she is gazing into space and I just happen to be in her visual line of fire.

Is she in my class? It's pretty early in the school year, so getting a lock on everyone's name is still a hurdle. For me, at least. I've always been terrible with names. Names and faces.

Do I have her? I think. I squint to see her. *Is that . . . what's-her-name. Her name . . .*

Sandy.

I almost say it loud out. To be honest, I'm not entirely convinced I didn't. Not from the way Mr. Dunstan is staring at me.

"The rabbit," he clarifies. He shakes his head and sighs. Such a solemn air. It feels a wee bit performative for my tastes, to be honest. Dunstan is just gunning to play the pipes at the wake. *Danny Boy*, I bet. Maybe he'll get his choir kids to sing a song they've prepared in class just for Professor Howdy. Perhaps even some choreographed dance routine. With scarves.

"How awful," he says, already humming the initial strains of some funereal dirge. Dunstan strikes me as a doughy Humpty Dumpty. His oval-shaped torso and bald pate glisten with the thinnest sheen of perspiration. The man is perpetually sweating. Always licking his lips. Always humming an ethereal strain to an unknown song, a symphony hiding behind his lips, seemingly unaware that he's even doing it. He has left me in suspense for long enough, leaning over and whispering into my ear that someone *eviscerated* our school's unofficial mascot.

"They're saying," he whispers, his eyes still on the kids, the warmth of his breath spreading down my neck, "it looked *ritualistic*."

He doesn't know I've already seen it for myself. That I was the one who discovered the body.

I bike to school. No car for me. I let my license lapse at some point a while back and still haven't renewed it. There's a well-furrowed bike path that cuts through the surrounding woods behind the building, allowing kids who live on the south side to Schwinn their way to school. They just have to cut through the soccer field to get here. I can bike to work in ten minutes flat.

This morning was no different. Not until I noticed that patch of white.

Braking, I turned to take in the glistening spectacle. My first thought was the groundskeeper must've run the rabbit over with his lawnmower without realizing it. An accident. But the longer I looked, taking in the fastidiousness of the display, the devout attention to detail, the more I saw it as sculpture. A work of art.

I couldn't shake the creeping feeling that, whoever did this, they'd made it just for me.

It's all for you, Richard, I heard the rabbit whisper. *All for you.*

There was a birthday card tucked in his guts. The corners of the cardboard stock were softening with blood, held upright within the ribs' grip.

Nobody knows it's my birthday. I choose not to celebrate it, haven't celebrated it, not even with Tamara, for years. I figured the day had faded by now. Nobody knows. And yet, this sacrificed rabbit felt like a gift. A present someone went ahead and unwrapped without me.

I carefully plucked the card out from Professor Howdy's rib cage, making sure not to touch any of the blood. It was an old card, printed years ago, yellowing around the edges.

The picture on the front was of a dimple-cheeked baby emerging from a head of lettuce. Leaves unfurled around his pudgy body, this plump infant sprouting out from the soil itself.

A Cabbage Patch Kid.

I haven't seen one of them in years. These dolls were all the rage when I was a kid. They flew right off the shelves every Christmas. Children were given an adoption certificate with each doll. You had to take an oath to raise them. Kids were instructed to hold up their right hand in front of an adult and pledge, *I promise to love my Cabbage Patch Kid with all my heart.*

I remember these dolls kicking up some dust in my hometown. Boys and girls suddenly weren't allowed to bring their Cabbage Patch

Dolls to school anymore because some fundamentalist mother on the school board believed they were possessed. By signing that contract and taking that oath, children were bringing the devil into their homes. It seems so silly now—but back then, people believed, *actually believed* these toys were vessels for the devil.

Can you imagine? The local church even hosted a Cabbage Patch burning. They tossed dozens of dolls into a pile and lit them up, the flames swallowing that patch whole.

Just some stupid-looking dolls. Dimples and blank eyes, bovine smiles. That's all they were.

So why were my wrists shaking?

I opened the card. In red crayon, the letters loose and crooked, as if a child had scribbled it, it read—

SEAN: 1982

Sean couldn't believe his ears. Had Mom just ordered two Happy Meals? He swore he heard her say two! Just like the Doublemint jingle sang—Double your pleasure, double your fun—all Sean could think about was who would be getting that second toy.

"What would you like to drink with that, ma'am?" said the crackling voice from the drive-through speaker.

"Orange soda and—" Mom turned back to face Sean in his booster seat. "What're you thirsty for?"

Sean took in the monolithic menu looming just outside his window. It towered over his head, an ancient pillar etched in fast-food hieroglyphics. He had to lean back to take in the mysterious alphabet he couldn't quite decipher. Even though he still wasn't quite old enough to read, Sean was positive there were many yummy foods to choose from. He knew the options: Big Mac, Chicken McNuggets, French fries, Filet-O-Fish swaddled in its special blue paper wrapper.

Eating at McDonald's was a treat. Mom only brought him here if there was something worth celebrating. This had to be one of those moments, even if he had no idea what he and his mother were commemorating. He certainly wasn't going to ask. He didn't want to ruin the surprise.

When Sean and Mom had said goodbye to their old home and driven the endless stretch of interstate to reach their new—and smaller—house, he assumed he'd never eat at McDonald's again. But now he was elated to learn that Ronald McDonald had followed them all the way to Greenfield, Virginia.

How had Ronald found him?

Maybe the move wouldn't be so bad after all. If he could still eat Happy Meals, just like he had back home, perhaps life wouldn't be that much different here after all.

"Sean?" Mom's voice snapped him back to the car. "Earth to Sean. What do you want to drink, hon?"

Sean pressed his luck. "Can I have a . . . a vanilla milkshake?"

The corner of Mom's eyes pinched just a bit. "How 'bout a Hi-C? You like the orange drink, right?"

"Okay." Sean nodded, trying to hide his disappointment. He knew milkshakes cost twenty-five cents extra but he tried anyway. All these changes. This *fresh start* Mom kept mentioning. Who knows? Maybe drinking milkshakes could be a part of this *fresh start*, too?

Mom leaned out from their Mercury Colony Park wagon with simulated wood siding. "Make that two Hi-Cs."

"Will that be all today?"

"That's it." Mom's left arm rested along the rolled-down window, her head leaning against the door. A wisp of her hair caught the wind and drifted across Sean's window. He watched it whip about on the other side of the glass, a string on a lost balloon lifting into the sky.

"Two cheeseburger Happy Meals with Hi-C," the menu crackled. "Drive up to the first window, please." This last part sounded like *cry up to thirsty no knees* to Sean.

Mom turned to face Sean again, bringing her finger to her grinning lips. "If the cashier asks," she whispered, "just tell them the Happy Meal's for your sick sister back at home."

Why was she whispering? Was the voice still listening to them? Were there people eavesdropping? What would happen to Sean if the voice found out he didn't have a sister?

Sean knew Mom was ordering herself a Happy Meal because it was cheaper than the regular adult meal and instantly felt a twinge of guilt.

"You can have my toy." Mom arched an eyebrow, giving him a mischievous wink.

Sean's face brightened. Of course he'd play along with Mom's game for two toys! Ever since they began the Big Move, this *fresh start*, he felt like he'd become Mom's sidekick. The two were on the lam now, making their big escape. The rear of the station wagon was filled with cardboard boxes, each labeled CLOTHES. TOYS. KITCHEN.

Mom had kept the radio on for most of the ride, cranking up the volume until they were drowning in sound, the station wagon filled with music. "Come on, Sean," she'd cajoled him, leaning forward just enough to find his reflection in the rearview mirror. "Sing with me!"

Sean had shouted, "I don't know the words!"

"The real words don't matter!" she'd said. "Make up your own!"

To prove her point, she'd crooned through her own rendition of whatever tune was playing on the radio. Wham's "Wake Me Up Before You Go-Go" became something entirely different: *Take my nose, before you blow-blow . . . Don't sneeze before you bring a tissue up and flow-flow. Take a breath, before you blow-blow . . . I don't want your snot on me toniiight . . .*

Sean couldn't help but laugh as Mom murdered the lyrics. She knew they were wrong but Mom put her all into her mangled version. She hit the high notes right alongside George Michael, bobbing her head to the beat, dancing in her seat and drumming her palms against the steering wheel. She'd smack the horn at the end of each verse, just to get the station wagon in on the fun, too. He imagined her dancing along with Mr. Michael, wearing a white sweatshirt with GO-GO printed in black block letters across her chest.

Mom was doing everything in her power to make this *fresh start* feel like fun. Like an adventure.

Just you and me, she always said. *Nothing else matters.*

When they pulled up to the first window, Mom had to count out exact change, taking her time to pick through the pennies until she got the right amount.

"You said two Happy Meals, right?" It was the voice Sean had heard through the drive-through speaker. A bored high schooler eyed Sean's mom, still holding both cardboard boxes in his hands, the handles of the Happy Meals shaped like golden arches. He was hesitating.

"It's for my sister," Sean spoke up from the back, leaning forward in his seat to speak through his mother's rolled-down window. "She's back at home. She's really sick."

The cashier sniffed before handing over their Happy Meals. "Sure. Have a nice day."

"You, too," Mom said.

The toy inside both Happy Meals was a cloth doll of Ronald McDonald. What a rip-off! Sean had his heart set on adding another Hot Wheels to his collection. There were fourteen in all, *while supplies lasted*. That was way too many visits to McDonald's. More than Mom would ever allow. He only had three cars, so collecting the whole set was practically impossible now.

Today's take was an utter bust. Lousy twin clowns. There wasn't much Sean could do with a pair of dumb dolls. They were like puppets without any place to put your hands. Both Ronalds simply grinned back at him. Each had a loop of red thread attached to the top of its head, for slipping on the Christmas tree, even if Christmas was still months and months away.

The two ate their Happy Meals in the parking lot in silence. Mom let Sean crawl up into the front with her so they could dine together, using the dashboard as their dinner table.

Mom pulled down her sun visor and checked her makeup in the mirror. Sean hadn't realized she'd been wearing makeup until she reached over to the glove compartment and pulled out a tube of mascara and eyeshadow, touching up the charcoal accents along her eyelids. Seeing her perform this ritual in the mirror brought her face into sharper focus for Sean.

"We've got to hurry. Mom's got a job interview in. . ." She glanced at the radio's clock. "Oh, jeez, thirty minutes! Think you can finish that cheeseburger, Big Man?"

"Will you pick out my pickles?"

"What're you talking about?" she said in mock horror, even though Sean always requested that she perform this culinary exorcism. "The pickles are the best part!"

"Pleeeease."

"Tell you what—I'll eat your pickles if you finish my Hi-C for me."

"Deal." The two pinkie-swore, making the transaction official.

Mom peeled back the bun on his cheeseburger, as if skinning some small woodland creature. A rabbit flashed through his mind. He could hear the tacky sound of ketchup unsticking the bread from the patty. She plucked out the pair of pickles between her fingers and plopped them in her mouth.

"Onions," Sean reminded her.

Mom swiped her pinkie across the patty, the same pinkie she used to swear by, now sweeping away the diced onions. She brought her finger up to her mouth and sucked the onions away. All that was left was a scab of melted cheddar. "I can eat the rest if you want . . ."

"Nooo!" Sean reached for his cheeseburger, still in Mom's hands.

"You sure?" She reeled back, holding the burger just out of his grip.

"Give it to me!"

"You're probably not hungry anymore . . ."

"Give it back, give it back!"

Eating in the car was one of their little rituals. Watching the world outside the window as if it were a movie. Life's own drive-in theater.

Sean knew not to ask about the ball pit. He glanced out the rearview mirror, spotting the Play Land inside the restaurant. It was so close. All he had to do was step out of the car, cross the parking lot, and dive in. But Mom had sworn off McDonald's Play Land on account of sanitary reasons. *There's germs all over those balls*, she'd said. *That place could make you sick.*

There had been that one time when Sean got to go to Play Land, tumbling through the ball pit with a bunch of other children. Somebody else's kid got sick and vomited all over everything. Mom had to fish him out before he touched those wet orbs. No more Play Land.

She must've sensed what was on Sean's mind. Mom lined up a row of French fries along the dash, just above the glove compartment. As soon as Sean took one to eat, she would lay down another. Then another. A greasy line of train tracks leading directly into Sean's tummy.

"I know this is a lot of change," she eventually said. "It's going to be hard at first. But it's for the best, Sean. Trust me. For both of us. We get to start over again. Start clean."

Clean. Sean wanted to be clean.

Greenfield was supposed to be the answer to all their problems. Whatever their problems were. Sean wasn't sure he knew, not exactly, but it felt like the move was only making things worse. Greenfield felt smaller. Their new home, smaller. Everything was small now. She swore his new school would be special, calling it something different. A *private* school. Sean imagined a building filled with secret rooms and hidden corridors. A labyrinth of classes. *You've got a real opportunity here, hon,* she'd said. *A chance I never had when I was your age.* Even he knew they couldn't afford a school like Greenfield Academy, but Mom had bandied about a new word—*scholarship*—to anyone willing to listen. *Scholarship.* The answer to all their problems. *Scholarship.* The magic password into the secret chambers of this private school.

"Wait here," Mom said. An idea had taken root in her head. Whatever it was, she couldn't shake it. "Keep the doors locked until I get back. Don't open them for anyone else."

And just like that, Mom slipped out the car. She closed the door behind her, knocking on the window to get Sean's attention. She pointed to the lock on the driver's side door. Sean had to crawl over the center armrest to reach the lock, poking it with his index finger until it sunk into its secured position. Now nobody could get in.

"I'll be right back," she said.

Sean's elbow hit the steering wheel, accidentally honking the horn. *Whoops.* Mom laughed as she spun around. Where was she going?

Sean watched her slip through a crowd of adults standing in the parking lot, disappearing among them. Moms and dads, or so he assumed. They held signs made of posterboard with scribbled pictures and bold words, angry words, written all over them. Some were even underlined. Even though Sean couldn't read what they said, he understood the pictures. He saw the devil, only it wasn't quite the devil. Sean recognized the Sharpied fangs and horns, but this devil had puffy red hair. A red button nose. Wide-arcing eyebrows and bone-white skin.

This devil looked more like a clown than an outright demon.

Like Ronald McDonald.

Why were these moms and dads waving their signs? What were they so mad about that they had to shout? He couldn't hear what they were saying.

Sean glanced at the stuffed Ronalds still in his hands. They had the same smile as the devils on those handmade posterboard signs. His twin clowns didn't have horns or fangs, but the resemblance was there. Their plush bodies suddenly felt hot in his hands.

Sean rolled down the passenger side window. Just a crack. Just wide enough for him to slip his right hand out, still clutching one of the Ronalds, and drop it into the parking lot.

The doll fell out of view, landing somewhere below.

Sean took the other Ronald and released the clown into the wild along with his twin. Once both diabolical brothers were out of the car, Sean quickly rolled up his window and sank into his seat. The leatherette squealed beneath his body as he slid beneath the horizon of the dashboard. He sat there, submerged from view, wondering if any of the protesting parents had noticed. Had they seen what he'd just done? Would they come after him now?

Sean crawled up in his seat. Just a bit. Just to peer between the headrest and the shoulder of his seat. Where was Mom? What was taking her so long? Why had she left—

Mom emerged from the crowd, pushing her way through with her elbows. She was holding a clear plastic container. A sundae just for him. Mom held it up to the window with both hands as an offering. The tip of vanilla curled over at the end.

"Found this just lying around. You don't know anyone who'd want it, do you?"

Sean nodded vigorously. *Me, me, me mememememeeeeeeeee!* He unlocked the station wagon door.

"All yours," Mom said as she slipped back inside. "Happy birthday, baby."

"It's already my birthday?" Sean was surprised it had crept up on him like that.

"Close enough. Now that it's just you and me, we can celebrate whenever we want." She leaned over and whispered, "And I wanted to be the first to wish you a happy birthday."

The world was going to be okay. Everything was going to be okay. No matter what came their way, Sean knew his mother would always be there for him. *Just you and me*, like she said.

Mom never asked about the dolls. She probably forgot. Sean never mentioned them, but as she turned the ignition and backed the station wagon up, forcing the protesting parents to part, he could've sworn he felt the passenger-side tire running both Ronalds over.

RICHARD: 2013

"Hear that?" Tamara asks. "Please tell me I'm not imagining it."

"Trust me, I'm hearing it, too."

Angels singing.

The grating strains of Enya's "Orinoco Flow" drift across the plucking strings of a harp. You would've thought the pearly gates had opened up in the gym. The song is practically flooding into the hall. The music only grows louder as we walk. "Guess we've all died and gone to heaven," I say.

Tamara moans. "If this is your idea of heaven, we're in trouble." She has been waiting for me in front of her classroom, wearing what I like to refer to as her Office Goth look. Subtly shadowed accents. A sooty half-pleated skirt. High-collared jacket that hides her neck. Her charcoal sleeves conceal the ink that wraps around her arms, over her left shoulder, the telltale tattoos of her after-school life obscured from her kids. Not to mention their parents.

"Hold your books?" I offer.

"Sooo sweet," she says in her highest-pitched pom squad impression. A part of our intra-school romance is to pretend we're other people. Role-play the Jock and Cheerleader, Chazz and Jenny, hitting on each other in the hallway between classes. "See you after practice?"

"Can't," I say in my best bro-brogue. "I'm totally stuck in detention again."

"Oh, Chazz . . . What'd you do *this* time?"

"Condrey just won't get off my back," I huff. "She keeps riding me and *riding* me."

Tamara laughs, drawing the attention of our wandering faculty pack. Mr. Dunstan turns toward us, his watery eyes widening, as if he's hoping to be included in our game. We both drop our act and walk in silence. Tamara dips her chin, concealing her grin.

"How's the day been?" I whisper. "Break up any riots?"

"Half my kids have come down with something." She moans. "My class feels like such a petri dish. I can already feel another cold coming on."

"We should get our flu shots together. We'll get a babysitter. Make it a date night."

Tamara stops walking. "I already got mine. We talked about this."

I feign heartbreak. "You went without me?"

"I asked you, like, *five* times."

She had. I'd just forgotten. Can I go the whole school year without inoculating myself against these rugrats? Danvers is its own hot zone. The bell rings and the outbreak begins.

"Hey." Tamara elbows me. "Where'd you just go?"

"Still here."

She clearly doesn't believe me. "What'd I just say?"

"You said . . ." *Find the thread, Richard. Come on, you can do it.*

She rolls her eyes and lets me off the hook. "Miss Castevet. Professor Howdy. Who'd do something like that?"

"She probably left his cage open. Just snuck out and some wild animal attacked him."

"That's your best guess, Sherlock?"

"Why? You got a better theory?"

She gives me her best interrogator impression: "*Where were you the night of...*"

I want to turn back. Break out of this building. "Wanna ditch?"

"Too late now."

"No, it's not." I stop walking, tugging on her arm. "Come on."

"You can't be serious."

"I'm completely serious. *Pleeease*?"

"Rich..."

"What? It'll be fun! We can ask someone else to fill us in on what we missed."

I tug on Tamara's arm again, harder this time. A confused expression surfaces, as if she isn't quite sure if this is still a game or not. She gently pulls her hand away. "Quit it."

"Your loss," I say, trailing after her. I do my best karaoke rendition of Enya as we immerse ourselves within the song's reverberations. "Sail a-*way*, sail a-*way*, sail a-*way*."

"Keep your day job," she suggests.

I pretend to be wounded. Her words hit me in the heart. "You don't like my singing?"

"Sorry..."

The gym doesn't quite have the acoustics to pull off an Enya concert. It's all rafters and no phonics. What's meant to lull the teachers into a calm, soothing stupor before kicking off our first faculty meeting of the year seems to simply set everybody on edge. Maybe it's just me.

A set of folding chairs is arranged around the center of the basketball court, forming a ring. No backs to the staff. There's a little pop psychology at play here. Condrey can sit amongst us as our peer. No leaders here, even though she's clearly the one in charge.

Tamara heads for the other side of the circle.

"What? You're not gonna even sit with me?"

"Not happening," she says.

"Why not?"

"You know exactly why. You're going to get bored after a few minutes and you're going to look for something to distract you, and then you're going to start bugging me for your own personal amusement, and then we'll both get in trouble . . . I'm not getting dragged in, sorry."

"It's going to be pretty boring over there, next to Mr. Lumbard."

Tamara glances over her shoulder to our beloved science teacher. Mr. Lumbard quickly catches Tamara's eye and his face brightens. "I'll take my chances," she says to me. "Thanks."

"Last chance. All the fun's gonna be over on this side, with the *cool* teachers."

"We'll see about that."

"You'll miss me."

"Keep dreaming." Tamara saunters to the other side of the circle.

Donuts had been voted down because Condrey was concerned they would make us sluggish. She prefers complex carbohydrates. Trail mix. Whole grain breads, lean meats. Some yogurt cups and granola parfaits. Coffee is nonnegotiable. Condrey will have a riot on her hands if she doesn't have a travel pack set up with paper cups and sugar packets.

A stack of photocopied agendas is passed around the circle. The itinerary is evenly divided and subdivided into bite-sized brackets for easy digestion. The whos, whats, wheres, and whens are all laid out. No whys, though. Never the why—as in, *why am I here?*

Or the how. *How is this even happening to me? How did I get myself into this?*

If Tamara was sitting next to me, I'd lean over and whisper about a few particular bullet points on the agenda that immediately catch my eye.

Halloween will be now officially be called "Character Day." *Oof.*

Active shooter drills. Parents are bound to kick up some dust over that one.

The recent uptick in graffiti. The inner walls in the stalls of the boys bathroom look like a Mötley Crüe video. Sharpied pentagrams. 666 in bold black letters. How do our kids even know this sort of stuff already? Aren't they too young for this crap? Save it for high school.

Mr. Dunstan slips into the chair next to mine. "Is this seat taken?"

He's already sitting so it doesn't seem kosher to say it's not available. "All yours."

Dunstan hums to himself as he peruses the agenda. "No discussion of budget cuts, I see. I do believe that means you and I are safe." He sneezes. He pulls out a handkerchief, monogrammed and everything. P.D. *Do I even know what his first name is?* He blows.

"Forgive me," he says between discharges. "Got a bug going around this week."

It's true. I discovered another runny nose in my class today. Timothy Haskell's upper lip was glistening all through first period. *Use a tissue, Timothy,* I say almost every day.

"Madame Condrey is fashionably late, I see," I say. "Anybody got eyes on our fearless leader?" This solicits a few charmed snickers from the faculty. Any opportunity to lightheartedly mock our esteemed principal in private is always appreciated. I could always earn a few points from the other teachers by getting a good jab in that didn't cross the line into crassness. Condrey could take it. Hell—she might even laugh herself. There's bound to be a funny bone somewhere in her body.

The Danvers School eschews the traditional educational model for something a little more "hands on." Our mission statement claims we look at the "whole student"—not just their reading, writing, and arithmetic, but their social, emotional, and cognitive development.

You won't find many desks set up in even rows here. Most are in circles. Mrs. Condrey, our beloved principal, wants to foster a *collaborative* relationship between educators and students.

Amplify their voice. Let them be heard.

The faculty represents a mix of pedagogies. There's the younger generation of hipstructors, intermingled with the old school, Old Testament–type teachers. There are twenty of us on staff, all told. Not a huge roster, but Condrey considers us all to be one big, happy academic family. As in, arguing-with-your-right-wing-uncle-about-whether-or-not-Obama-was-born-in-the-USA-during-Thanksgiving-dinner type of family. That's what kind of family our faculty is.

I notice Miss Castevet is absent. Her empty foldout chair is taken away. Our circle tightens. Enya's last chant suddenly halts. *Sail a-way. Sail a-way. Sail a—*

"All righty, everyone," Condrey calls out as she presses STOP on the portable CD player. Her heels clack over the basketball court, echoing throughout the gymnasium as she joins us. She has an aerodynamic demeanor. Short, sandy blonde hair. No jewelry, unless you count her wireless glasses. She seems to go through a rotation of hip-length blazers. Today is turquoise. "Sorry to keep you waiting," she says as she glances over her own agenda. "Quick addendum. I'd like to address the elephant in the room."

I would've said *bunny*, but that's just me.

"I'll have a card for Ruth tomorrow. If you could all sign it, that'd be wonderful. Just a little something to say we're all sorry for her loss. I'll leave it in the faculty lounge."

No mention of Professor Howdy or what happened to him. No suspects.

Our faculty meeting begins with a team-building exercise. The agenda even says so. Just a fun activity to bring teachers together. "This is a great game to play with students," Condrey says. "Especially on the first day. Nice icebreaker."

I'm imagining tossing a beach ball around the circle to see how long we can collectively keep it in the air or some version of Zip-Zap-Zop.

"Two Truths and One Lie," she announces. "In class, I always prefer Two Truths and One Tall Tale, just so I'm not advocating for kids to fib . . . but we're all adults."

The rules are simple. Each teacher has to share three things about themselves. Two are true, the third is a total fabrication.

Condrey zeros in on me from across the circle and smiles. Something about her stare makes me feel the slightest bit on edge. Had she heard me mocking her? Why do I suddenly feel like she caught me doing something I shouldn't? "Why don't you go first, Richard?"

"Sure." I feel the spotlight shining on me. I glance through its imagined glare and find Tamara. She leans back in her chair with one eyebrow arched as if to say, *This should be fun.*

"Hi. I'm Richard, your friendly neighborhood art teacher. Okay. Let's see . . ."

My mind goes blank. This is harder than I'd expected.

"Okay. Uh. . . Got it. This summer I married the love of my life."

(True.)

That statement earns me a few *aah*s from the circle, several teachers turning to Tamara to give their nod of approval. Only I seem to notice Tamara rolling her eyes.

"In college, I got to hike the Grand Teton and I broke my leg coming down."

(True.)

"And . . . I have never eaten at McDonald's before."

(Lie.)

Condrey surveys the circle to see if anyone might know where the fib is hidden. "Which one's the tall tale?" She tries her best not to look at Tamara, who now bows her head just enough to silently state that she will not be contributing.

Dunstan raises his hand, his fingers grazing my shoulder. "Breaking your leg?"

All eyes are on me. Staring. Like I am the guest on some talk show and this is my big interview. I can feel the initial beads of sweat pebbling my forehead, rising from my skin.

"Sorry," I say. "That one's true. Still have the scars to prove it . . ."

"I'm guessing," Condrey cuts in, "that it's McDonald's. Unless there's something you want to tell Tamara . . ." The faculty all laughs. Well, chortles anyway. *Huh-huh-huh.*

"You got me."

Got me. Condrey seems pleased. *Yes—I've got you.*

She's onto the next teacher, and almost immediately, I find myself having a hard time focusing. Her words loosen, fading away. Tamara was right, of course. I'm bored out of my gourd. *That didn't take long.* This meeting is only supposed to take up sixty minutes of our lives. Sixty mind-numbing minutes of bureaucratic jibber-jabber. Figuring out parking spaces. Prep for the annual bake sale. The book fair. It's exhausting, but I keep my eyes open. I don't doze.

I'm simply not . . . present. I find myself glancing at the nape of Tamara's neck from across the circle. I can just make out the hint of scales peeking from beneath her collar. I remember the first time I saw the snake for myself. Tamara has mastered this trick of flexing her bicep so that it looks as if the serpent is coiling around her arm. Reminds me of those old hula girl tattoos on septuagenarian sailors, faded hips of blue ink dancing the hukilau with every twist of their wrist. Whenever I looked at Tamara's tattoo, I could have sworn I saw it writhing on its own. Alive.

"It's traumatizing." I snap back to hear Tamara's voice lifting. She sounds agitated. Something's riling her up. "We're doing more damage than good."

"I appreciate your point of view on this," Condrey calmly responds. "I do, but this is happening statewide. It's not just us, it's all through Virginia."

"I can't be the only one who feels this way. Am I?" Tamara searches the circle.

What are we talking about here? I couldn't have drifted for that long. I have to catch up before I'm called on.

Too late. Tamara glances across the ring of teachers and locks her eyes directly onto me, cueing me to agree with her. I nod. It's the best I can do given the circumstances.

"I'm well aware of how parents feel," Condrey says, clearly in politician mode. "But this is coming from the superintendent. We need our students to be prepared."

Tamara shakes her head. "Prepared for . . . what? Are we really saying a third-grader is going to bring in a semiautomatic and start shooting up their classmates?"

Some of the older teachers recoil. Even Condrey winces.

This is one of the many things I love about Tamara. Watching her get all riled up, like a firefighter racing into a burning building while everyone else stands back and stares. Most of us mere mortals have beliefs. Tamara has *convictions*. I always dread getting into an argument with her. I have made a practice out of avoiding conflict at all costs throughout my life, but she dives right on in, headfirst. Her parents are the same way. Holidays are a blast, believe me.

"How do I explain this to Elijah?" she asks. "He'll be afraid to come to school, because what I'll be saying—what we're all saying—is this is a place to be afraid of. It's no longer safe."

Condrey matches her. "What about someone we don't know? A man with a gun finds his way into the building? What if we're the next Sandy Hook? How prepared should we be?"

Tamara considers this. This type of heated discussion, these debates, is meant for her to reach some sort of understanding on the subject. It's never about being right or wrong, not to Tamara, but about achieving a level of knowledge, of truth, that she can only obtain after these intense, in-your-face, voices-raised, heated deliberations. It terrifies me at times how much the truth matters to her. How far she is willing to go to find it. Understand it. Believe it.

"I just wish the lockdowns weren't necessary," she eventually says. "I . . . I just wish all of this wasn't happening now. That we even need to do this to our children horrifies me."

"I heard Sandy Hook was a hoax."

The voice comes from somewhere else in the circle. At first, I don't know if I actually heard it or if I am just imagining it. A mouse squeaking under our feet. It pipes up just as Tamara lapses into her own thoughts, lost to the terrors of school preparedness programs.

Someone else has spoken.

Tamara turns her head, confused by who said it. We are all a little taken aback, to be honest. Even Condrey seems thrown.

Miss Gordon inches forward in her seat, clearing her throat. "The government wants to take our guns away. They have an agenda, so the only way they can get their bill to pass through Congress is to make up—"

"What are you talking about," Tamara cuts her off. It's not a question.

Miss Gordon is one of our special ed teachers. She wears a pink sweatshirt with an iron-on decal of a kitten printed across her chest. The image has faded from a few too many spins in the washing machine. That cat has deteriorated around the edges, but its paw still reaches up to wave hello at the rest of faculty. Miss Gordon has never struck me as being an outspoken individual—or, more to the point, I don't think I've ever really heard her state her case about much of anything, staunchly political opinions or otherwise. I always greet her in the hallway—*Mornin'!*—filing in with the rest of the teachers before school starts each and every day.

What nobody is willing to say, not even Tamara, is that the biggest difference—the key difference—between Miss Gordon and herself is that Miss Gordon has lived here her whole life. She is old-school Danvers. In fact, she first taught here when there still was a school in town. That one closed down, decades back. It wouldn't reopen until the rebirth of Danvers commenced and the heretical pedagogy crept in. Before everything became *touchy-feely* here. So when Tamara asks point-blank—well, not asks, *demands* to know what in the hell Miss Gordon is talking about, it's not much of a stretch to see where this is heading. Careening.

Miss Gordon sits up and speaks directly to Tamara, her double chin lifted. "I was listening to the radio and I heard it wasn't proven that the shooting actually—"

"You can't be serious." Tamara again. I can hear the disbelief in her voice. The incredulousness of it all. "Are you serious?"

"I'm agreeing with you," Miss Gordon offers. A misguided olive branch. "I don't think we should do lockdowns, either."

"But do you really, genuinely believe that Sandy Hook *didn't* happen?"

Miss Gordon glances around the circle of chairs, searching for someone to speak up. To join her. Most eyes, save for Tamara's, are now staring at the floor. "I—I heard it. On the radio."

"But it's not true," Tamara says. "You know that, right? What you're saying isn't true."

Condrey clears her throat. "We're getting off topic here . . ."

Tamara's head turns sharply toward Condrey. "I feel like this is something we should discuss. If there's a member of the faculty that actually *believes* Sandy Hook didn't happen—"

Miss Gordon sure isn't happy with Tamara's tone. "I'm just telling you what I heard. You might not agree, but those are the facts as I believe them."

"Does anybody else agree with her?" Tamara's spine is ramrod straight. "Anyone else want to chime in? Because if something like this happens here, heaven fucking forbid, I want to know who to depend on for help and who thinks it's *just a hoax—*"

"*Please.*" Condrey holds out her hands, aiming her palm at Tamara, as if she is a conductor signaling to a particularly loud violinist to tone it down. She is losing control of her faculty meeting. The music is slipping right through her fingers. This shitty symphony.

"I just think it's wise to hear all sides of the story," Miss Gordon says, crossing her arms, ready to be done with this. Probably praying for the next bullet point on the agenda.

Tamara's face sours. "*Sides?* What are you talking about? There are no *sides* to this story. It *happened*. It's *real*. Twenty students *died*. Six faculty members *died*. It's not a *hoax*."

"Well." Miss Gordon shifts in her seat, sinking just a bit, like a turtle retreating into her pink sweatshirt. "Everybody is entitled to their own opinion."

"My God," Tamara practically shouts. "I can't believe I'm hearing this! Will somebody else say something? Anyone? Am I the only one who thinks this is insane?"

"That's enough, Tamara." Condrey is on her feet. "The school board has put active shooter drills into effect and that's that. You don't like it, you can take it up with Mr. Slonaker."

We still have four bullet points left on the agenda—four fucking more—and you damn well better believe Condrey is going to make us sit through them all, addressing each and every one until we've reached the bitter end.

Tamara sits across from me with her arms crossed, muted for the rest of the meeting. Sulking. She won't look at me. See that I'm on her side.

The next thirty-four minutes are quite painful. I fold—and refold—my agenda. Before I'm aware of what I'm doing, I've origamied my sheet into a fortune teller. I hadn't made one of these since I was a kid. I'm amazed I even remembered how, folding on reflex. Kids ask it a question, and in a matter of numerical combinations, fitting your fingers into the slips, opening and closing its Venus flytrap mouth—*one, two, three, four*—your fate is revealed.

What do I want to ask it? Most kids test the fortune teller's grasp of the future with soapy questions like *Will I get married*? Or *How many kids will I have?*

In my head, staring at the fortune teller in my hands, I ask it—

Who am I?

I open and close the paper, its mouth segmenting in one direction, then bifurcating in the other, as I count—*One . . . Two . . . Three . . . Four . . . Five . . . Six . . . Seven . . . Eight.*

When I flip open the fold, the answer is . . .

. . . *will now be called Character Day.*

Marquis de Condrey, sadist that she is, won't put this meeting out of its misery until we perform one last teambuilding exercise. Or "team celebration," as she calls it.

"We're going to play Jump In and Jump Out."

Tamara's eyes finally find mine from across the circle for the first time since Condrey shot her down, imploring me to escape. *Told you so,* I psychically say back.

Everyone pushes their chairs back but we all remain in our circle, now holding one another's hands. Mr. Dunstan squeezes my hand a little too tight, his palms sweating. I feel the clamminess of his skin slide over mine. Meaty fingers. Cold-cut flesh.

We no longer need chairs to complete the ring. We are the ring. The circle has integrated itself into our bodies. Condrey calls out one of the following four commands:

Jump left, jump right, jump in, jump out.

"When I call out the instruction," Condrey says, "not only does the group have to do the command, but we have to call it out while we do it. Easy, right?"

Easy peasy.

But for round two, when Condrey calls out a command, the group has to repeat the instruction while doing the opposite. Jump left now means jump right. Jump in means jump out.

Not so easy.

Round three reverses it. Now we have to say the opposite while doing whatever the hell Condrey calls out. She presses PLAY on the boom box, Enya setting an angelic rhythm to our haphazard hokey-pokey. This circle of teachers, clutching one another's hands, hops in and out, left and right, creating a rhythm, a clumsy cadence of dancing bodies.

We're dancing. All of us are dancing. Spinning in a circle. An impenetrable ring.

Sail a-way, sail a-way, sail a-way . . .

DAMNED IF YOU DO
SEAN: 1982

Miss Betty cranked the can opener along the rim of a Del Monte can. Sean stared at the purple veins lacing her hands as she flipped the jagged lid back and poured a bland mix of cubed potatoes, diced carrots, green beans, peas, corn, and lima beans onto a slice of white Wonder bread. She slipped the plate into the microwave and heated it up for one minute. Her finishing touch was a pinch of sugar. "My secret ingredient," she called it.

Sean's stomach grumbled.

"Sounds like somebody's hungry," Miss Betty exclaimed. "Let's say grace." She always insisted on saying grace, even if she wasn't the one eating. She closed her eyes and bowed her head. Sean stared back at her. What was he supposed to do? He mirrored Miss Betty without closing his eyes, dipping his own chin to his chest, watching her pruny lips mouth the words. Even though he'd been through this ritual before, he still didn't know the words. Was he supposed to?

"Amen."

"Amen," he echoed.

Miss Betty opened her eyes and smiled. "Dig in."

Mom was late. Again. The sun had already sunk below the surrounding tree line on their block. The other children from the street had gone home, leaving Sean behind with Miss Betty. It wasn't the first time. It was becoming something of a habit, actually.

Sean didn't mind. He kind of liked it, to be honest. The vegetable medley. The stillness that settled over her kitchen. The grandfather clock down the hall that gave her home a pulse.

The houses along their street were mostly small, one-story rentals choked by weeds and made of cracked concrete. Each yard either had a rusted swing set or a cinder-blocked car out front, hood open, its chest cavity missing its most vital components.

There were four houses between Miss Betty's home and theirs. Sean could walk door-to-door in less than a minute but he'd have to turn the corner at Shoreham Street to reach his house. That meant Miss Betty couldn't see him open his door. A lot could happen in that blind spot. She'd seen a white van with no windows slowing down along their block, as if the driver were fishing through the neighborhood for kids playing on their own. Miss Betty had called the police several times to tell them about the van with its corroded underbelly, insisting the mysterious vehicle had driven around her block five times in the last few days. She was able to write down the first three letters on the out-of-state license plate, if the authorities wanted it. Could've been Florida plates. Or Colorado. Miss Betty wasn't sure. The police never sent anyone out.

All the kids loved to visit Miss Betty because she let them watch TV. Her twenty-one-inch Zenith color television set, embedded within a varnished maple console, was a tank. As long as her soaps were done for the day, Sean and anyone else could come over and watch whatever show they wanted. After-school cartoons were decided upon democratically. That usually meant *Masters of the Universe* or *Scooby Doo* if it was mostly boys—or *Monchhichis* if there were more girls there.

Miss Betty never stepped in. She didn't care what the kids watched, as long as there wasn't any foul language.

Miss Betty wasn't a babysitter. She made that clear to Sean's mother from day one. "I don't change diapers or burp babies," she warned. That Sean was five and well beyond his diapering days didn't seem to make much difference. Miss Betty was the proxy daycare for most families on the block. She never left home, save for her Wednesday hair salon appointment, so for a few dollars a week, she opened her door to any child who needed a place to play until their parents picked them up.

"By six, you hear?" Miss Betty reminded Sean's mother on countless occasions. "Not six-oh-one and certainly not six thirty. You show up late again and your boy's on his own."

"Yes, Miss Betty," Mom had said, properly chastised, time and time again.

Everybody called Miss Betty *Miss Betty*. Even the adults on the block. Was *Betty* Miss Betty's last name? Or was it her first? Did anyone around these parts know for sure?

Miss Betty's experience included raising four children of her own—three sons and a daughter, who collectively gave her a dozen grandbabies to dote over. Their christening photos lined the hallway on every inch of available surface area. Their smiling faces were everywhere.

But it was a boy who only appeared in a few pictures that Sean was curious about.

This lonesome child remained hidden farther down the hall, where the overhead lights had a hard time reaching him. When Sean found his black-and-white photograph, he paused long enough to take the child in. The boy looked to be close to Sean's age. His skin looked gray. He wore a suit, his Sunday best, most likely on his way to church. His shoes were the darkest part of the photograph, while the rest of the picture had begun to fade away.

Who's that? Sean had asked Miss Betty, pointing to the gray boy.

Oh, she replied. *That's my first son.*

How come he's only in this picture?

He wasn't long for this world. He's with Jesus now.

Since Sean attended Greenfield Academy, he rode a different bus than the rest of the kids from his block. They teased him for it, calling him "Richie Rich" to his face. Sean hated that nickname. It made him feel awkward when his mom was always counting pocket change. During commercial breaks, the other kids asked Sean—*Hey, Richie Rich, what makes you so special that you get to go to Greenfield? Your mama fucking the headmaster?* Miss Betty would kick those kids out of her house if she ever heard them speaking to Sean like that, but they still called him Richie Rich under their breath.

Sean was usually the last to leave, even when Mom was on time. Miss Betty would wait until the second to last kid was picked up before leaning over and checking to see if he was hungry.

"How is it?" Miss Betty asked, bringing him back to the present moment.

"Good," he said between bites. "Thank you, ma'am."

"*Ma'am*, nothing. Please—Miss Betty's just fine."

"Yes, Miss Betty."

At six o'clock on the dot, Sean heard *ding-ding-ding-ding-ding-ding*. His body tensed.

Miss Betty excused herself. "You keep on eating."

Sean waited in the kitchen, straining to hear their conversation. His dinner turned in his stomach. Sean always sensed the tension between Miss Betty and Mom whenever she picked him up. But today was different.

Sean didn't want his mother to find out about what happened earlier that day. He'd had an accident on the bus coming home from school. Before boarding the bus, he'd felt the initial ticklings in his bladder but figured he could make it to Miss Betty's in time. Using the bathroom at school came with problems, like Tommy Dennings. Sean preferred to hold it in whenever he could, but the longer the drive home took, the more the pressure mounted. That tickling became an itch, which soon grew into a burn.

And just like that, his corduroys turned warm. Sean froze in his seat at the rear of the bus, hoping nobody would notice. But as soon as the bus reached his stop, he had to stand. He had to walk down the never-ending aisle past all the other kids.

With each step down the aisle, Sean's corduroys made a *zip-zip* sound as the fabric rubbed together. It was surprisingly loud, like claws on cardboard—*skrk-skrk-skrk*.

Tommy Dennings noticed the dark spot on Sean's pants immediately and pointed. Tommy whispered to his pal Matt Saperstein just loudly enough for everyone to hear. *Sean pissed in his pants!*

Soon every kid onboard turned to see.

Pissy pants! they all sang. *Sean is a pissy pants, Sean is a pissy pants!*

Who had taught them this song? How did these kids all know the lyrics, just like that? It's like they knew beforehand, ready for the moment when Sean would wet himself.

Sean was sobbing by the time he reached Miss Betty's door. He fell against her soft stomach, pressing his face against her. She shooed all the other kids away. "Go play outside. No TV today."

Miss Betty promised she wasn't going to say anything—but still. Would she? He did his best to eavesdrop but could only catch scraps.

—*not like him at all. Sean never wets his—*

—*has something happened that would—*

—*of course not! Not at home—*

Both their voices dropped even further, until the conversation disappeared altogether. Sean knew they were still talking. Especially

Miss Betty. Lecturing Mom. What was she saying?

Sean Crenshaw is a pissy pants . . .

S ean had never seen anyone on the freestanding swing set sinking on Miss Betty's lawn. *Whose swing set had it been?* he wondered. *Had it been the gray boy's?* None of the neighborhood kids went near it, except for the long-haired teenagers in the jean jackets and studs when they smoked cigarettes in the middle of the night while Miss Betty was asleep. Its metal posts buckled inward, like a knock-kneed daddy long-legs about to collapse in on itself.

The swing itself eased back and forth in the evening breeze, the rubber seat drifting on its chains. Sean imagined there was a ghost sitting on it right now, watching him walk by.

"You're awfully quiet," Mom said as they turned the corner. "Penny for your thoughts?"

He slowed just enough that Mom's arm stretched back, tugging on his own. "Is your name really Jezebel?"

Mom stopped and turned. "Excuse me?"

"You always said your name was Susan."

She kneeled before Sean so they were face-to-face. The streetlamp illuminated the back of her head, the light seeping into her hair. "Who said that?"

Before Sean could answer, Mom shot back up to her feet, dragging him down the sidewalk.

"Ow," Sean cried. "You're hurting me . . ."

"That's it. No more staying at Miss Betty's. I don't want you going over there after school anymore. You understand me?"

Miss Betty had read to him that afternoon instead of letting him watch TV. The book had a leather cover and the onionskin pages were very thin. Not like a regular book. Miss Betty had flipped through until she found the appropriate passage, underlined in blue ballpoint pen.

"Thou sufferest that woman Jezebel, which calleth herself a prophetess, to teach and seduce my servants to commit fornication, and to eat things sacrificed unto idols."

These words were completely lost on Sean, save for *eat things*. He could understand that. Sort of. But what did *eat things sacrificed unto idols* mean? What was Miss Betty saying?

"I want you to pray with me," Miss Betty had said. "It's not too late, son." She had squeezed his hands tightly between her own and wouldn't let go.

His mother's hands gripped him even more tightly. Everybody was pulling him around.

Tugging.

Yanking.

He felt like a puppet. Like Raggedy Andy getting dragged everywhere. Sean felt the tug in his shoulder as his mother pulled harder. His arm was about to pop by the time they reached their house.

Once they were inside, Mom tossed her keys onto the counter. She helped Sean out of his puffy coat, dropping it to the floor along with his backpack. "I'm sorry," she said. "I . . . I just got angry. I had a long day and the last thing I need is a goddamn bible lesson from Miss Betty."

It sure didn't sound like an apology. Not a real one. Not to Sean.

"Hey," she said. "What's up, mister?"

Sean said nothing. He was mad. He was hurt.

Mom kneeled in front of him, searching his face. "Hey . . ."

One eyebrow arched upward, almost in an *I got you now* kind of way.

Sean resisted.

"Hey . . ."

His frustration was ebbing but he tried hard to hold on to it. He wanted to stay angry. It was unfair of her to do this. He liked Miss Betty. Or her TV, at least.

Before Sean could shrug away, Mom brought him into her arms and whinnied like a pony, making him giggle. She pressed him against her until he felt her heartbeat through his own chest. "Just you and me," she whispered into the top of his head, the warmth of her breath seeping into his hair. "We can do anything, as long as we stick together. Okay? You and me."

"You and me," he echoed.

If he said it enough times in his head, *you and me*, it almost sounded like he believed it.

You and me.

You and me.

RICHARD: 2013

D anvers is a renovated relic. I call it a refurbished town. Nobody wanted to live here for years. This unincorporated community had gone to seed ages ago. You couldn't find it on a map, even if you were looking for it. The straightest shot was to cross the truss bridge that spanned the Rappahannock River, serving as a crossing for State Route 3. Once you were over the bridge, you still had about fifteen miles to go before spotting the first hints of habitation.

Quiet doesn't even begin to describe it. *Sleepy* is a bit closer. *Coma* is more like it. Boarded-up storefronts blighted the main drag for decades. Amazon killed all the mom-and-pop shops. A cancer of foreclosures spread through, most homes dying a slow death of debt. If anyone tried to sell their house, it never helped that two or three homes on the block were sealed up with plywood sheets.

Then the antiquers came. The domestic treasure hunters dusted off the cobwebs, polishing this parish right on up until it sparkled again—for twice the listed price.

What most likely happened is this: Some young professional couple from D.C. took a wrong turn too many, pulling into Danvers for a pit stop after their cell service faded and the little blue dot on their Google Maps veered way off course. Then they spotted the local secondhand shop. Probably bought themselves a pre-Victorian dresser for a steal. Now that they were here, taking in the quaintness of their surroundings, well ... *Why not putter along the main drag and see what else we might find?* Sniffing through town, this couple caught wind of the empty four-square colonials going to waste just down the road. *Can you believe this? Look at these gorgeous homes! They're stunning!* They just had to bring their contractor down. A few new floorboards, a fresh coat of paint, and these homes would be good as new. *Better than new.*

Reborn.

This couple went ahead and probably whispered to their friends back in Georgetown how they uncovered buried treasure—*An honest-to-God real estate gold mine!*—less than two hours from the Beltway. Those friends probably went ahead and bought the shuttered colonial next door. Then their friends plucked up the next. Next thing you know, a pilgrimage of newlyweds seeking to escape city living swooped in, ready to raise a family with a sprawling backyard all their own.

More than 164 properties had been listed online during Danvers's decline and nobody noticed. Dozens of foreclosed homes were just wasting away. Empty manses sinking into disrepair.

And then, just like that—*Sold!*—all gone. Not a single house left. Scooped up in a realtor feeding frenzy. How long before a coffee shop opened in one of those shuttered storefronts? What about an organic grocer taking over the former Piggly Wiggly? A microbrewery?

The lifers, the elder set who had always called Danvers home, whose roots were tethered to this soil for generations, watched their town undergo a transformation before their eyes. What could they do but simply sit back as the young mothers jogged by with their aerodynamic strollers, a travel mug of ethically sourced fair-trade coffee tucked into a cupholder. This was no longer their town. Not with the flood of new blood rushing in. Danvers became a theme park. Norman Rockwell Land.

A group of civic-minded parents were motivated to incorporate Danvers and improve its services. A layer of local government made way for better education. Rather than drive their kids twenty miles to the nearest "good" school, they could start one right here in town.

The Danvers School was a remnant of the old school building that closed back in 1979 due to redistricting. It had high ceilings. Massive windows. Sturdy masonry. There just hadn't been enough students to fill it. Not only did it need infrastructure upgrades, it needed children.

And an art teacher.

By the time I moved here, the Disneyfication of this town was well underway. I didn't ride that initial wave of gentrification into Danvers. The coffee shops were already here. The artisanal delicatessens. The farmers market. This place had the veneer of Small Town, USA—but even I knew it was a mask, more a replica of a bygone era than the actual artifact. Families could have the *feel* of the good ol' days, but with all the modern accoutrements at our disposal. The greasy spoon with Wi-Fi. The gluten-free soda fountain.

Danvers was now home. My home. I just had to find my place within it. Put down roots.

I have very lofty goals for tonight's dinner. Vegetable stir-fry with peanut sauce. Tamara never imposes her vegetarianism on me—which I appreciate, thank Christ—but I have to fend for myself if I ever want to eat meat. She won't cook it, won't touch it, not one single fork tine, not for me and certainly not for Eli. Maybe there will be a fillet o' fish on the rarest of occasions, but that boy is growing up in a meat-free household . . . and now so am I.

Tamara texted to say she and Eli were running late. No explanation, which is perfect.

Time to shine . . .

The recipe suggests it will only take twenty minutes, but I'm thirty-three minutes in and nowhere near done. I should have followed the instructions and used precut vegetables—but nope, *no sir*, I chalked that up to cheating. I want this to be homemade all the way. Every slice and dice has to come from these hands, not some preprocessed package. Just the way Tamara likes it. Little did I know most of the cooking time is for cutting.

Full confession: I am not a cook. Or, more to the point—pre-Tamara, I rarely cooked for myself. I remember when Tamara first realized this. It was early in our relationship. Maybe the first or second time I spent the night at her place. Their place. One morning, after we all woke up, Tamara suggested we take a stroll to the farmers market—Eli included—and pick up some fresh veggies to make omelets. I was all for it. Why not? But we could also, you know, just go to the local diner. The greasy spoon makes perfectly fine omelets. Less hassle, fewer dishes.

Do you even like *food?* she had asked, point-blank, almost offended. The Culinary Inquisition had begun.

Who doesn't like food? I had shot back, already on the defensive.

But if you had a choice between eating an actual, home-cooked meal you made yourself or—I don't know—popping a pill, you'd be just as happy swallowing the pill, wouldn't you?

I wasn't about to cede any ground and admit that yeah, sure, I'd probably be just as happy popping the pill.

Didn't your mother cook for you as a kid?

Of course, I said, on reflex. Then I started thinking about it, sifting through my memory for my favorite meal. Pasta. I vaguely remembered loving Mom's spaghetti, I think . . .

Now I have something to prove. I've had a year to crash-course my taste buds, expanding my flavor palate. I have to learn how to cook. Not only cook, but cook *vegetarian*.

A fresh start, I think. Some very distant memory tickles at the stem of my brain.

Weegee hops onto the counter, startling me. "Jesus—"

Fucking cat.

If there's one thing I wish I'd pushed back against, it's Tamara's goddamn tabby. The cat has somehow outlived every conceivable catastrophe that could befall him. Kitty cancer. Heartworms. Diabetes. He just won't die.

Weegee squats on the counter, his flaming mane of unkempt fur ready to shed and contaminate my meal. "Shoo." I raise the spatula. I've never been a fan of Weegee, nor has he ever been a fan of me. He was here first and he always goes out of his way to make a point of it.

Weegee just stares back, indifferent to my threats.

"Hellooooo," Tamara calls from the front hall. I hear the door shut, the keys tossed into the dish on the console table. "Uh . . . What's that smell?"

"I'm burning the house down," I holler back.

"Should I call the fire department?" Tamara halts in the doorway, struck by the green sprawl before her. Her expression suggests she has come upon a stranger in her home. Who is this man making a mess of her kitchen? She mugs for my sake, pleasantly impressed—if not a bit bewildered. "*Wow*. What's going on here?"

"Surprise," I say, grabbing the knife. "Hope you two like stir-fry."

"Is that what we're calling it? Interesting . . ."

Elijah races into the kitchen, slipping past me and reaching for the cabinet.

"Mister Man!" I say. "How was school?"

"Okay," he says in a way that makes it sound clearly not okay. He opens the cabinet and pulls out a bag of Sun Chips.

"*No snacks,*" Tamara says sternly. "Straight to your room."

"But . . ."

"No buts. *Now.*"

Eli looks to me to help bail him out. I'm about to toss the kid a lifeline, which is clearly not the right call as far as Tamara is concerned. She drops the hammer. "Upstairs until dinner."

"Fine." He huffs, storming out of the kitchen.

"I'm grilling steak," I call after him. "How 'bout some juicy red meat tonight, Eli?"

"Okay!"

"Hear that?" I ask Tamara. "I'm making a convert out of him."

"Nice try." She stands behind me, flossing her arms through mine to steal a carrot. She chomps it just next to my ear. It sounds like the thinnest femur fracturing.

"So what's up with the big guy?" I ask. "Why send him to his room?"

Tamara plops down at the table where a freshly uncorked bottle of merlot waits, purchased by yours truly. "Elijah had to stay after school."

"What for?"

She takes a big gulp before answering. "He hit someone."

I put the knife down and give Tamara my undivided attention. "Seriously?"

"Apparently he was sticking up for someone else. A girl from his class was getting picked on in the hall by a couple of third-graders, so . . . he just took a swing."

I can't believe it. "Who did he hit?"

"Condrey wouldn't say. She doesn't want parents to 'take matters into their own hands.'"

"Did Eli tell you who it was?"

Tamara looks at me. It's a difficult expression to decipher. "What? You want to hunt them down tomorrow? Give them a hard time?"

"Maybe I do." I'm trying act manly. Dadly. Or something.

"That'd go over well," she mutters. "That's exactly why Condrey won't say. She doesn't want you pulling out the pitchfork and torches."

"So Condrey's protecting these dipwads? Fuck *that*. And fuck her for protecting *them*."

Tamara puts her glass down and holds up her hands in surrender. "I'm not taking her side. School policy. I'm just worried Elijah's going to be bullied by these creeps now."

Eli is already a prime target, considering his mother teaches at Danvers. Tamara has always been the cool pre-K teacher. The Doc Martens. The highlighted hair. The subtle punk accents suggest she can throw down on a Sunday night and still show up Monday morning and power through her lesson plan without puking. You better believe my inner soundtrack was blasting the Ramones as soon as I laid eyes on her.

"Here's the thing." She pours herself another glass. "You can't get mad, okay?"

"You can't tell me not to get mad at something before you tell me what it is."

"Promise me or I'm not going to tell you," she says, a little too matter-of-factly.

"You saying that makes me know it's something that's going to make me mad."

"This isn't coming from me, I swear. It's from the little man himself."

"Fine," I say. Annoyed. "I promise I won't get mad."

Tamara takes another sip. "He doesn't want you to know."

That stings. "Why not?"

"He . . ." Tamara searches for the right way to articulate this, how best to thread this parental needle. "He doesn't want you to feel like you *have* to talk to him about it and . . . you know. Make it into *a thing*."

Some invisible force presses against my rib cage. "And what did you say to him?"

"I told him okay."

"That's it? *Okay*?"

"What else was I going to say?"

"You could've said—I don't know, 'Hey, maybe Richard could help out. He's a guy.'"

"Oh, *is* he now?"

"You know what I mean."

"No. Please. You're a guy. Tell me."

"All I'm saying is . . . Maybe he could use a different perspective on this."

"From *who*, exactly?"

"Someone to help him navigate what he's going through. Help him understand it from a—from a guy's perspective." As I am saying this, I am keenly aware of how wrong it sounds, but the only course of action is to keep on talking.

Tamara is ready. "What you mean is, because he's been raised by a *woman*, it'd be helpful for Elijah to finally have a dude to step in and tell him how it *really* is?"

"That's not what I meant."

I abandon my burnt meal, the scabs of scorched peanut butter and wilting vegetables, to kneel before her. "You are, hands down, the best mom I ever met. You raised a kickass kid."

She doesn't respond so I pry her legs open just enough that I can ease between her knees. I press myself against her chest, kissing her between my effusive compliments.

"Elijah's a rock star," I continue. My hand slides under her shirt, snaking its way along her rib cage. My fingertips scale each rib, climbing until I feel the coarsened skin along her chest. Even now, it still startles me. "He stuck up for a classmate because you raised him right."

"Damn straight." Her breathing deepens at my ear, catching itself.

I run my index and middle finger along her scar tissue, tracing the textured flesh that spreads over the bulb of her shoulder and down her arm.

"I'm just here to fuck things up," I say. "Ruin the amazing work you've already done."

Tamara pulls away. "Are you trying to get out of cooking? Should I fix it?"

"No. I started this meal, I'm going to finish it, and you're going to like it, damnit."

"Good luck," she says into her glass, teeth biting the rim. I don't know if I believe she is forgiving me, but still—she is choosing to move on, letting me pull my foot out of my mouth, which is a relief. She takes another sip, swishing the wine in her mouth before swallowing.

"Who was the girl?" I ask.

"I don't know. He wouldn't say . . . I could kill those third-graders, though. Little shits."

"Got any thoughts on who they are?"

"Still want names?" Tamara grins, her cheeks warm with wine. "What're you gonna do, tough guy?"

"I'm going to find them in the hall. Drag them outside and—"

"Elijah!" Tamara says unnaturally loudly.

I turn and see him in the doorway, eavesdropping on my master plan, eyes wide.

"Hey, Eli," I say. "You hungry?"

SEAN: 1982

here did these bruises come from?

W   It was such a simple question. The answer was already there, perched on the tip of Sean's tongue. All he had to do was say a name. One simple name.

Tommy Dennings.

That wouldn't be so hard, now, would it? It was the truth, after all. The bruises were Tommy's fault. He had zeroed in on Sean at the beginning of the school year, targeting him on the playground. In the boy's bathroom. The cafeteria. The hallway. Sometimes even in the classroom, in front of all the other boys and girls, whenever Mr. Woodhouse had his back turned. Word had finally spread among the other kids that Sean wasn't actually a Richie Rich; he was a charity case, and he didn't have a dad like all the other kids in class. The perfect target.

Now he had the bruises to prove it. Mom spotted them in the bathtub and gasped.

"Where did these bruises come from, Sean?"

He wanted to tell her. He really did. But there was something about the sound of his mother's voice that worried him. An elevation in her pitch. It sounded urgent, like she was worried. Scared, even. Sean got afraid of his mom in moments like these. When her voice lifted to this level—*Code red! Code red!*—Sean knew giving her the answer wouldn't be the end of his worries with Tommy Dennings. It would be only the beginning. If he told her The Truth, Mom would get on the phone. She would call the school and demand to speak with the headmaster.

Or worse . . . What if Mom called Tommy Dennings's mother? *His goose would be cooked*, as he'd heard adults say. Sean would never survive to see the end of the school year.

"Talk to me, Sean," she implored. *"Please."* Mom's voice always sounded like this lately. Ever since Sean brought home that letter—The Letter—from school. Sean had watched her read it, witnessing the low-grade fear take over her face, but she never told him what The Letter said. She balled the paper up and threw it away, as if she were sickened by it.

When Mom talked to Sean now, her words were always urgent. She had never been good at hiding her feelings, especially when she was afraid of something. And Mom was afraid of a lot of things. Boring things, mainly. Like bills. Or work shifts. Or getting Sean to school on time so she could make it to her job. Dinner, bath time, story time, bedtime, wake up time. But something else was bothering her now. Something new.

Their *fresh start* was starting to feel like a bad start. They lived in a constant state of code red. There was a time when Mom wasn't afraid but now she acted like something terrible was going to happen to him at any moment. She had even changed her schedule so she could pick him up from school. Sean didn't understand where this was coming from. If the world was so scary, why couldn't they stay together forever? Why did he even have to go to school? Sean hated school.

Well, Mr. Woodhouse made it okay, he guessed. He was fun. He was always making up cool new games for the students to play in class. Sean knew these games were actually lessons, but he still liked them. He was becoming sensitive to the intentions of adults.

Mom had been asking Sean a lot about Mr. Woodhouse lately, wanting to know what he did with the rest of the students. She kept asking the same question, only with different words.

Had Sean answered the wrong way? It didn't seem like she was happy with his reply, even if it was the truth. What did she want to know? What was she looking for?

How could Sean give her what she wanted?

"Did Mr. Woodhouse give you these bruises, Sean?"

What a strange question. Mr. *Woodhouse*? His *teacher?* Of course he hadn't! Mr. Woodhouse always wore brightly colored sweaters, each with a different picture knitted across his chest. Turkeys or reindeer or hearts, depending on the holiday. How many sweaters did he own? A hundred? *A thousand?* He was a lot younger than Sean's other teachers. He was always excited to talk through their lessons, like he was learning these things for the first time himself. There was a spark in his eyes, and his red curls bobbed as he nodded enthusiastically whenever a kid answered a question right. He had more energy than any of Sean's other teachers. Even more than his classmates. He laughed at his own jokes. Sang louder than everyone else. To Sean, he was like a clown without makeup. Always smiling. Eyes wide. Ready to entertain.

"No." Sean shook his head. It seemed so silly to even think for a second that Mr. Woodhouse would hurt him. Sean *liked* Mr. Woodhouse. Everybody did. Didn't they?

Mom only stared back. It seemed like she didn't believe him. But Mom always believed him. Why doubt him now? That was their one rule. *Don't lie to me,* Mom would say whenever a glass broke in the kitchen or there were crayon scribbles on the hallway wall. He knew adults put value in The Truth. A version of it, at least.

"Are you sure?"

Sean didn't know what to say. He'd already told her that it hadn't been Mr. Woodhouse—*why would a teacher do that?*—but Mom wouldn't accept his answer.

He saw it in her face. Her beautiful face.

Sean always knew his mother was pretty. He thought so, of course, but he knew other people thought she was pretty, too. Men. Customers at the restaurant she worked at. Mom brought him straight home from school most days, but sometimes she would bring him to the diner while she finished her shift. He would eavesdrop on the men telling her that she had a pretty smile. That she should smile more often. *See, that wasn't so hard, was it?* She would laugh as she brought them their check, but her smile would fade the moment they left. Sometimes her face would crumple the way Sean's did before he cried.

Her face was crumpling now.

The water in the bathtub had gone cold. How long had he just been sitting in there? He felt like a California Raisin now, his skin completely pruned. How did that song go? Something about hearing something?

Sean looked down at the water. He really wanted to know what was bothering Mom, but he couldn't focus if he was looking at her face. He thought of the conversations she had with other adults whenever they came to the house. Dressed-up adults who seemed interested in asking Mom all kinds of pokey questions. Proddy questions.

Are you finding time to manage part-time work and parenting? Are you still on food stamps? What's the home environment been like since your husband left?

It was all Mom ever talked about anymore. Never with him, but with everybody else.

But Sean heard everything.

"Sean? Sean?" Mom leaned in closer, taking hold of his shoulders so he was forced to look directly at her. Only her. For a moment, he had forgotten he was in the tub. "Talk to me, baby. You need to tell me what happened. *Please*." Her voice kept climbing.

What was worse than code red? Black and blue?

More. She always wanted more from him. She wanted to get beneath his skin. Beneath his face. Her grip kept tightening. She wouldn't let go, no matter how much he squirmed, until she found whatever it was that she was digging for. Which was confusing to Sean. There were times when she didn't want to know the truth. Not really. Like whenever he got sick. If he ever complained of feeling under the weather, Mom would ask him if he was *really-really* sick. Or was he just pretending? She didn't want to hear The Truth in those moments, because Sean knew a sick day for him meant a sick day for her. She wouldn't be able to go to work, and not going to work was a major code red. But isn't that what she wanted? For them to be together?

"Listen to me, hon." Her voice strained.

Code blue!

"I need you to tell me if there's anything happening at school . . ."

Code purple!

"It's very, *very* important that you tell me the truth . . ."

Code black!

"If—if your teacher—if he's touched you. Hurt you in any way."

Code burst capillaries!

Sean just wanted to give her whatever it was that she needed from him. He wanted to give her everything. To make everything right. To make all the bad stuff go away.

He just had to figure out what the right answer was. What would make her happy? Should he tell her it was Tommy Dennings? Or did she want him to say it was Mr. Woodhouse?

The truth—or this other thing. Not a lie. Not exactly. An answer that made everything safe again. That brought code black back to purple to blue to red to orange to yellow and all the way down to the way life used to be. Back to when Mom wasn't always afraid.

That's what Sean wanted. To take her fear away. Make the world a safe place for her.

Just her and him.

Alone, together.

Sean could do that for her, he was sure of it. He had that power.

By the power of Grayskull, He-Man always said, *I have the pooooower . . .*

All Sean had to do was tell Mom exactly what she wanted, *needed,* to hear.

A game, he thought. *That's all this is. Just a game.*

And the name of this game was to say the right thing. Figure out the secret message that protected Mom, the meaning hidden within the words that would defend them both.

The Truth.

DAMNED IF YOU DON'T
RICHARD: 2013

I hesitate outside Eli's room, peering through the cracked door, just to see what he's up to before I barge in. This is all about respecting boundaries. "Got a sec, big man?"

Weegee hops off Eli's lap at the sound of my voice and hides underneath his bed. The boy eventually nods—or, I think he nods. I enter his shrine to paleontology, keeping the door open a comfortable gap. Still figuring out our footing here. *Dances with Stepdad.* Every exchange that doesn't involve Tamara is a self-conscious crossfire of questions and murmured answers that never quite hit their mark. I don't want to put him on edge straight out of the gate.

"Heard there was a little scuffle at school today. I'd hate to see the other guys . . ."

"Mom *told* you?" Eli flops back on his bed, surrounded by plastic dinosaurs, an impenetrable ring of prehistory. Pre-me. If Elijah could have his way, I reckon he'd be content to stay in the Jurassic period with the rest of his prehistoric pals, all those centuries before I rocketed into his life and destroyed everything. In Elijah's eyes, I am the meteor that wiped out the dinosaurs. I am the domestic asteroid that caused the extinction of life as he knew it. "Do we have to talk about it?"

"Not if you don't want to."

"Okay." He's back to his dinosaurs. *That's all she wrote.* Case closed.

"Who was the girl? The one you were sticking up for."

"I'm not supposed to say." Eli doesn't look at me when he says it, smashing a stegosaurus against a . . . diplo-something-or-other-acus.

"How come?" I try keeping my curiosity in check. Seems strange he'd hide this sort of thing.

"She told me not to tell."

"If somebody's getting bullied, it's good to let a teacher know. Maybe I can help?"

"Are you helping like a *teacher* or like a . . . *dad*?" He swallows the last word, unfamiliar with its taste.

"Uh-oh . . . You said the 'D' word. We're in trouble now."

"I mean," he tries. "You wanna be a dad?"

"What do *you* want?" I had practically written out a script in advance of this, practicing all afternoon, like rehearsing for some role in our fall play.

Eli shrugs. He's clearly not comfortable navigating his way through this conversation.

"You and your mom have talked about when I was your age, right? She's told you about my childhood? How I was adopted?"

There. First hurdle down. Now the "A" word is finally out there in the ether.

In front of an adult, raise your right hand and say: I promise to love my Cabbage Patch Kid with all my heart. I promise to be a good and kind parent . . .

Elijah glances up at me while keeping his head tilted down so his eyes can hide behind the cover of his hair. It is a simple trick he has perfected since I've known him. He dips his chin so that the curtain of his bangs covers his face, shielding his eyes beneath that auburn mop top.

"The truth is," I say, "I don't really remember that much about my family before. I was five, just like you are. Maybe a little older. But a lot of it is a blur for me."

This is new information for him. Is he finding any of it even remotely interesting?

"I never knew my father. My real father. He left when I was young. For the longest time, it was just my mother and me and we—well, we had a hard time making it on our own."

Liar.

"My mother loved me, just like yours. But there came a point where she couldn't—"

Stand you.

"—take care of me anymore. I had to move in with a new family, called a foster family, and they were—"

Afraid.

"—amazing. Like superheroes, really. They moved heaven and earth for me. They knew I was really sad, that I missed my mom, but they wanted me to feel loved. It was important to them for me to know that they would never replace my mother. Nobody ever would. *Could.*"

Elijah hasn't run out of the room. Hasn't brought his hands up to his ears and started humming some tune to drown the sound of my voice out. I call that progress.

"They knew a family can be made up of more than just your biological parents. A family can be made up of whoever you want it to be." *This is it*, I think. *This is the moment. Here it comes.* "So they asked if I wanted them to be my family. To be my parents. And I . . . I said yes."

Elijah keeps his chin dipped, but I can tell he's listening. The words are sinking in.

"When your mom and I first started seeing each other, we talked a lot about you. When it might be the right time to tell you about me and what my childhood was like. I told her I wanted to wait a little while. Until it felt like the time was right. And I guess now is the time. To tell you. Because . . . Here's the thing, Eli. There's something I've been wanting to ask."

Too late to turn back now.

To run.

"I know it's been hard, adjusting to this new life with me and your mom. But I think we're finally hitting our stride and I was wondering if . . . if you'd think about me adopting you."

Elijah stiffens. Becomes a human fist.

"Now I want you to know nobody will ever replace—"

That asshole.

"—your father. That's not what I want to do. That's not my intention here at all."

Isn't it, though? Isn't that my intention? Blow that fucking fucker out of the water so Elijah can finally have a fighting chance at a decent male role model in his life? Someone to look up to? Someone who won't bail on him? Someone who won't cheat on his mother? Who won't stumble in drunk beyond belief after a night out with the boys? Who won't forget which door leads to the bathroom and piss on his own kid's bed?

Elijah squirms. The weight of all this, the pressure of it, pushes him down. Does he want to make a break for it?

He's looking for his mother. Why was Tamara letting this happen? Where was she?

Where's Mom?

"All I want, Eli, is to be someone who's there for you. Whenever you need it. Your father will always be your father, and nobody's ever going to replace him. I promise."

Liar, liar.

"All I want is . . . Well. All I want is to be a family. *Your* family." I can't shut up. I can't stop myself from filling in the silence, the suffocating sound of nothing. I'm just blathering on like some idiot because I'm afraid he'll say no. "Only if it's okay with you. I don't want to do it unless you're cool with it. If you think it might be a—"

"Okay."

Elijah doesn't look at me when he says it, but I'm pretty sure I hear him correctly. His eyes are still shrouded. I can't be sure if his *okay* is an acknowledgement of what I'd said, *proof of receipt*, or if he's giving me the thumbs-up. I am a grown-ass man struggling to parse out the possible interpretations of a five-year-old's *okay*.

"Think it over. Totally take your time. If you wanna talk to your mom—"

"No. I want to."

I don't know if I'll ever be able to express this feeling. The downright relief of it all. That release of pressure, a dam cracking in my chest.

I promise to love my Cabbage Patch Kid with all my heart . . .

The subsequent flood of blood.

I promise to be a good and kind parent . . .

The absolute joy.

I will always remember how special my Cabbage Patch Kid is to me . . .

Tamara is going to absolutely lose her mind. I hope she's been hiding in the hall, eavesdropping on us. "Okay," I say, letting out all the pent-up air. "Let's make it official."

Make me a Dad.

Dad. Kinda has a ring to it, doesn't it? I want to say it over and over again, to anyone willing to listen. Race through the streets and shout it to the heavens. *I'm a dad! I'm a dad!*

"It was Sandy," Eli says.

I have no idea what he's talking about, still running my mental victory lap. "Sorry?"

"Sandy," he repeats. "From our class. She was the one getting picked on."

This house isn't mine. Not yet. The memories made within these walls are Tamara and Elijah's. The divots are filled with their days, the dust of their skin. Their fingerprints cover the walls. It will take time for me to become one with their home.

I feel like an intruder most days. A houseguest who never left, freeloading off their life.

But Tamara invited me in, hadn't she? Into her home? Their life?

When will I start feeling like I am a piece of it?

A part of them?

The dishes are hers. The glasses. The cutlery. The cookware. All hers, all acquired in the years prior to my arrival. Their kitchen was already stocked with all the necessities, so when it came time to move in, I didn't have to bother bringing my sad bachelor set of forks and knives. My chipped plastic plates. My one good wineglass. Tamara and Elijah already had everything they needed, everything I needed, so I simply donated my kitchenware to Goodwill.

All I brought into this house, their home, was . . .

Me.

It'll take time to rid myself of this feeling that I'm some kind of domestic parasite. But from the very beginning of our relationship, whenever it came down to *my place or yours*, it was always going to be hers. There was never a question. My cramped apartment never stood a chance against Tamara's cozy farmhouse. It is situated in a small grove of cedars, giving the illusion that the house is tucked into the woods, even though the neighbors are a baseball toss away. There's even a weeping willow in the backyard, just outside the kitchen window. Tire swing and all.

Tamara has been killing time in the kitchen. The bottle of wine I'd opened is now half empty. Not that I'm keeping tabs. Her glass rests on a stack of printouts. We're going to fill out the adoption forms together, plow through them one of these nights. I'm not going to say anything, but I notice the thinnest dribble of wine has formed a red ring around the top page. I'll have to reprint that sheet before we fill it out. Nothing says ADOPTION DENIED quite like a merlot stain bleeding through your application, front and center.

"So," she says, stretching the "o" out. The suspense is killing her.

"So," I volley back, milking it.

"Sure were up there for a long time. I was about to send a search party."

"Worried?"

"Of course not."

I join her at the table and pick up where I'd left off drinking, catching up to her. The alcohol hits my blood.

"You're going to make me ask, aren't you?"

"Ask what?" I grin. The cat who totally killed the canary. Weegee ain't got nothing on me. I'm feeling pretty proud of myself, I must admit, now swirling in a tide pool of wine.

I'm a dad! I'm a daaaaad! I'm—

"Such an asshole," she says, rolling her eyes. But she's smiling. Definitely smiling.

This is our life now.

We are making a family together, cobbling the bits and pieces of our previously shattered lives, stitching them together into a cuddly, huggable Frankenstein's family.

Tamara had Elijah when she was twenty-six. Her playlists of Black

Flag and Minutemen turned into lullabies and the sounds of rain or ocean waves to get Elijah to fall asleep. If we ever had friends over for dinner and used her iPod for the evening's soundtrack, the shuffle option would quickly shift from Slint to "Baby Beluga."

"It was terrifying," I say. "I just yammered on and on . . . I couldn't stop. But he said—"

My cell phone abruptly chirps, cutting me off. *Probably a robocall,* I think. Nobody calls me at this hour. But the caller ID lists a familiar area code. One I haven't seen in a long time.

I answer. "Hello?"

No answer back. It takes a moment for the automated recorded voice to click in, but I swear I hear a layer of white noise from the other end of the line, as if someone is listening.

"Who is it?"

"Telemarketer," I lie as I hang up.

Tamara's hand finds mine across the table. "What'd he say?"

"The salesman?"

"*Elijah.*"

"Oh. He . . ." My throat hitches. "He said *yes.*"

"I knew he would. Here . . ." Tamara lifts her glass. "To making it official."

"To making it official," I echo, clinking her glass with mine.

"Welcome to the family." Tamara leaves her chair and slips into my lap. Her arms wrap around my neck, embracing me. When we kiss, she tilts her head down until her hair falls over my face.

She bites my bottom lip.

"*Ow* . . . Be careful."

"Almost forgot." She leaps off my lap and runs to the counter to open the cupboard. She glances back at me. "Turn off the lights."

"Why?" I run my tongue over my bottom lip, tasting the slightest hint of blood.

"Just do it! Hurry! It's almost midnight and then it'll be too late."

I do as I'm instructed, turning off the switch. The kitchen is swallowed in darkness.

I hear a scrape—the strike of a wooden match—and slowly, the outline of Tamara's body begins to glow.

It's a candle.

Tamara slowly turns toward me. One hand cups the flame so that it won't extinguish.

"Happy birthday to you," Tamara sings.

She holds a single red velvet cupcake in the palm of her hand. The candle casts its low glow across her skin, as red as the icing itself, leaving her looking bathed in blood.

My entire body feels as if it's about to unravel. Everything that had been clenched suddenly releases itself.

"What? You think I'd forget?"

"*Tam*. We talked about this."

"I know, I know . . . I couldn't let it slip by. Not without celebrating just a little bit. Just between us, nobody else. You and me, I promise. It's bad luck to not celebrate your birthday."

"Says who?"

"Me." She straddles me again, holding the cupcake between us. The flame flickers.

"I don't even remember how old I am anymore."

"*Old*," she says. "Now make a wish."

The flame vanishes. Darkness sweeps over the room. The dimensions of the kitchen are undefined in the absence of light. The space feels larger somehow. Endless.

I don't feel like I'm here anymore.

"What'd you wish for?" Tamara's voice whispers in the dark.

"I'll never tell."

"Take a bite." Tamara guides the cake to my mouth. The icing is sweet, but just underneath that frosting, I can taste my blood. "How is it?"

"I bit my lip."

"Poor baby. Here." She presses her lips against mine, searching for blood, licking away the icing. "You know, witches were asked to bake a cake during menstruation. Sometimes . . . they'd even put a drop of their own blood into the batter. To hypnotize whoever ate it."

"Is that what this is?" Tamara's mind always goes to the weirdest places. It's part of her charm, but I can't help wondering how her thoughts led her there. "You casting a spell on me?"

"You tell me . . . Is it working?" I can see her smile as the moonlight coming through the kitchen window hits her face. Her snake tattoo.

I remember when I first saw Tamara's scars. As she described it, her mother had been frying chicken cutlets when the phone rang, leaving a pan full of oil simmering on the stove. Little Tamara, just six years old, wandered into the kitchen and reached for the handle . . .

I had three skin grafts before I turned eight, she'd told me. *The scars never went away. At some point, I decided to turn all that scar tissue into something powerful.*

Tamara's serpent slithers along my fingertips. I feel the scar, the scales of the snake's body gliding up, winding around my neck, finally reaching my chin, my lips, forcing itself through.

SEAN: 1982

It began with a game of telephone.

Mr. Woodhouse called it something else to his kindergarteners. *Whisper down the lane.* That made him sound *old*, like some kind of fuddy-duddy. Then again, Mr. Woodhouse always had a funny way of talking. He made stuff sound more important than it was. He found poetry in the little things nobody else seemed to care about. You just had to look deeper. Look closely and see the potential for *more*.

The rules were simple: During circle time, everyone in class sat in a ring. One student whispered a phrase—*Sean only eats the marshmallows in his Lucky Charms*, for instance—into the ear of the student sitting next to them. That student then whispered what they heard into the ear of the next person. Then onto the next, and the next, a daisy chain of whispers, until the last student in the circle said the sentence to the student who initiated it. That first student then said the sentence out loud for the whole class to hear—*Sean eats marsh men on the farm.* Then the kids would all laugh and laugh at how a sentence could become something new. *A fresh start.*

These kids didn't know that there had been a letter campaign against Lucky Charms. Some of their mothers had complained to the local Safeway that the marshmallows included symbols mixed in among the horseshoes and clovers. What kind of supermarket sells a breakfast cereal that peddles pagan propaganda? It's right there on the shelves, next to the more wholesome cereals—like Frosted Flakes. These motivated mothers demanded that Safeway pull this satanic brand of breakfast food. They spent their Sunday afternoons after church in the parking lot, passing out flyers.

HOW SAFE ARE YOUR CHILDREN AT SAFEWAY?

SAFEWAY IS NOT THE ONLY WAY.

SAFEWAY IS NOT SAFE.

There was a different game of telephone going on with the parents of Greenfield, spread through actual telephones. And the sentence had consequences.

Mr. Woodhouse bad-touched Matthew Saperstein.

When Matthew complained to his mother that Mr. Woodhouse had been mean to him in class, she sat her son down and insisted he explain. Matthew—Matty, as his mom always called him—was irritated at first. He had assumed he could gripe about Mr. Woodhouse and his stupid way of talking at the dinner table. She asked him if Mr. Woodhouse had yelled at him. Matty said no. She asked if he had been unfair. Matty said no. She asked if he had touched him. At that point, Matty asked if they could talk about something else, but Mrs. Saperstein was on high alert. She had been watching the news lately.

Matty's best friend, Tommy, was also in Mr. Woodhouse's class. Mrs. Saperstein and Mrs. Dennings were relatively close acquaintances, tied together by the occasional Saturday afternoon playdate. Mrs. Dennings's phone number was written on their refrigerator door, along with several other mothers from the PTA. After *The A-Team* was over and Mrs. Saperstein had put Matty to bed, she picked up the phone and called straightaway.

Mrs. Saperstein and Mrs. Dennings talked for close to an hour. Tommy had wet his bed a few nights ago, which was so unlike him, and now Mrs. Dennings wondered out loud if Tommy might be anxious about something.

"Has anything changed at home?" Mrs. Saperstein asked.

"Not a thing," Mrs. Dennings said. But as soon as the words left her mouth, she changed her mind. "You don't think . . ." She couldn't finish the sentence, the words curdling.

Mrs. Dennings knew two other mothers in their class, thanks to their tennis socials. She spoke to both Mrs. Cardiff and Mrs. Gilmore after she'd dropped Tommy off at his bus stop the following morning.

Mrs. Dennings's conversation with Mrs. Cardiff didn't last longer than twenty minutes. She mentioned Mr. Woodhouse, then asked if Mrs. Cardiff had noticed anything *peculiar* in her daughter's behavior. Mrs. Cardiff thought it was *strange* and rather *coincidental* that Mrs. Dennings would mention it because, *yes*, as a matter of fact, she had noticed the *slightest* shift in Jenny's behavior lately. She had begun waking up in the middle of the night from terrible dreams. Two nights in a row now. Never mind that Jenny had just watched Michael Jackson's *Thriller* on MTV in the basement of her friend's house while her parents were upstairs. The girls had asked if it was all right to watch it together. And why shouldn't they? It was one of the Jackson 5. Wasn't he that talented boy who sang "ABC" and "I'll Be There"? Completely harmless.

Mrs. Dennings waited until after lunch to call Mrs. Gilmore, but Mrs. Cardiff got right on the phone with her husband at work. She pulled Mr. Cardiff out of a meeting in a complete panic. Mr. Cardiff did his best to calm his wife down, cooing soothing words into the receiver, but she was adamant that he call the headmaster immediately. No, she wouldn't *take it easy*. She wanted Mr. Cardiff to fix this!

This was their daughter's safety they were talking about!

Mr. Cardiff had never been a fan of Mr. Woodhouse. He considered his daughter's kindergarten teacher to be, as he explained to his golf buddies . . . well, a bit *swishy*. He griped on the green about what the headmaster should do about it. This fruity fella in their children's midst. Teaching them lord knows what. Was he just going to let some *faggot* manhandle their kids?

By the time Mr. Cardiff had put in a call to the headmaster at Greenfield Academy, Mrs. Gilmore had personally phoned Mrs. Dellacort, Mrs. Blackmer, and Mrs. Evans.

By the time Mrs. Dellacort had gotten on the phone with Mrs. Kelly, Mrs. Blackmer had called Mrs. Cook, while Mrs. Henry and Mrs. Evans had phoned the school three times, demanding the headmaster reach out to them at once with answers about Mr. Woodhouse.

By the time Sunday services were underway, there wasn't much else for these mothers to discuss. The pews simmered with whispers about Mr. Woodhouse and his class.

Well, yes, Gloria couldn't keep her meal down just the other night . . .

Now that you mention it, I've noticed Craig has been acting rather remote . . .

Who'd blame Michael Jackson for Jenny's nightmares? This has to be something else . . .

I noticed a few bruises on Alice's leg. I thought it was just horseplay, but now that I think about it, they were a little too far up her thigh for my comfort . . .

There were twenty-one students in Mr. Woodhouse's class.

The number twenty-one represents the Union of the Trinity. The number twenty-one appears in the Bible seven times.

Seven multiplied by three is twenty-one. The number twenty-one is a symbol that represents the union of unknown superiors—or the great spiritual *masters* of humanity.

Tommy Dennings's favorite after-school cartoon was *Masters of the Universe*. His mother hadn't realized the show's main character was a boy—a prince, just like her Tommy—whose secret identity would be conjured up after he lifted his mystic sword and recited an incantation:

I haaave the pooooooooower.

Several mothers had written to the local television channel to encourage programmers that they should no longer air *Master of the Universe* due to its, as they claimed, "pagan undertones." Their letter campaign had little sway over the channel, so Mrs. Dennings merely switched the television off during that particular half hour after school, no matter how loud Tommy griped.

There was power in unifying their voices, these mothers learned. A combined strength.

Unity.

They could harness their concerns and make it one voice. One loud, determined voice. These mothers were legion—and they demanded to be heard. Reckoned with. They were not going to simply sit by as their community corroded—*downright decayed*—underneath them. Certainly not when it was their children at risk. Their little angels.

Their one voice spoke louder. More forceful. It gained strength as their numbers grew.

They would be heard.

By Monday, more phone calls were pouring into the school. It wasn't parents anymore. Concerned citizens were picking up the phone. *What exactly is happening in Mr. Woodhouse's class? What's he doing behind closed doors? What the hell's going on in your school?*

Local authorities logged ten official complaints. The headmaster assured detectives there was nothing untoward happening in their classrooms. Mr. Woodhouse was happily married. They had a child of their own, a lovely daughter. She was enrolled at Greenfield Academy as well. Mr. Woodhouse was one of the school's most prized teachers. Just last year, he'd received a regional award commemorating his commitment to academic excellence. He *inspired* his students. He was a *shining* example for all teachers to follow. The school was lucky to have him.

Greenfield stood by Mr. Woodhouse, the headmaster told detectives.

That was last week.

This week, the escalation in complaints was too steep to be written off. There was something foul happening at Greenfield, *something rotten*, even if no one could quite say exactly what. All anyone knew for certain was it had to do with Mr. Woodhouse. His name was consistently whispered among the parents, and their voices were growing louder.

The calls were coming into the school at an even clip. The administration couldn't answer them all. They needed to bring in an additional secretary just to log all the complaints.

Now other members of the faculty were being accused of following in Mr. Woodhouse's footsteps. The school had to act. Had to get out in front of this story before it was too late. This wasn't stopping. If anything, the whispers were only getting worse. Parents were organizing now. A phone tree was distributed. Parents met in the evenings to discuss and compare notes.

I heard he keeps a bag of candy in his desk to give kids who do special "favors" for him . . .

My daughter told me he likes to massage the students' backs . . .

My son says he has them play "touchy" games in class . . .

By Tuesday, only eighteen students were in attendance in Mr. Woodhouse's class. On Wednesday, it was fifteen. Ten the next. Then six . . .

Six . . .

Six.

Greenfield was hemorrhaging students. Their parents were keeping them at home. And it wasn't just Mr. Woodhouse's class anymore. It was all of them now. A letter had been hastily written by the headmaster to quell the rising tide of concerns. It was dictated, typed, and mimeographed, then sent home with each student. Not just Mr. Woodhouse's class. This was schoolwide. An epidemic. Everyone knew what was happening in Mr. Woodhouse's room.

Everyone except Susan Crenshaw.

Sean remained in Mr. Woodhouse's class even as his classmates began to vanish. Mr. Woodhouse was the first to sense there was promise in Sean. The depth of the boy's developing imagination was on full display from the beginning, even at age five. His capacity to create worlds. His questions. He was, as far as Mr. Woodhouse was concerned, a star pupil.

A bright boy, Mr. Woodhouse called him at the first parent-teacher night. *A shining child.*

When Miss Crenshaw received a note from school informing parents about an ongoing investigation regarding one of their teachers—Sean's teacher—she was utterly paralyzed. She was working herself to the bone, losing sleep just to keep her family under one roof. Now this?

Where were the warning signs? Had she missed something? *How blind could she be?* she imagined the other mothers whispering behind her back. Sean told her he'd had a tummy ache the other day, but she thought he was just trying to get out of eating his broccoli.

Now, during bath time, she noticed the berry patch of black-and-blue skin on his thigh.

Where did these bruises come from? Such a simple question. *Who did this to you? Was it your teacher?* Sean nodded. So slowly it was imperceptible at first. *Yes*, the nod said. And just like that, their precariously balanced life, constantly teetering upon collapse, came crashing down around her. Miss Crenshaw—Susan, a single mom—had let this happen to her own son.

How? It was a strange way to phrase the question, she realized later. Mainly because when she asked it, it could have meant so many things. Could be interpreted so many ways.

How could it happen? How did he hurt you? How did I let it happen? How can I stop it? How could the school let this happen? How can I protect my son? How? How? HOW?

Sean decoded the question the best way a five-year-old could. He told her the first thing that popped into his mind, a blend of both fib and truth.

Mr. Woodhouse had taught them how to play *horsey*.

December 2, 1982

Dear Parent:

As some of you may already know, the Chesterfield County
Police Department is currently conducting a potential
criminal investigation involving an employee of our school.
This undoubtedly raises some concern and serious questions
regarding the safety and well-being of your children.

In respect of the police department, and those involved in
this investigation, the school administration has agreed
to allow the authorities to proceed with their inquiry with
our complete support.

Our school records indicate that your child has been
or is currently enrolled as a student at Greenfield. If
you believe you have any information regarding this
investigation that you would like to offer, please contact
our office.

If you believe your child may have witnessed any wrongdoing
relating to their teachers or on-campus activities, please
contact our office as soon as possible. We only ask that you
please keep any information regarding this investigation
under the strictest confidence. Please do not discuss the
details or any potentially incriminating aspects of this
investigation with anyone else other than your immediate
family.

Please bear in mind that there is no evidence to
indicate that any other employee at our school is under
investigation.

Your cooperation in these matters is greatly appreciated. If
you have any further questions or concerns, please contact
our office.

With regards,
Jim Cunningham
Principal

RICHARD: 2013

Forty blank eyes stare back at me. Glassy things, like marbles, empty of emotion. They could have been dolls. Stuffed animals. Puppets, quietly waiting for me to say something.

"Who's ready to get messy?"

I never wanted to be a teacher. Never imagined I'd be standing in front of a group of kids—*my kids*—all of them waiting expectantly for me to begin our lesson for the day.

What is my plan, exactly?

What am I doing here? It's a question I've been asking myself more and more lately.

The plan is to make papier-mâché piñatas, apparently. With a little flour and water, I mixed up some homemade glue—totally nontoxic—to dip our strips of newspaper into.

This particular project is a perfect distraction for when the other teachers crank up their assessments. My kids need to blow off a little steam and clobber the shit out of something.

Condrey decided today is the perfect opportunity to survey my class. "Don't mind me," she says, as if she were merely passing by. Completely impromptu. I can't help but feel like I am under her microscope, being examined. It's becoming difficult to hide my unease around her.

We have high hopes for you here, I remember her saying during my interview, taking my hand and squeezing. *We want you to feel like you're a part of our family here at Danvers*...

I never thought I stood a chance at landing this job—what with my complete lack of teaching credentials. Yet, lo and behold . . . Now Condrey won't stop observing me. Always popping in for an unannounced visit. Sure seems to me like she never does this for any of her other teachers. Does Dunstan get this type of treatment? Am I the only one being studied?

"Just pretend I'm not here," she says over my shoulder, to the class, for my students' sake—even though I'm the one being observed, not them. "What are we making today?"

"Piñatas!"

"Sounds like fun." It doesn't sound like she thinks it's fun. "Just don't hit anyone, okay?"

At the very beginning of the school year, when Mrs. Condrey took to the intercom for morning announcements and welcomed everyone back from the summer, she introduced herself to the new students by saying, *I am Sylvia Condrey, your principal. The best way to remember how to spell "principal" is to remember I am your prince-ee-PAL. Friends till the end.*

I couldn't help but wonder . . . end of what?

My kids gather around the table as I stretch out a balloon, letting it snap against my fingers. "Whose got some strong lungs?"

Several hands shoot into the air. Not Eli's. He keeps pretty quiet in my class, not wanting to draw attention to the fact that we're now tethered together. I give him plenty of space, as per Tamara's request. He stands in the back, behind everyone else. Right next to Sandy. I've noticed the two of them hanging out a lot more lately. Wherever Sandy is, Eli's not far behind.

"Give this a go." I hand the rubber intestine off to Arvind. "Now for the messy part . . ."

Condrey steps back. Her smile remains in place, but her masked pleasantness slips a bit.

"Stick your gluey newspaper all over the balloon, like you're making a mummy." My kids squeal as I drape a slimy tendril of newspaper over the balloon. "This is the main body of your piñata. Once you're done, we can make arms and legs to create whatever you'd like. Maybe a pet? Who's got a pet at home?"

I thought about using Weegee as an inspiration, but the last thing Eli needs is to batter his own tabby. I made a horse instead. I glance over at Condrey, feeling her eyes press down on me. I have to steer my kids clear of the notion of whacking animals with a broomstick. That'll get me in a heap of shit with our princiPAL.

"Once the papier-mâché is dry, we cut through the hardened shell . . ."

I hold up the piñata I made the night before at home.

"And we pop the balloon!" I demonstrate by stabbing the scissors through the exterior, puncturing the rubber beneath. The newspaper shell remains intact. "See? All hollow."

I notice Eli lean over and whisper into Sandy's ear. I can't dwell on it, not at the moment. I clock the developing rapport between those two so I can mention it to Tamara later.

I promised Tamara I wouldn't give Elijah any preferential treatment in class. He's had a hard time of it this year. We knew it was coming. Once the others caught on that I was married to his mother, well . . . you know how kids are. Always looking for their way in to needle you.

Tamara and I married over the summer. A small backyard service just next to the weeping willow. Nothing fancy. But now there's no getting around the fact that Elijah's stepdad is also the art teacher.

It kills me. For all its progressive pedagogy, Danvers is just like any other school dealing with peer pressure. *Kids'll be kids.* The students surrounding Elijah right now, the boys and girls home-birthed from parents who moved to this quaint Southern town, dragging Danvers out from its blue collar decrepitude, are just like any other kids. Bullies.

Sandy is a target, too. I haven't quite figured her out yet. She's a bit of an odd bird. She even *looks* like a bird, a hatchling fresh out of the egg. No feathers yet. Just pale skin, her veins starkly visible. She's new to school. Just moved to Danvers over the summer. She doesn't have many friends from what I gather. Until Eli. But when I see her in class, working on her art, I swear I can spot that *spark*. I don't want to go too far. She's only in kindergarten. Lord knows I've slogged through enough shitty stick figures to know what most kids draw like. But Sandy's work is different. There's a hint of something fundamentally *other* to her sketches. Yes, they're still the drawings of a five-year-old. And yet . . . I see it. Maybe she'll rub off on Eli a little.

And who knows? Maybe their burgeoning friendship will be a good thing. For both of them. Perhaps they'll drag each other out from their shells.

I've prided myself on establishing our classroom as a safe haven. Our own clubhouse. No judgment. Each kid gets a sketchpad at the beginning of the year. It's theirs, nobody else's. They can take it home or to their other classes. All I ask is that they fill it up. Each and every page has to have its own drawing by the end of the year. Doesn't matter what. No critiques.

All I'm after is the art. I want them to take in the world around them and try to capture it on the page. I want to see life through their eyes. See the world how they see it.

The walls of my classroom are covered in kids' drawings. The Museum of Modern Masterpieces, I call it. I want my kids to take pride in their work. Hanging them up gives the students a sense of contributing to something special. To history. They're adding to a legacy. Each kid writes their name at the bottom of their painting, along with the date. That's their timestamp, so subsequent students can see how far back their legacy goes.

For as long as I can remember, I always doodled. I had a lot of time on my hands when I was younger, so I found my way to the page, sketching whenever I had a free piece a paper. If there was a blank space, I'd fill it with whatever was in my head. Let it possess the emptiness.

The images I sketched had an *unsettling maturity* to them, Mrs. Kittle, my seventh-grade art teacher, said. *He seems to have a wealth of imagery to pull from. Where does it come from?*

Then the real clincher: *Did something happen to him? When he was younger?*

Tim and Nancy caught on and started subsidizing my passion right away. Buying me blank notepads. Colored pencils. Magic markers. Anything and everything. They noticed that fledgling bit of talent within me and started to nurture it at whatever cost, no matter what.

They even paid for a two-year art program. *Watch out, Basquiat...*

Look where it got me.

"All right, gang." I pull out the sawed-off broomstick. "Who wants to take a whack?"

All cheers. Even Eli lets out a rebellious yell along with Sandy. No wonder I'm considered one of the more popular teachers around here. I let my kids hit things.

"Care to join us, Mrs. Condrey?" I hold out the broomstick for her, almost as a challenge.

She demurely laughs off the invitation, but her eyes tighten. Her face, the surface of herself, remains completely congenial—but I swear I can see something pinch. "You all have fun. But be safe! No accident reports."

I find myself breathing a bit easier as soon as Condrey's gone. It's just me and the kids again. I have a bag of candy stashed in the bottom drawer of my desk for special occasions such as this, filling my horse up with it like stuffing inside a Thanksgiving turkey. "Follow me, everybody!"

Professor Howdy is still fresh in everyone's minds, so it seems ever-so-inappropriate to take the kids over to the soccer field. I could still see where the blood had seeped into the ground when I biked through, the grass vaguely stained in a ruddy hue. The hose hadn't rinsed all the red away. We string our piñata up from the basketball rim instead. The horsey dangles a good foot over everyone's head, spinning through the air as if it's dancing. The kids all try to grab it with their hands, but it's just out of their reach. They look like they're dancing with it. Spinning.

"Is that a goat?" Sandy asks behind me. I turn around, taken aback by the sound of her voice. I didn't know she was standing so close to me.

"Good question." I examine my papier-mâché horse, or whatever the hell it is. "I thought it might be a pony. What do you think? Help me out here."

Sandy studies it for a moment, taking her time to make an astute assessment. "A goat."

"A goat it is!" The goat hovers above their heads, springing up and down with each smack of the broomstick, prancing about as the kids circle around and laugh, leaping along with him. Each kid takes a turn to break him apart. I blindfold them one at a time with a bandana, guiding them along. The sawed-off broomstick I place in their hands is now their mighty sword.

"Time to slay the bleating beast!"

Watching each student swing—and usually miss—gets the kids giggling. It takes several turns before someone finally establishes contact. Nobody deals the death blow just yet.

Trey misses. Sam misses. Larissa isn't even close.

"Who's up next?" I call out. "Eli! How 'bout you?"

He tenses. I did it again. I called him the thing—the name—I'm not supposed to. Allowed to. *Shit.* The other kids egg him on, chanting, "Eee-liiiii, Eeeee-liiiii, Eeeeeee-liiiiiiiiii!" as I blindfold him and spin him around. I can see he's blushing under the bandana. This might be more attention than he's comfortable with.

I don't see the broomstick coming right for my thigh.

You would lose your head if it wasn't attached to your shoulders, Tamara would say if she were here to see this, and she'd be right. *It's a surprise you haven't walked off a cliff yet . . .*

Laughter from his classmates swells all around. Cheers, even. Elijah pulls off his blindfold. Elation spreads all over his face, that look of anticipation. He thinks he's just busted the goat . . . but then he realizes what he's really hit. *Elijah, the Teacher Slayer.*

The other kids think it's downright hilarious. Beating up his own stepdad. Bunch of bloodthirsty pricks. Elijah lowers his chin.

"It's okay," I say, playing down the pain. "I'm okay. Don't worry about it."

I have to keep things moving.

"Who's next? Sandy—how about you?"

Sandy timidly steps forward. She runs her hands along the sides of her floral print dress, straight out of the Mormon sewing pattern catalogue, wiping the sweat from her palms. Some students exude overparenting vibes. Sandy has them in spades. Something about the way she engages with the others, students and teachers alike. Always hesitating for just a breath. It's barely noticeable, but to the trained teacher, you can sense a litany of questions going through Sandy's mind: *Am I allowed to eat that? Does it have gluten in it? What artificial additives are—*

THWACK.

Sandy takes the head straight off my goat. Its body bursts open in a ripe explosion of hard candy, bleeding Tootsie Roll intestines all over the asphalt. *Didn't see that coming.* The mob drops to their knees and scavenges for sweets. Even Eli takes the plunge, rummaging about its guts. Sandy stands back, watching the class grab fistful after fistful of candy.

"Nice swing, Sandy," I say. "You sure you don't want a jawbreaker?"

She tilts her head and squints. "My mother doesn't allow me to eat processed sugar."

"I won't tell if you don't." I want to offer an olive branch. *Just between you and me.*

"No, thank you."

"Suit yourself." To the rest, I call out, "One more minute and we're heading back in, guys. Fill up your pockets!" The other teachers are not fans of my piñata project, given that they have to contend with the sugar shock rocking their classrooms for the rest of the day.

There's still time left on the clock before the bell rings, so I let the kids doodle in their notepads back in the classroom. I busy myself by picking up the damp piñatas to take back to the drying racks. Each student has a placemat with their name on it, making it easier for me to remember whose project is whose. Too many names, too many faces. They all blur together after a while.

When I pick up Sandy's piñata—a bunny—I notice it's crushed. "What happened here?"

Sandy doesn't answer. She merely dips her chin, afraid to say. The shell has collapsed in on itself, as if someone stepped on it, and I'm suddenly filled with a low-grade rage.

"Who did this?" I ask the other students at her table, but none of them respond. The best I can drag out of them is a shrug. *Snitches get stitches.* I can't believe this.

"It fell on the floor," Sandy offers. I know she's lying. Protecting her oppressors.

"Sandy. Come on . . . You put a lot of work into this. Who stepped on it?"

"It fell," she repeats, her voice a dull monotone.

"Nobody's gonna to own up to it?" I ask the entire class, hoping one of them will weed out the asswipe who did this. "Nobody? Guess that means I'm keeping everybody's piñatas . . ."

A collective cry of injustice rises up from the kids.

"Sorry." I go about the room, picking up the last of the piñatas. "You don't disrespect your classmates like that. I won't tolerate destroying each other's artwork. Until someone—"

One piñata is left out, even though the drying rack is full. There seems to be an extra. *That's odd*, I think. Everybody's project is already on their own mat. *Whose is this?*

It's a man. Boy? He has gray skin. The kids aren't painting their piñatas until tomorrow, after the papier-mâché dries, but this one already has eyes. There's an uneven line rippling across his mouth. A grimace. An expression someone makes after tasting something sour. Something yucky.

Mr. Yucky. The name pops into my head—*plip*—and I'm immediately brought back to—

The bell rings. Students leap from their seats and head for the door.

"Whose project is this?" I call out over the commotion, but nobody answers. My kids are already caught up in the stream, riding the current to their next class.

Maybe Eli knows. He's already heading out the door with Sandy. "Elijah. Hold on a sec."

He turns, doing his best to suppress his embarrassment.

Better make this quick, I think. "You know who made this?"

He stares at the man in my hand. The effigy. The doll. Whatever it is.

Mr. Yucky.

No.

It's Mr. Yucky.

Elijah shrugs. Sandy takes his hand and the two enter the flow of students before I can say anything more.

The papier-mâché has yet to harden, so the figure feels damp in my hand. Like flesh. Actual flesh. But without warmth. Without life. The clammy skin of a cadaver. I close my eyes, and in that darkness, for just a moment, I feel like I'm holding a dead man's hand in my own.

Maybe somebody just made two papier-mâché projects? But then why not claim it.

I turn it over to see if anyone wrote their name on the underside.

There, scrawled across the sole of its right foot—what would've been this faceless person's foot—is a name written in purple magic marker.

SEAN.

I throw the piñata into the trash can.

There's no Sean in my class.

SEAN: 1983

The stitching within its left eye had come undone. The threads had frayed, unraveling from the quartet of buttonholes. It looked like he was bleeding out.

The sock puppet refused to blink. It only stared back at Sean.

Mr. Yucky.

Peach-colored plush. Its slack mouth wrapped around the entirety of its head, its lipless grin far larger than any normal mouth should ever be.

Maybe it was more like a bear trap. That's what the puppet's mouth reminded Sean of. *A trap.* It hung open, waiting to capture his words, yearning for somebody's voice to fill it.

At the center of the therapy puppet's overalls, resting upon its heart, was a fluorescent green sticker. Printed along the top of the sticker, in bold block letters, was the word POISON. And in fine print, barely legible from this distance: IF INGESTED, DIAL 911 IMMEDIATELY.

Sean couldn't read those words. Not all of them. *Ingested* felt foreign to him, like another language. But Sean knew that sticker. He had seen it plastered on the bottles and boxes hidden beneath their kitchen sink at home. It was an unhappy face, neon lime green skin, eyes pinched tight into lightning bolts of anguish. Its tongue stuck out from its frowning mouth.

Poison. Sean knew how to read that word because Mom had made him repeat it, a household incantation, pointing the word out wherever it materialized in their home.

In the bathroom cabinet.

In the broom closet, amongst all the things he wasn't supposed to touch.

In the garage.

The sticker was a warning: *Don't ever drink me. Don't ever touch me. Don't ever let me inside. I can kill you, if you ingest me . . .*

Whatever was brewing inside those bottles, those plastic containers with complicated names, was never, ever to be *ingested*. The creamy pink and blue and green liquids were toxic.

So what did that mean for this puppet? Was it harboring noxious toxins inside its plush body? Was its blood poisonous like the sticker said? What kind of thoughts did Mr. Yucky have?

What were his secrets?

Sean couldn't help but dwell on the broken thread inside its left eye. What if he plucked it? Would the artery untangle itself? How far did the vein go? How long would it take for Sean to pull on that string before that button eyeball popped out from its socket?

The puppet was supposed to be a boy, just like Sean, but calling him a "he" didn't feel right. Didn't feel *real*, no matter how much Miss Kinderman insisted Sean should consider this lifeless object was just like him. *He's just like you,* she had said. *You two could go to the same school. He could even be in your class! I bet you have a lot in common. Why don't you say hello?*

Miss Kinderman used her fingers to comb its tangerine-colored hair. It wore a pair of overalls that tapered off at its torso. It had no legs. Everything below the waist was gone. Its arms flopped limp at its sides.

He, Sean reminded himself. *It's supposed to be a he. Not an it. He.*

A boy, just like him.

Was Mr. Yucky waiting for Sean to say something? To break the silence? The office was so quiet. Full of dolls. Puppets of all kinds, suspended from the walls. Doctor puppets. Mommy and daddy puppets. Police puppets. All of those open mouths. Silently gaping. A muted chorus.

Some dolls looked more lifelike than others. *Anatomically correct* was how Miss Kinderman described them. Those puppets had no clothes on at all. Their boy parts and girly parts were completely exposed. Sean couldn't help but blush. His cheeks felt hot from just glancing at them. He knew he shouldn't look, turning away, still aware of their presence.

Sean scanned the office while Miss Kinderman busied herself with her notepad, scribbling something. She was always taking notes. He would say something and she would nod, looking very, *very* interested, like he had just said the most interesting thing in the whole wide world. So interesting, in fact, that she wanted to make note of it. Write it down.

Was Sean really that interesting? Were the things he said actually that special? Miss Kinderman always made him feel special. The things he said were *noteworthy,* she explained.

He liked feeling special. He wanted to make Miss Kinderman think he was important. If he could just keep saying interesting things, *noteworthy* things, he might feel special forever.

Sean had something to say. Something *noteworthy.*

Now people wanted to hear.

Listen to *him.*

First, he'd told his mom. Then she made him tell the police. Then another type of police officer who didn't have to wear a blue uniform. He still had a police badge, but he kept his in his pocket, hidden away from everyone. That officer had a lot of questions for Sean.

The more people Sean talked to, repeating what he'd said to his mother—or what he thought he remembered saying, it was getting harder to recollect exactly what he'd told her—the more other people wanted to hear him say it. Repeat it. *Tell us again what happened . . .*

These adults made Sean feel like he had something special to share. *Just like the teachings of Jesus,* Miss Betty had said. *When he spoke, the world stopped. Everybody listened.*

This was the first time Sean had ever been listened to. Truly listened to. Before, nobody other than his mother and Mr. Woodhouse really cared about what he had to say. Now adults were asking him to *tell them more.* Now they were *all ears.* He'd never felt that kind of power before.

I haaaave the pooooower . . .

Sean just had to remember what to say.

Keep his story straight.

Now it was Miss Kinderman's turn to listen. She was nice enough. She reminded Sean of his mom, only . . . sunnier. More smiles. He felt bad for thinking it, but it was true. His mom couldn't keep still. Her eyes were looking more red. *Bloodshot,* that's what it was. Her hair was a bit frizzier. The things that made his mother so beautiful, so special, were chipping away.

Not Miss Kinderman. Her hair curled into golden waves. It reminded Sean of a poster in his classroom at school. It was a photograph of a surfer barreling through a clear blue tunnel of water. At the bottom, it read HANG ONE, TWO, THREE, FOUR, FIVE, SIX, SEVEN, EIGHT, NINE . . . *TEN!* The poster was a counting game. A play on words.

Sean liked to play word games. Maybe that's what this was all about.

Just another game.

Looking at the waves that cascaded across Miss Kinderman's temples, he couldn't help but count to ten to himself. It was a force of habit. Whenever he saw waves, he automatically started ticking off in his head—*One, two, three, four, five, six, seven, eight, nine, ten.*

Miss Kinderman looked like she could've been the same age as Mom, but all adults looked old to him. Miss Kinderman wore makeup, though, in a way that made him realize she wanted people to know she was wearing makeup. Her skin shined. Glimmered, almost.

Their first interview had been a downright disaster. Even Sean knew that. It only lasted a few minutes before he broke down crying. Miss Kinderman had dressed up like a scarecrow. "I thought you might need a friend," she'd said in this nasal, high-pitched voice. It didn't sound real at all to him. "Everybody likes Cabbage Patch Kids . . . Do you like Cabbage Patch Kids?"

Sean didn't know what to say. He only stared at this grown woman wearing a Halloween costume. Overalls and a wig made out of yarn. Talking in a funny voice. "Think of me as a pal!"

Miss Kinderman might have wanted to look like a Cabbage Patch Kid, but the dimples and stitchwork resembled a scarecrow. The expanded smile, her lips painted beyond their normal proportions, stretched across her cheeks, all the way to her ears. Sean had slipped into a crying fit that promptly ended their first session before it even started. No interview that day.

Miss Kinderman didn't have to dress up in a costume to make Sean feel safe. All he needed was someone to listen. Miss Kinderman was always excited to hear what he had to say.

So why was Mr. Yucky here?

There was a large mirror that took up nearly the entire length of Miss Kinderman's office. Sean gazed into his own reflection. He spotted the reflection of the puppets behind him.

Over his shoulder. Staring at him.

The room was beginning to make him feel scared.

Miss Kinderman slid her fingers into Mr. Yucky. Suddenly he gasped to life and smacked his lips, opening and closing his mouth until finally finding his voice. "Heya, Sean!" Mr. Yucky beamed. He sounded like Mickey Mouse with a head cold. "Whatcha thinking about?"

Miss Kinderman receded into the shadows. She wasn't there anymore. Just Mr. Yucky now.

A boy. Sean could see him.

Sean and Mr. Yucky could tell each other anything. *Everything*, just like Miss Kinderman had suggested. But Mr. Yucky had no ears. How could he really listen to Sean? Mr. Yucky had the same funny way of always asking the same exact thing, just like the adults did, only in different ways, changing the words a little bit to make it sound new. But it wasn't.

Tell me about Mr. Woodhouse . . . What was it like in Mr. Woodhouse's class? What did Mr. Woodhouse do during naptime? What did Mr. Woodhouse say to you when he took you to the supply closet? Did Mr. Woodhouse bring any other teachers into class?

Woodhouse, Woodhouse, Woodhouse! How many ways could Sean answer the same thing? Bread crumb questions—that's all this was. A game. Maybe Mr. Yucky and Sean were playing the same game he had played with his mother. If Mr. Yucky asked the same question, over and over again, that meant Sean had to figure out the right answer. Until he answered correctly, he'd be stuck in the same spot, unable to move on to the next round.

He just had to listen closely. Listen to the clues. The answers were there, somewhere, embedded within Mr. Yucky's questions. It wasn't easy. Sometimes the questions led to a dead end and Mr. Yucky would give up and move onto a different riddle. Sean always felt like he was letting him down in those moments. Like he'd failed. He didn't like that feeling. Failing. Losing.

So he tried harder. *Harder*. As hard as he could. Winning was the best feeling. Mr. Yucky's voice would lift even higher, saying, *Great job, Sean! You're doing great! So brave!*

He did feel brave. Powerful. Mom would be so proud of him.

Just a game. A puzzle. It was all a matter of listening for the clues, the hidden meaning within the words, and answering back. Echoing. Hear whatever Mr. Yucky wanted Sean to say.

The game may have started with Sean and his mother, but now they were inviting others to join in on the fun. How many other people could he get to play along? A hundred?

A thousand?

A million?!

He suddenly thought of a song, that song from the commercial, singing it to himself—*I'd like to teach the world to sing . . . in perfect harmony . . . I'd like to buy the world a Coke . . . and keep it company . . .*

DAMNED IF YOU DON'T
RICHARD: 2013

What do you think? she asked when I first moved in.

It's great, I managed.

The standalone garage was built to look like a barn. Its wood-paneled sidewalls faded into elephant skin. The rolling door no longer rolled, its runners rusted in their tracks, so we entered through the side door. The air was heavy with mildew, waiting for release.

You can use it as a studio, she said. *Your own workspace.*

The garage was stacked with boxes four or five high, full of artifacts from her and Eli's life before me. Out of sight, out of mind.

You're just giving me the garage? No strings attached?

Why not? Not like anybody else is using it. My wedding gift to you.

All these boxes, just for me? Aw, honey . . . You shouldn't have.

We could bring out a space heater when it gets colder. Maybe we could even winterize it. Some insulation and I bet . . . Tamara stopped when she realized I was staring at her. *What?*

I appreciate the push, but . . .

This was all a not-so-subtle way of suggesting I should get out of my head and back to doing something, *anything*, vaguely creative. Just the gentlest of nudges.

Am I pushing?

Not at all. But she was. A cattle prod to my ass. *Sometimes I just have to stay stuck, you know? I'll crawl out of my skull when I'm ready.*

I want the house to feel like it's yours, too. I thought having your own studio might help.

I love it, I said, hooking one arm around her neck and drawing her near, kissing her on the side of her head. *It's perfect. You're the best. Thank you.*

Now you're just patronizing me.

No—I'm serious. Having a studio is just the kinda kick in the pants I need.

I'm just relieved you're not demanding a man-cave . . .

That was an option? I take it back.

Not happening, sorry. Tamara peeled back the lid on one of the cardboard boxes and peered in. *You can get back to your work whenever you feel up to it. No pressure.*

No pressure, I echoed.

I can't remember when I gave up on my art. It didn't happen overnight. It was by degrees, over the course of years, with a series of the simplest sacrifices—*do I stay in and sketch or do I go out to the bar*—until eventually, there wasn't any inclination to draw left.

My last exhibit—if you could even call it an exhibit—was some god-awful group show in Richmond. A friend was the manager at World Cup, and she wanted to fill their evenings with poetry readings and God knows whatever else, so she hatched the bright idea to have monthly art exhibits. I hung a couple self-portraits up in the back, just next to the bathroom. I was, what, twenty-eight at the time? Christ, *twenty-nine*? Was this what my art career had amounted to? A gallery in some tucked-away corner, the sound of flushing toilets providing some on-the-nose atmosphere? (Literally. You could smell emana-tions of Lysol.)

I didn't consciously give up art. My ambition just faded away. How long had I been telling people I was an artist, even when I hadn't picked up a stick of charcoal for months? It was how I had identified myself at dinner parties. It was what I told Tamara when we first met.

Now I had inherited her garage. Partially to make her happy, par-tially to try to rekindle that spark. First things first, though—I had to clean it out. Purging their past became my summer project. Which soon became my fall project. Which was increasingly inching toward becoming my winter project. Somebody had to empty all the boxes. The landfill of their family. Nobody had set foot amid the clutter of cardboard and cobwebs. I felt like Tamara had lived twice the number of lifetimes I've lived.

I spotted a TV/VCR combo in the far corner. I wondered if it still worked. Maybe there was a box of dusty workout VHS tapes out here, as well. My reflection stretched across its obsidian screen, almost as if I were dancing. I noticed, just above the television set, a paper wasp's nest where the wall met the ceiling.

I chipped away at the garage on weekends. I would drag out one box at a time, open it, and assess the value of the belongings inside. After a few hours of cleaning, I was coated in a dusty layer of sweat and cob-webs. But I could finally spot the back wall of the garage. I couldn't stop now.

What to toss? What to keep? All the Halloween decorations, the knots of Christmas lights. There were no instructions from Tamara on any of this. She probably would've been happy for me to throw it all away. That way, she wouldn't have to know what I'd gotten rid of.

Skrch.

A box shifted on its own. In the rear. I swore I heard it.

Skrchskrch.

From the corner of my eye, I thought I spotted a box move. I stopped and turned, staring at the skyline of cardboard and waiting for whatever it was to move again.

I wasn't going to play this game. I wasn't going to let my imagination get the best of me.

Skrch.

I saw it shift this time. The bones in my body locked. All I could do was watch the box jostle on its haunches. Something was inside, scraping against the cardboard. I forced myself, willed myself, to hold out my hand. Reaching for the flap, I flipped the lid back and—

A pile of possums was nestled inside.

There had to be about a half dozen newborn possums huddled together, writhing about in the box. Pink, hairless bodies. They hadn't opened their eyes yet, craning their necks toward the shift in light. Mewling at me with thin voices, as if I were their mother. *Where's Mom?*

I left the box outside. Let nature take its course.

I uncovered an unmarked box buried deeper in the cobwebbed stacks. Peeling the flaps open, I was met with the musty smell of mildewed clothes. Men's sweaters. I pulled one out and held it up. Motes of dust swirled out from its sleeves, spiraling in tight rings through the sunlight reaching into the garage. It had a home-stitched essence to it. Certainly not something bought at the J. Crew down the street. Someone sewed this. Tamara, no doubt. Moths had made a meal of this moss green turtleneck, a few stray veins of yarn unraveling at the cuffs.

Eli's father.

What was left of him. This must have been Hank's box. All the artifacts that had been left behind had made their way here, buried among the plastic pumpkins and Santa hats.

I dug in, hoping to learn a little bit more about this man. I'd only heard stories. Tales from Tamara of the Man Before. Maybe there was something else to glean from him in here.

What was Hank like? I'd ask.

Believe me, she'd always say, *the less you know about him, the better.* She never wanted to talk about him. If he ever came up, she'd steer the conversation as far away as possible. Almost like she didn't want him to exist. Certainly not in Elijah's life.

Tamara and I never dug into each other's past. I didn't ask her about her childhood and she didn't ask me about mine. There was an unspoken agreement between us about the lives we had led before we found each other. Who we were before we met, our ups and downs, were behind us. All we had were our scars—some more visible than others—and that was enough to tell the story. Our past didn't need to define our day-to-day, as long as we were honest about who we are now.

So why had she kept all of her ex-husband's crap? How could she not have thrown his things away? I wasn't about to get jealous over some box, but it was strange to me, meeting this man this way, learning about him through his discarded belongings. A lost and found for one.

I kept Hank's box. What if he came back for it one day? I'd have to explain that I'd been the one who tossed him out, which wasn't something I felt ready to do. The others ended up by the curb on trash collection day, while his box stayed in the corner, under the wasp's nest.

Next step was to set up my studio.

Before school started, I had cleared the floor and put up some shelving units. Tamara was pleasantly pleased with herself for assigning me a house project, which, in all honesty, I had begun to suspect was some sort of pretense for me to clean out their goddamn garage.

No matter. The space was mine now.

After the whole papier-mâché incident, I told Tamara I was going out to the studio for a bit before dinner. Just to wash the day away. Class left me a little rattled.

I can't put my finger on it, but I can't stop thinking about—

Mr. Yucky

—that papier-mâché puppet. Who could've made it? I decide to get my mind off things and finally christen my new workspace with a charcoal sketch. Just a little drawing to limber up the ol' imagination. See if I still have it in me. Tamara would complain about how everything I touched had blackened fingerprints all over it if I ever sketched, but that's the price of inspiration. Secretly, I think she liked it. It's her way of keeping tabs on me. She'll know I've been working.

So what am I going to draw? I stare at the white space on the sketchpad, losing myself in the vast expanse. When working with charcoal, you bring darkness to the page. The shadows come first. Before the image clarifies, before you even see what you're drawing, it's all black.

I prefer charcoal because of its impermanence. It's a delicate substance but there's a brittle quality to it as well. It allows for quick sketching to capture an image before it disappears from the mind's eye. But charcoal fades faster than most other materials. Without a fixative, the charcoal particles won't adhere to the paper. Not permanently. They will fall off, like dust. The image itself drifts away from the page over time, until it's gone altogether.

It's cold out here. Tamara is right—I should winterize this place. The temperature's only going to drop the deeper into the year we go. Winter is on its way and without a heating system, I'll freeze. Just over my shoulder, I spot a cardboard box in the corner and remember what it is. I reach in and pull out what I know is already there.

The sweater fits perfectly.

Beside a few loose threads, it's still a good sweater. Snug. It's strange to be wearing it, but let's just consider it a quick remedy for the cold. I'll take it off before I head back to the house.

I saved all of Tamara's CDs, stuffed in a box along with a dinged-up Discman. I sift through her old albums until I find the perfect soundtrack for tonight's endeavor.

The Police. *Synchronicity.* I haven't listened to this in ages.

I slip on Tamara's headphones, the foam disintegrated but still usable, and press PLAY. Let The Police take me away. Track one kicks off and I pick up a stick of charcoal.

Sketching has always been a somnambulistic act. I don't want to think. Don't want to be conscious of what I'm drawing while I'm working on it. I tend to shut off and let the work take me away, as if in a trance. I'll eventually wake up to an image. Music helps.

I wait for the shadows. Wait for an image to rise from my mind. One stroke. Then two. I'm conducting a sort of séance here.

Skrch.

Skrch.

Skrch.

The charcoal scrapes over the sketchpad.

Skrch.

Skrch.

Skrch.

Shadows seep into my peripheral vision, the charcoal dust blotting out everything around me, until I head off somewhere. Somewhere else. Far away from here.

Skrch.

Skrch.

Skrch.

The image materializes over time, like conjuring a memory. What am I drawing? Even I don't know. Not yet. Not until I snap out of it.

At some point I realize I'm more than halfway through the album. Where did all that time go? I step back and take in the image.

Mom.

Her hair fans all around her head, as if she's drifting underwater.

There's someone else. Someone hiding just over her shoulder. A boy. The shading is faint, as gray as a wasp's nest. His eyes are two black slashes. He has no mouth to scream.

INTERVIEW: January 10, 1983

KINDERMAN: I'd like to introduce you to someone, Sean.
  A friend. I think he could probably be a friend to
  you, too. Would you like to meet him?
CRENSHAW: Okay.
KINDERMAN: This is Mr. Yucky. That's a funny name,
  isn't it? Mr. Yucky isn't really yucky. It's his name
  because he helps boys and girls like you talk about
  all the yucky stuff that they don't want to talk
  to anyone else about. Have you ever had any yucky
  stuff happen to you that you didn't want to tell
  anybody, Sean?
CRENSHAW: (Nods.)
KINDERMAN: Well, I'm glad I get to introduce you two
  to each other! Mr. Yucky and I have been friends
  for so long. I've introduced him to a whole bunch of
  other boys and girls, just like you. He's helped so
  many kids. He loves to help. When I first met you,
  I thought, *Oh, I bet Sean could really use a friend
  like Mr. Yucky. They'd had so much fun together.
  They would have so much to talk about.* What do you
  think? Do you think you'd like to be friends with
  Mr. Yucky?
CRENSHAW: Okay.
KINDERMAN: Good! That's great to hear . . . Mr. Yucky,
  this is Sean. (Modulating voice:) *Hey, Sean!* (Voice
  returning:) Don't be shy . . . Did you know Mr. Yucky
  has already met your classmates? He's talked with
  them about some of their yucky stuff . . . You can
  tell they feel so much better already. It's nice
  to have somebody to talk to. Who'll listen to you,
  don't you think? That's what Mr. Yucky does best. He
  listens. Listens to everything. Even the stuff you
  think you're not supposed to talk about. Okay?

CRENSHAW: Okay.

KINDERMAN: Do you think you have something you want to say to Mr. Yucky?

CRENSHAW: (Shrugs.)

KINDERMAN: It's okay. There's nothing to worry about. Mr. Yucky is your friend now. We're all friends here. And that means we can talk about anything and everything. The good stuff, the bad stuff. Because that's what friends do, right? They tell each other everything. No secrets. You don't have to keep any secrets from Mr. Yucky, okay? Even the stuff you don't think you should tell other people. Even your mom. Are there things you don't tell your mom?

CRENSHAW: Yeah.

KINDERMAN: Oh yeah? Like what?

CRENSHAW: (Shrugs.)

KINDERMAN: You want to tell Mr. Yucky? You don't even need to look at me, if you don't want. I'm not even here. It's only you two, okay? You and Mr. Yucky. (Modulating voice:) *Hey, Sean! Whatcha thinking about? You got something you wanna tell me? Something that happened to you at school? With your teacher?*

CRENSHAW: (. . .)

KINDERMAN: *You like to play games? I heard you're really good at games.*

CRENSHAW: Yeah.

KINDERMAN: *You ever play a game called horsey?*

CRENSHAW: Yeah.

KINDERMAN: *How do you play?*

CRENSHAW: You get on your hands and knees and pretend you're a horsey and another person gets on your back and rides around like they're a cowboy.

KINDERMAN: *What about your teacher? Have you ever played horsey with your teacher, Mr. Woodhouse? Did he show you and your friends how to play?*

CRENSHAW: No.

KINDERMAN: *Huh. That's weird . . . Because when we talked to Samantha, she said Mr. Woodhouse showed the class how to play horsey during naptime. Do you think Samantha made that up? Do you think she lied? Are you calling her a liar?*

CRENSHAW: No . . .

KINDERMAN: *Are you lying, Sean? Are you a liar?*

CRENSHAW: Mr. Woodhouse said it was quiet time and . . . he turned off the lights.

KINDERMAN: *Does he always turn off the lights?*

CRENSHAW: At quiet time, yeah.

KINDERMAN: *Then what?*

CRENSHAW: He, um . . . He told us to find a spot on the floor.

KINDERMAN: *And then? Sean? What happened next?*

CRENSHAW: He, um . . . He got on the floor and pretended to be a horse.

KINDERMAN: *Are you sure?*

CRENSHAW: He let us ride him like a horse.

KINDERMAN: *Who? You? Your classmates?*

CRENSHAW: We took turns riding around the class and—and sometimes he'd pretend to be a horse and make sounds.

KINDERMAN: *What kind of sounds?*

CRENSHAW: Horsey sounds.

KINDERMAN: *Can you pretend to make the sound now?*

CRENSHAW: Yeah, it was like . . . like . . . like . . . like this. (Grunts.)

KINDERMAN: *That doesn't sound like a horse. Don't be stupid. Are you stupid?*

CRENSHAW: No.

KINDERMAN: *'Cause that sounds more like somebody getting an ouchy.*

CRENSHAW: No, it wasn't an ouchy sound. It was a good

sound.

KINDERMAN: *A good sound?*

CRENSHAW: Yeah, a happy sound.

KINDERMAN: *Have you heard adults make that sound? A man and a woman?*

CRENSHAW: (. . .)

KINDERMAN: *Sometimes parents make that sound together. Have you ever heard your parents make that sound together? Your mommy and daddy?*

CRENSHAW: Sometimes.

KINDERMAN: *When Mr. Woodhouse made these sounds, did he seem happy?*

CRENSHAW: Yeah.

KINDERMAN: *Did he seem to be having fun?*

CRENSHAW: Yeah.

KINDERMAN: *A lotta fun?*

CRENSHAW: Yeah.

KINDERMAN: *Was Mr. Woodhouse wearing any clothes when he was playing horsey, or did he take them off?*

CRENSHAW: He took them off.

KINDERMAN: *Were you wearing your clothes?*

CRENSHAW: Yeah. I mean, no.

KINDERMAN: *Were other students wearing their clothes?*

CRENSHAW: No.

KINDERMAN: *Was Charlotte wearing her clothes? Craig?*

CRENSHAW: No.

KINDERMAN: *What did Mr. Woodhouse do after he took off Charlotte's clothes?*

CRENSHAW: He—he made her ride him like a horsey.

KINDERMAN: *Was that all he did?*

CRENSHAW: Then he started making the sounds.

KINDERMAN: *The horsey sounds?*

CRENSHAW: Yeah.

KINDERMAN: *And what did you do? What were the rest of your friends and classmates doing while this was happening?*

CRENSHAW: We watched.

KINDERMAN: *You watched?*

CRENSHAW: Mr. Woodhouse made us watch and wait our turn to ride.

KINDERMAN: *Then what?*

CRENSHAW: He'd ride around the class and then it was somebody else's turn.

KINDERMAN: *You took turns?*

CRENSHAW: Some were asleep.

KINDERMAN: *Because this happened during nap time? Quiet time?*

CRENSHAW: Uh-huh.

KINDERMAN: *Seems hard to sleep while there was so much horsing around . . . Don'tcha think? How could your friends sleep through all the loud horsey sounds?*

CRENSHAW: Because they were tired?

KINDERMAN: *Did Mr. Woodhouse give you and your friends anything to drink?*

CRENSHAW: He gave us cups of Hi-C. Orange. Orange is my favorite.

KINDERMAN: *Did you see him make the Hi-C, or was it already made?*

CRENSHAW: He, um, he made it.

KINDERMAN: *So it was the powdery kind? He gave everybody in class a cup?*

CRENSHAW: Yeah. Waxy cups. The kind that you can crumple with your hand.

KINDERMAN: *Did you ever drink the Hi-C?*

CRENSHAW: Yeah.

KINDERMAN: *How did it make you feel?*

CRENSHAW: It was sweet.

KINDERMAN: *Did it ever have a chalky undertaste?*

CRENSHAW: Chalk?

KINDERMAN: *Powdery. Like there's too much drink mix at*

the bottom of the cup. That it's not stirred all the way. So it tastes a little chalky.

CRENSHAW: Yeah. Chalky.

KINDERMAN: Did it ever make you feel sleepy?

CRENSHAW: Uh-huh.

KINDERMAN: And then you'd take a nap?

CRENSHAW: Then we'd play horsey and then we'd take a nap.

KINDERMAN: Then what happened? It's okay, Sean. It's me! Your pal, Mr. Yucky! You can tell me anything. I'm not gonna tell anybody, I promise!

CRENSHAW: I don't remember.

KINDERMAN: Don't be stupid! You remember. Don't you?

CRENSHAW: He—he would lay down with us.

KINDERMAN: How'd that make you feel? Were you sad? Scared?

CRENSHAW: Silly?

KINDERMAN: Did it make you feel uncomfortable?

CRENSHAW: I don't think so. It was just a game. We all played it.

KINDERMAN: The class? Your friends and Mr. Woodhouse? Were there others?

CRENSHAW: Others.

KINDERMAN: Other who? Adults? Teachers?

CRENSHAW: No.

KINDERMAN: Are you sure? Really, really sure?

CRENSHAW: I mean, yeah.

KINDERMAN: Yeah, what?

CRENSHAW: It was teachers.

KINDERMAN: And were the teachers wearing clothes or no clothes?

CRENSHAW: No clothes?

KINDERMAN: And what were the teachers doing? Were they watching?

CRENSHAW: Watching.

KINDERMAN: *Is that all they were doing? Are you sure? Were they making the happy sounds?*

CRENSHAW: Some of them, yeah.

KINDERMAN: *Were they playing horsey, too?*

CRENSHAW: Yeah.

KINDERMAN: *All of them?*

CRENSHAW: All of them. And when it was over we'd put our clothes back on and take a nap.

KINDERMAN: (Voice returning:) What a brave boy you are, Sean. Don't you think Sean's a brave boy for sharing that story with us, Mr. Yucky? I think you're very brave! Thank you, Sean. I bet your mother is very proud of you.

(END OF INTERVIEW.)

RICHARD: 2013

I swear I didn't lose Elijah. Not exactly.

He was with Mr. Stitch.

The Fall Harvest Fair has always been a big draw in Danvers. For three days the freshly cropped soybean fields surrounding Hal Tompkins's farmhouse turn into grassy parking lots. Slightly stoned teens don fluorescent-yellow vests and use air-traffic-control batons to direct a steady stream of SUVs into an evenly segmented grid. From there, the flannelled families of Danvers follow the colored lights and the sweet hint of cotton candy drifting in the breeze. In the background, you can hear the shuddering of portable roller coasters weaving along their rickety tracks. You can hear the screams.

Eli was in a bit of a mood during the ride because Weegee had gone missing. He refused to get in the car, standing on the front porch and calling out, *Weegeeeee? Weeeeeeegeeeeeeeeee!*

I figured he was out roaming the neighborhood. Can't say I'm heartbroken over the cat's absence, but it's probably best I keep it to myself. But now Eli's sulking in the back seat.

"Don't worry, baby," Tamara offers. "Weegee will come home."

"No he won't," he mumbles. It's not like Eli to be so fatalistic about this sort of thing.

"Have faith, mister," I say. "He's probably just made a friend. Speaking of which . . ." Terrible segue—but you take what you get. "Looks like you and Sandy are becoming pals."

"Who's Sandy?" Tamara asks the rearview mirror.

"Nobody." Eli sinks deeper into his seat, his eyes never breaking from his window.

"A girl from class," I say. "She's been having a tough time, but Eli's looking out for her."

"That so?" Tamara seems impressed. To me, she softly asks, "Is she . . ."

The girl Elijah punched a third-grader over? she implies with silence, which I readily receive. I nod. It's unclear how much Eli picks up, but he doesn't seem to notice. Or care.

"Want to invite her over one day?" Tamara asks. Even I know that's not gonna happen.

"We're not friends," Eli says, killing the conversation.

It's unclear if Hal Tompkins grows corn for the purpose of feeding anyone anymore, or if he keeps his farm around solely for this one weekend out of the whole year. By Sunday night, his entire property will be flattened from the foot traffic, the cornstalks pressed against the ground, grass trampled into muddy submission.

The harvest fair has your regular autumnal draws. Funnel cakes. Hot apple cider. A pumpkin-carving contest. Face painting. Pint-sized pumpkin heads run rampant through the fair, cheeks streaked in orange, as if they're a bunch of headless horsemen racing around your ankles. There are even haunted hayrides on Hal's ancient tractor.

But the real draw has always been Hal's corn maze. He spends the months leading up to October mapping out a web of intertwining paths. Every year, he comes up with a new configuration—three endless acres' worth of tangling footpaths, spiraling corridors, and dead ends that confound the whole community.

Mr. Stitch remains at the heart of the field. You know you've reached the maze's center when you come upon the scarecrow perched upon his post, staring down with his impassive button eyes. There are stories about how Mr. Stitch is possessed by the ghost of a dead Confederate soldier. This field had been the site of some Civil War skirmish, long forgotten by now. Hal says he's still picking bones of Union soldiers out of the mud. When he first assembled Mr. Stitch, the spirit of one particular Johnny reb rose from the soil and slipped inside that ratty husk. This ghost won't let go, haunting this cornfield ever since.

At least that's what the high schoolers say. *Watch out for Mr. Stitch! Don't get too close! And whatever you do, don't ever say his name three times. You'll wake him up!*

Tamara told me the story on my maiden foray to the Fall Harvest Fair. I was, I guess, what you might call a Fall Harvest virgin. This was my official induction into Danvers.

Tamara got a babysitter for Elijah so we could go alone. We role-played high school sweethearts all night, playing overpriced games that would go toward the community's coffers. The fair is staffed with volunteers, a loose organization of civic-minded moms and dads more commonly known as the Friends of Danvers. More like a cult, if you ask me. These parents offer up their time and energy to help maintain the Rockwell vibes all year long, keeping our town's historic patina intact.

You've never heard of Mr. Stitch? Tamara had asked between bites of caramel corn.

What? Is he an ex of yours?

Oh yeah, she said, playing along. *Best boyfriend I ever had. I'll introduce you two. Just be careful. He's a real jealous type.*

Am I gonna have to take him down?

Mr. Stitch? Tamara laughed. *Oh, hon, I love you and all but nobody can take Stitch.*

We kissed on the carousel, practically in front of the whole town, thereby announcing our relationship to the rest of Danvers. Sure, there had been whispers, but rumors are just rumors that can always been denied. We shot them down all through the previous school year. But here we were, finally making it public. Coming out of hiding. *Follow me*, I remember her saying, taking me by both hands and dragging me into the maze. The outside world washed away. There was nothing to hear but the winding channels of cornstalks bristling in the breeze.

Better block out an hour before braving the maze. An hour, *at least*. Ol' Hal prided himself on crafting an expansive labyrinth full of twists and turns. This wasn't a simple in-and-out affair. I learned that the hard way, losing myself alongside Tamara in its meandering corridors. Losing ourselves. But we held each other's hands the whole time. I sensed everyone's eyes on us, neighbors and coworkers processing this new bit of information: *They're a couple.*

Tamara wanted to flaunt it. *Be loud and be proud*, she insisted. Kissing me at every corner, electric with this revelation. She pulled me further into the maze, until I felt completely discombobulated, losing my sense of space. Of time. How far had we gone? Tamara kept leading the way, as if she knew exactly where she was going. The spider luring in the fly.

When we reached Mr. Stitch, I remember feeling the tug in my arms as Tamara pulled me up to his post, until we were standing directly before him. His burlap sack of a head slumped over his right shoulder. Tamara grinned, still out of breath, and asked, *What if we tied the knot?*

I laughed, unsure if she was kidding or not. *You mean like, right here? With him?*

I'm sure Mr. Stitch has officiated plenty of weddings. She leaned into my ear and whispered, *Dare you to say his name three times.*

For real?

Everyone in Danvers does it. It's the rules. Now it's your turn.

Okay, I said, playing along. *Mr. Stitch.*

Tamara grinned.

Mr. Stitch . . . Just as I was about to say his name a third time, my throat caught. I couldn't say it. Not two breaths before, I would have laughed at myself for feeling afraid, but now, out here, in the cornfield, sensing Mr. Stitch's button eyes pressing down on me . . . I couldn't do it.

That was last year.

Tonight, Elijah tags along. He's insisting he's ready to finally brave the maze, demanding from the back seat that we take him. Tamara is indecisive, but Elijah begs for the entire ride. When begging doesn't work, he moves to whining. And when whining doesn't do the trick, he shifts to shouting. "I wanna go in the maze! I wanna go in the maze! I wanna go in the—"

"Funny," Tamara says from behind the wheel. "I didn't hear a magic word, did you?"

"Please! Please! *Pleeeeeeeease!*"

Opening night is always the most crowded. That's when the high schoolers take over the fair for the night. All the seniors, out on their dates, making out in the maze.

I campaigned for opening night.

You sure we shouldn't wait till Sunday? Tamara asked. *It'll be hormone central.*

That's exactly the point . . . We might as well be eighteen. Sixteen! I'll take feeling any other age again before the oppressive weight of adulthood starts to weigh me down . . .

I didn't know you were feeling so weighed down, Tamara said.

That's not what I meant . . .

She didn't say anything for a while, lost in thought. *Know how they used to kill witches?*

Uh, burning them at the stake?

Pressing, she says. *They were made to lie on their backs. A wooden board was place on their chests and weighed down with one rock after another. Their chests eventually collapsed . . . Is that what parenthood feels like to you?*

Clearly I had said the wrong thing. Putting my foot in my mouth is nothing new, but Tamara has a rather novel way of making me twist in the wind whenever I do this.

She turns into the lot, letting the air-traffic-control kids guide her Cherokee toward the designated lane.

"Please, Mom?" Elijah whimpers. "Can we? I really wanna go."

"I already said no, hon. Not tonight. It's too spooky in the dark."

"What's it gonna hurt?" I ask. "Maybe he's ready."

"Whose side are you on again?" Tamara side-eyes me. "Don't you dare team up on me."

"If *Dad* says I'm ready, then can't I go?" The name rolls right off his tongue.

"I'm sold," I say.

"I'll make a deal with you," she says to Eli through the rearview mirror. She's always making deals with him. "We'll come back on Sunday. You and I can do the maze then, okay?"

"Nooo! Sunday's boring!"

Sunday afternoon is "family day," which is to say the church-going crowd, of which the surrounding county still has its fair share. Opening night might be when all the teens come out, sneaking flasks topped off with peach schnapps pilfered from their parents' liquor cabinets, but Sunday is a much more, well, *chaste* affair, for the stroller crowd. The maze will be full of families guiding their tykes through in full daylight.

Not like tonight. Not in the dark.

"Please, Dad? Pleeease?"

This kid is good, I'll give him that. I glance at Tamara before answering to see if she caught it. I almost miss the look in her eye that very clearly states: *Don't you fucking dare, pal.*

"Sorry, bud," I say, defeated by Look #34. "We'll come back first thing on Sunday before church gets out. We'll have the corn all to ourselves, I swear."

"It's not fair," Elijah mutters under his breath. Cursing us. The silent treatment is new. Something he's testing out on us. Only time will tell if he keeps this one in the tool kit.

It's not that the Fall Harvest Fair feels exactly like a flashback to better times. It's more like waltzing into some idealized version of the past we all want to believe in. Imagine a whitewashed rendition of yesteryear, filtered through an Instagram lens of yellowing leaves crackling under our feet, the wistful scent of autumn in the air. A real Bradbury throwback.

The Friends of Danvers who specialize in face painting offer up a trio of prefab faces: Pumpkin. Skull. And to honor our signature seasonal mascot, the scarecrow himself—Mr. Stitch.

Eli chooses scarecrow. Painted centipedes skitter across his cheeks, twisting stitches winding over his smooth skin. I don't like it. Something about it—I don't know—unnerves me. He looks like a doll. A Cabbage Patch Kid. Can't he pick pumpkin, like all the other kids?

I notice a mother in a burgundy sweater walking with her own family. She's staring at me. When we make eye contact, she smiles. I can't help but turn as she passes, just to see if she keeps looking. Why is she looking at me like that?

"You're looking pretty proud of yourself," Tamara says, snapping me back.

"How's that?" Truth is, as a matter of fact, yes, I am feeling rather proud of myself. I can't help but replay what Elijah said back in the Jeep: *Please, Dad . . . ?*

"You two are going to conspire against me, aren't you? Boys against girl?"

"You set down the ground rules and I'll enforce them, I promise. I got your back."

Eli quickly fills up on funnel cake, dusting his chin and cheeks until he looks like the ghost of a scarecrow.

"He's beginning to trust you," Tamara says. "Open up."

"You okay with that?" I ask. Have to ask. It doesn't take a mind reader to sense she's thinking back to the years when it was just the two of them. She single-handedly raised Elijah—and now here I am, infiltrating their family dynamic and insinuating myself into their routine.

She swears she doesn't miss the single-parent period of her life. The struggle to make ends meet. The pity from other parents. *Poor you,* the married mothers all coo. She doesn't miss the coffee-shop gossip at all. But after carrying the weight of her family on her shoulders for years, it's been dizzying to suddenly have somebody else help. I have to keep reminding her that she doesn't have to do this alone anymore. *This is about us*, I always say. *We're in this together.*

A chill seeps into the air. I'm wearing a red-and-black flannel jacket, which I zip up to keep the encroaching cold away.

Tamara slows her pace, staring at my chest. "Where'd you get that?"

"Get what?"

"The jacket."

"This? I found it."

"In the garage?" She won't stop staring—not at me, but the flannel.

"Yeah." I spin around, arms out, modeling it for her. "What do you think?"

"It looks nice on you," Tamara manages to say.

Someone else is staring at me. A silver fox of a father volunteering at the cotton candy machine weaves a pink web around a paper cone for a group of kids. He grins as we pass. The salt-and-pepper bristles across his chin glisten with pink sugar crystals. Why is he looking at me?

"Richard?"

Do I know him? I've seen him before . . . But where? Why does he look so familiar?

"Richard."

That's when it dawns on me. It's Eli's biological father. *Hank*. But it can't be. Can it? I'm just imagining it. I've seen pictures of him buried in shoeboxes in my studio, so I know what he looks like. But as far as Tamara and I know, he lives in Richmond, two hours away.

"*Rich*."

I snap back. "What?" Tamara hasn't noticed Hank yet—*it's him, isn't it*—and I'm not sure I want her to. I'm suddenly second-guessing myself. Of course it's not him. Why would he be here?

Tamara's face has dropped. *Oh no, she saw him, too.* She spins around once, twice, three times. "Wait . . . where's Elijah?"

I scan the crowd around us. He was just behind us, eyeing the goldfish game not two seconds ago. I swear I saw him leaning over the railing of the game, peering into the dozen glass bowls holding their foregone fish, each one swirling in their own foggy body of water. Where did he go?

"Elijah?" A question desperate for an answer. Then it becomes a demand. "Elijah!"

The contours of his name sound strange to me. There's uncertainty in her voice. Fear. It only grows worse the louder she shouts.

Until it becomes an absolute scream. "ELIJAH!"

Other carnival-goers slow down, loosely gathering around us. I sense their awkwardness, and I know they're wondering if they should ask us if we need help. I smile gratefully but shake my head to ward them off. It'll be faster if we just start looking for him.

We agree to separate. She'll find a volunteer and I'll backtrack. Surely somebody has seen him. He couldn't have gone far. That's what people say in these moments, right?

He couldn't have gone far.

He was right here a second ago. That's what they always say. He was *right here.* A kid doesn't just disappear into thin air.

What if . . . ? The gnawing thought creeps into my mind. I shake it off, but it refuses to quiet itself. *What if somebody took him?*

That doesn't happen. Not here. Not in our town. Not where everybody knows everybody else. Impossible. That's why people move to a place like Danvers in the first place.

To be safe.

These swirling thoughts have already occurred to Tamara. It was probably the first thought that popped into her head: *Somebody's taken my baby.* Moms always imagine the worst. *Somebody's taken my baby boy.* My parental instincts haven't fully kicked in yet. I mitigate. I try to assess with a calm, cool head. What's the more likely scenario? That Elijah simply got distracted and wandered off on his own, when he should've been keeping up with the rest of us?

Even as I reason with myself, I feel like I'm failing him by *not* fearing the worst. That's what parents do. What *real* parents do. They fear everything. *Everything.* Until life proves otherwise, life itself is a threat.

I push through the crowd at a brisk walk that turns into a full sprint once I realize that I'm not seeing him anywhere.

I stop before the mouth of the maze. An archway of jack-o'-lanterns curves over my head. Each carved pumpkin has a battery-powered LED light flickering within, mimicking a candle.

"Elijah!" I call out. "*Eli.*" There's no peering over the towering stalks.

Hal's made sure of that. I have to plunge into the labyrinth, make my way through its rows like everyone else, navigate each twisting lane, suffer every dead end. But there's no time. I know that every slipping second is sending Tamara deeper into a catatonic state, the panic consuming her.

I'm going to find him. I have to find him. There isn't any other option. The second I saw the maze, I knew he was in there because that's exactly what I would've done if I were in his shoes. This is where I would've gone. Where every boy goes.

I run through the maze. I rush past all the other parents still with their kids, forcing my way through the clusters of teenagers.

"Watch it, *asshole*," some dipshit in a varsity jacket shouts as I pry apart his crew.

I spot a flash of blue through the stalks and think it looks like Elijah's T-shirt. Isn't he wearing a blue T-shirt? I can't remember anymore. The only thing to do is plow through the cornstalks and make my way into the neighboring lane.

"Elijah!" When I burst through the maze's wall, I stumble upon an unsuspecting family. Their son lets out a shout, startled by my abrupt entrance. I try to play it off, pretending I'm a part of the festivities, a volunteer minotaur that pops out and says *boo*. "Sorry . . . Sorry."

I swore I've already come this way. I'm so turned around. Now I have to backtrack. The maze is making me dizzy. The cornstalks seem to turn as I pass, like they're watching me.

Where am I? Where's Elijah? My pulse hammers against my temples. I feel my heartbeat full-on throbbing in my head, pressing against the inside of my skull. I need to think. Need to—

Pray.

I need to stop and get my whereabouts and just—

Pray.

I'm willing to do anything. Do whatever it takes to get him back. Do

I need to get down on my knees? Clasp my hands and say the words out loud? What do I need to do, what do I have to say, to make this all go away? Make it stop? *Please*, I beg, *please, just bring Elijah back.*

I halt before the body suspended from its post. Its arms are slung out at its shoulders. Its head is slumped to one side.

Mr. Stitch's bloated chest is disproportioned. The hay stuffed into his shirt settles into misshapen muscles. One arm is bulkier than the other. His head is a burlap sack, the faded letters SUGAR CANE printed across his forehead. But most unnerving is Mr. Stitch's new addition to his annual getup, something that'll surely cause a stir with the churchgoing crowd on Sunday . . .

A pentagram.

Red rivulets dribble down his flannel shirt onto the flattened corn-stalks below. Purely on reflex, I reach out and brush my finger along a wet tendril. Did I really think it was—what, blood? I recognize the bright crimson tincture right away. Red tempera paint. I use the same brand at school. The paint is still fresh against his chest, from the looks of it.

Do I want Mr. Stitch's help? Somehow, the spirit of this dead Con-federate will know where to look? Isn't that what kids do here? Come to Mr. Stitch? Let him whisper his stories?

Anything. I am willing to try anything. What do they all say? How does the story go?

Watch out for Mr. Stitch. Don't get too close . . .

"Mr. Stitch." I can't recognize the sound of my own voice.

And whatever you do, don't ever, ever say his name three times . . .

"Mr. Stitch." This doesn't sound like me.

You'll wake him up.

"Mr. Stitch—"

Just the faintest release of air spills out from his hay-stuffed chest. It's wet. Ragged, like damp burlap ripping. I take a step closer. To listen.

"Is this who you're looking for?" The voice comes from behind me, but in the vertigo of the moment, I swear, I *believe* Mr. Stitch says it.

I spin around and find Elijah. His eyes hide beneath his flop of hair. He can't stand still, shifting his weight from one foot to the next, as if he needs to pee.

I rush to him and kneel before him. "Oh God," I say. "You're okay, you're okay."

The ground is soft, the stalks pressing down into the mud, leaving me unsteady. I have to clasp Elijah's shoulders to balance myself. My grip is tighter than it should be, but I need to hold on to him, not just for balance, but to make sure I don't lose him again.

Then the slightest spike of anger wedges itself in. "You can't run off like that! We were looking *everywhere* for you! Your mom is scared to death." Funny how you can be so afraid one second, and then the next, something just switches. The current of emotion reverses course and some self-righteous sense of indignation takes over. *How dare you make me feel this afraid*, this roller coaster of emotion seems to say, as if this were all Elijah's fault. Am I blaming him? I don't think I had shaken him that hard, but he's crying now. "Don't you *ever* do that again."

In the blinding heat of the moment, I hadn't acknowledged—hadn't noticed—the woman standing next to him. I had launched directly into my parental tirade.

It was Mr. Stitch, right? I called him, conjured him, and he brought him back. Right?

Then who is this woman?

She looks familiar. She doesn't go for brand-name catalogue clothing like the other Danvers moms. I notice her gray-blonde hair. There's something all-natural about her. I spy a girl hiding behind her hip. *Sandy.* This must be Sandy's mother. I'd met her at the open house at school. I have a vague memory of her but can't remember if she's a

Mrs. or a Miss. All I know is that she bombarded me with quickfire questions, grilling me about my lesson plan. Art is never high on any parent's list of priorities, but Miss Levin was thorough. "Is this your son?"

"Yes." I manage to stand, the corn husks flexing under my feet. "Stepson."

I can't read her reaction. "You should be more careful."

"You're right." I pluck Elijah from the ground. "I should get him back to his—"

"It's not safe," she interrupts. "Even here, it's not safe. In the dark."

"No, I guess it's not." Eli wants to stay with Sandy, his legs locking, refusing to move. I start backing away, dragging Eli by his arm. "Thank you. Thank you for finding him." I take a moment to acknowledge Sandy, waving at her. "Thanks to you, too. See you in class?"

Sandy nods. It seems like she's afraid to look at me. Why would she be afraid? Of me?

By the time I wave and say one last thank-you, I spot Mr. Stitch hovering above her. His slumped head seems to take this all in, as if he's on their side. Even Mr. Stitch doesn't approve of my parenting skills. I swear I can see that burlap sack for a head shake on his shoulders.

"Come on," I say. "Let's find your mother."

INTERVIEW: March 3, 1983

KINDERMAN: Sean, your mother told me that you like to draw. She says you draw pictures all the time. In fact, she told me that your house is full of pictures drawn just by you. Is that true?

CRENSHAW: Uh-huh.

KINDERMAN: She even calls it the Museum of Sean because you're the only artist on exhibit. Your mom brought in some of her favorite drawings that you've done. She wanted to show me how much of an artist you are. I have to agree, Sean, they're great! You really do have a wonderful imagination. I was wondering . . . Would you do some coloring with me? I have a brand-new box of crayons that I was going to open and color with by myself . . . but then I figured, *Oh, wait, I'll share these with Sean*! What do you say? Can we color together?

CRENSHAW: Okay.

KINDERMAN: Great! Maybe you can show me how you draw such amazing figures. Whenever I draw, my people look all funny. I think I need your help.

CRENSHAW: Okay.

KINDERMAN: This is so exciting, Sean! I can't wait. Here's some paper and here are the crayons. Twenty-four colors. Which is your favorite?

CRENSHAW: Green.

KINDERMAN: Me, too! See? We've got a lot in common, you and me. I bet we're going to draw something really amazing together.

CRENSHAW: What should we draw?

KINDERMAN: Good question. What are some of your favorite things to draw?

CRENSHAW: I like—I like dinosaurs.

KINDERMAN: Dinosaurs are great! What's your favorite

kind of dinosaur?

CRENSHAW: Stegosaurus.

KINDERMAN: Mine, too! What else do you like to draw?

CRENSHAW: Um . . . Cars.

KINDERMAN: Do you ever draw stuff that's happened to you? I was thinking . . . maybe you could draw a picture of your teacher.

CRENSHAW: Why?

KINDERMAN: What? You're not good enough to draw a picture of somebody you know? Your mom told me you could draw anything . . .

CRENSHAW: I can do it.

KINDERMAN: Good! That's great, Sean . . . Thank you. Now, if somebody asked you to draw a picture of Mr. Woodhouse, what would you draw first?

CRENSHAW: His . . . head?

KINDERMAN: Okay. How about you show me? What color are his eyes?

CRENSHAW: Um . . . blue?

KINDERMAN: Are you sure about that? I thought they were . . .

CRENSHAW: Green?

KINDERMAN: Brown-green! That's what I thought. Here. What about his hair?

CRENSHAW: Brown.

KINDERMAN: Perfect. What about his body? How would you draw his body?

CRENSHAW: Like . . . this.

KINDERMAN: Sometimes people have different things on their bodies. Like pictures. Or words. Sometimes even numbers. Like the number 6. Does Mr. Woodhouse have anything like that on his body, that nobody really sees because he's always got his clothes on?

CRENSHAW: Like he hides it?

KINDERMAN: Exactly. Something not many people see.

Maybe he shows it to a few people. But not a lot. Has he ever showed you anything on his body before?

CRENSHAW: (Shrugs.)

KINDERMAN: It could be a picture on his skin—or maybe it's even a part of his body. Has Mr. Woodhouse ever showed you a part of his body before?

CRENSHAW: A secret part?

KINDERMAN: Yes, exactly. A secret part. Adults call those private parts. Has he ever shown you something like that? Could you draw a picture of his secret parts for me? Do you know where a person's private parts are on their body?

CRENSHAW: (Draws.)

KINDERMAN: When did he show it to you? In school? During class time?

CRENSHAW: (Shrugs.)

KINDERMAN: It wouldn't have been during recess, would it? When all the other kids are playing outside? Or was it on a field trip? A special field trip?

CRENSHAW: It was a field trip.

KINDERMAN: I thought so. I'm wondering if we could draw another picture. You can use as many colors as you want, okay? The whole box. Some of your classmates told me about how Mr. Woodhouse took a few students on a field trip.

CRENSHAW: To the zoo.

KINDERMAN: Yes, well, we already knew about the field trip to the zoo . . . but some of your classmates mentioned another kind of field trip. One that happened at a different time. Do you know anything about what field trip they mean?

CRENSHAW: Yes?

KINDERMAN: Did you go on this field trip? With Jason and Sarah and—

CRENSHAW: Craig was there, too.

KINDERMAN: Craig Richardson?

CRENSHAW: Uh-huh.

KINDERMAN: Interesting. Maybe you can tell me a little bit about what this field trip with Mr. Woodhouse was like . . . Do you think you could do that, Sean?

CRENSHAW: I don't know.

KINDERMAN: Know what? It's okay to talk to me about it. Or, better yet, you can draw a picture! When we asked Jason, he said it was pretty scary and he'd rather draw it than talk about it. He used a lot of the black crayon. And the red.

CRENSHAW: Because it was dark?

KINDERMAN: That's what Jason said! That it was dark. Why was it dark, Sean?

CRENSHAW: Because . . . Because it was at nighttime?

KINDERMAN: Jason told me the same thing! How do you think Mr. Woodhouse was able to take you on a field trip at night?

CRENSHAW: Because he waited until Mommy was asleep.

KINDERMAN: Where did he take you? Was it outside? Like, in a field? Or a cemetery? Where they bury people who have died? Was it near a church?

CRENSHAW: (. . .)

KINDERMAN: What if I said you were helping me, Sean? Helping a whole lot of people. By telling me what happened to you, you're helping to make sure nothing bad ever happens to you or any of your friends. But to do that, we need to know everything that happened. We need you to explain it to us. To show us. It can be with words, if you want. Or with pictures. Whatever feels better to you, okay? But you have to show me, Sean. You have to tell the truth.

CRENSHAW: Okay.

KINDERMAN: So. Where did Mr. Woodhouse take you? Do you want to draw it? Draw a picture for me. Show me. Can you show me what you did on these field trips?

CRENSHAW: (Draws.)

KINDERMAN: That's a great picture, Sean. Can I ask . . . Who is that?

CRENSHAW: Jason.

KINDERMAN: And that must be Mr. Woodhouse, then.

CRENSHAW: (Shakes head.)

KINDERMAN: No? Who is it then?

CRENSHAW: That's the gray boy.

KINDERMAN: Gray boy?

CRENSHAW: (Nods.)

KINDERMAN: Does the gray boy have a name? Is he a classmate? It's okay to tell me. You're safe now. Nobody's going to hurt you . . . Do you know him?

CRENSHAW: (. . .)

KINDERMAN: Do you know who the gray boy is, Sean? Is the gray boy another student? Is he a teacher? Sean? Who is he?

CRENSHAW: He doesn't live here anymore.

KINDERMAN: Why not? Where is he now?

CRENSHAW: He's with Jesus.

(END OF INTERVIEW.)

RICHARD: 2013

S creaming doesn't need sound, I realize. There is so much screaming in the car right now. Even though the drive home is in complete
silence, Tamara shrieks with her entire body.

Elijah's body wails in the back seat. Their emotions echo noise-
lessly through the car.

I try to play peacekeeper and turn on the radio to block out this
howling that has no sound. I find a song that I sort-of-but-not-really
know the lyrics to, doing my best to lighten the mood. "Oh—here we
go. Who wants to sing along?"

Nobody responds so I dive in with my best reinterpretation of Tay-
lor Swift. *"Everything will be all right if we keep dancing on like we're a
hundred and two."*

"That's not how the song goes," Eli says.

"Who cares what the real lyrics are? We can make up our own—"

Tamara turns the radio off, forcing us to sit in this thick stillness.

I peer over my shoulder and see that Elijah is asleep.

"He's out."

Tamara keeps her focus on the road, driving in ear-splitting quiet. She doesn't look at me. Her foot presses on the accelerator, gaining speed.

Everything blurs outside. The cornfields zipping past the passenger-side window blend into a sea of roiling green, barely illuminated by our headlights, churning in the dark.

"Everything's okay," I offer. "Eli's fine."

The speedometer keeps climbing. "What if we didn't find him?" I get the sense she's been having this internal conversation with herself the whole ride. All the *what if*s have been building up and now that Elijah's asleep, there's no holding her back from going volcanic.

"But we did find him," I say. "I found him." A little white lie on my part, but still. The gist is essentially true. I brought him back to her. An offering.

"What if it had been somebody else?" Tamara persists, playing out the darkest possibilities in her head. Once she starts imagining the worst, it's hard to pull her back. I can see the shadow play of child abduction flittering across her mind. "What if they took him? Kidnapped him? What if we were still looking for him now? What if . . . ?"

What if . . . ? I know those gnawing thoughts. I've had my own. Chewing on my ear.

Whispering.

"Tamara," I say, as evenly as possible. "Slow down."

"What if . . ." Either her imagination peters out, or the grim finale of her fantasy is too much to say out loud. Best not to let Tamara stew too long in these morbid thoughts. She needs to get out of her head, away from the gruesome worst-case scenarios.

"At least we don't have to tell him he can't ride Satan's Taint this year."

"Don't." The arrow on the speedometer starts to lower, the miles winding back down.

"The Devil's Dickcheese."

"It's not funny . . ."

"Lucifer's Scrote."

"Don't try to make me laugh. I don't want to." I swear I see her smile but she still wants to role-play Panicked Parent.

Fine. I give up. Let her have it. That leaves me with the corn outside my window.

Drifting.

I'm in the station wagon on the interstate. I remember the car's wood siding. The flip bench seats in the rear cargo. I'd crawl back there and fall asleep on the longer drives. It's raining. My window is rolled down just a crack. Water drips along the lip of the door and soaks into my sleeve. Mom hasn't said much these last few hours. Her hands grip the steering wheel as if it's the only thing holding her up. Every time a pair of headlights reach into the car, her eyes immediately shoot up to the rearview mirror, taking in the encroaching vehicle behind us.

I remember finding the reflection of her eyes. That look of panic illuminated by high beams, framed in the rearview mirror. Every passing car held the possibility of someone following us. Of being whatever we were running from. That's what we were doing, yes?

Running away?

What did we pack? Barely any clothes. Not one toy. We'd been on the road since Saturday, crossing state lines. Eating McDonald's in the car all the time. It used to be a treat, eating fast food. But now there was a graveyard of hamburger wrappers at our feet. The stale husks of Quarter Pounder crusts, soaked in congealing ketchup. Empty milkshake cups. A thick miasma of grease hung in the air. It coated my throat every time I took a breath.

Mom had called it a road trip. *We're going on a road trip. Doesn't that sound like fun?*

Even as a kid, I knew the higher register in her voice was a dead giveaway that all was not fun. The lilt in her voice was testament that she was hiding something. That she was lying.

She was afraid.

Mom let me sit in the front seat with her. Even I knew kids weren't supposed to sit in the passenger seat, not until they were older. But this was a *special* adventure. *Just us,* she'd said.

I hadn't taken a bath since we'd left. Neither of us had. The car was beginning to ripen. The oiliness in the air, thick with French fry grease and body odor and breath, was only growing denser. Every time I rolled down the window, Mom would insist I roll it back up.

Don't, she said, almost shouting. *We can't let them in.*

How far were we going? Mom never said. Every time I tried asking her, she'd pretend like she hadn't heard me. *Where are we going, Mom?* I asked and asked. *Where are we now?*

An eighteen-wheeler barreled by, overtaking our car and blaring its horn. I could hear the rapid-fire attack of gravel kicking up and hammering the underbelly of our chassis as Mom momentarily let the station wagon slip off the road and onto the shoulder. She had to recover, yanking on the wheel, bringing our car back onto the highway with a stomach-turning swerve.

Another car quickly came up behind us. The moment Mom noticed it in the rearview, her hands tightened around the steering wheel, fingers knotting, knuckles about to burst. The engine heaved, sending the car forward. The car was straining under the weight of Mom's foot.

Glancing at the dashboard, I saw the arrow on the speedometer reaching seventy miles per hour.

Seventy-five.

Eighty.

A swirling hue of red and blue lights suddenly filled our car. The dancing spiral of colors spun over the ceiling and seats, as if we were at a carnival. Even my skin was speckled in red.

Get down, Mom said, glancing into the rearview.

I turned around in my seat before ducking down. Just to see who was behind us.

Someone was in the car. Behind me the whole time. Staring back at me.

The high beams of the police car shined right into my eyes, so all I could make out was the shadowy silhouette of our passenger sitting in my booster seat. Where I usually sat.

Their features hid in the dark. But they were—

There.

Their body was nothing but muck, shadow and grease, like they didn't want to be seen.

The gray boy.

He reached out for me. He called out my name: *Sean* . . .

I closed my eyes. Squeezed them shut. Blotting it all out. *Make it go away*, I thought to myself, *make it go away go away go away* . . .

The siren wailing through the rain. The hammer of the storm against the roof of our station wagon. Mom's voice as she kept saying *everything's going to be okay everything's going to be fine just don't stop don't stop stay down don't move.*

But all I could think about was the gray boy in the back seat of our car, the gray boy who knew my name who whispered to me who knew my name the gray boy reaching out for me—

The gray boy knows my name—

The gray boy—

The gray—

When I open my eyes, all I see is Elijah fast asleep in the back seat.

The windows are full of green once again, a sea of stalks bristling in the dark. The smell of hay is still in my skin. I bring my hand up and take a deep breath, filling my lungs with it.

It's okay. Everything's okay. I had simply drifted off. Just a bad memory.

Just a dream, as they say. Don't they say that? *Just a bad dream.*

When we pull into our driveway, the headlights barely brush over a creamy tangle hovering in the air, just visible above the backyard fence. Something is dangling from the willow tree bough where Eli's tire swing hangs. I only see it for the split second the high beams pass over it before it sinks back into blackness. Tamara doesn't mention it. She must still be lost in her litany of worst-case scenarios.

I extract Eli from the back seat. It takes some maneuvering to unbuckle him, scooping him out from the booster without his limbs tangling in his seatbelt.

Tamara opens the front door for us. We never lock up the house. Not here. None of our neighbors do. Nobody in Danvers does. But lately I've been wondering if that's wise.

I carry Elijah upstairs. He feels so light. A doll. Raggedy Andy. He doesn't wake in the transition from my arms to his bed. I don't know how long I sit there staring at him.

My phone buzzes in my pocket. I fish it out and silence the ringer.

The area code. I know it. It's—

I'm not going to pick up. I let it go straight to voicemail. Once I know Elijah isn't going to wake, I tuck him in and close his door.

I sidestep the kitchen. Tamara's waiting for me in there but I have to go out back. I slide a box cutter from the hallway table into my pocket and slip outside.

I need to see.

We added the tire swing to one of the weeping willow's branches only a few months ago, during the summer, giving Eli something to do whenever we were out back. I would give him a push if he ever asked for one, sending him higher into the air, his feet piercing the sky.

But the tire isn't where it's supposed to be. Someone cut the rope that tied it to the branch.

In its place is a body.

Weegee is hanging upside down, his tail tied to the severed rope. His tawny body spins in the evening breeze, intestines dangling out from his gaping torso. Blood drips on the grass. I spot Elijah's tee-ball bat propped against the tree. The bulb of the bat glistens.

Someone tied Weegee to the tree, alive, and beat him until he burst open.

A living piñata.

The weeping willow is directly outside our kitchen window. I see Tamara on the other side of the glass, opening a fresh bottle of wine. She can't see me, not out here in the dark. If she were to step up to the sink and glance out the window, she might notice movement outside. Just shadows, but still. I have to act fast.

Weegee's body twirls in a gust of wind. I cut him down and stuff him into the inner rim of the tire and quickly roll the whole thing to my studio until I can come back with a garbage bag. I'll need to hose down the lawn. All that blood dripping over the grass. The bat.

I notice the tree trunk is smeared in red as well. Finger-painted, more like it. I step closer to make out its shape.

A pentagram. In our yard.

Our home.

Somebody's fucking with me. The thought is crystalline, so clear in my head. First Professor Howdy, then the pentagram symbol on Mr. Stitch. *Who, though? Who would do something like this?*

And then, just like that, it comes to me: *Hank.* Eli's father. As far as I know, Tamara hasn't seen or spoken to Hank since he left her. He didn't even show up to the hearing when the court terminated his parental rights on grounds of abandonment. Had he changed his mind? Did he want back into this family and see me as a roadblock? It's absolutely batshit to consider, but once the idea starts to take root, I can't stop myself from thinking it.

Hank knows. He is trying to scare me away. Mess with my head.

Tamara is on her second glass of wine when I enter the kitchen. "Hey," she says.

"Hey," I echo. I can't recognize my voice. It sounds distant, hollow.

"Where've you been?"

"Just went out to the studio," I lie. I know I should tell her about Weegee. Now's my chance. I can feel the opportunity to say something slip away. It's easier to say nothing.

Nothing at all.

"About before. I think . . ." She stops herself, as if she's still working out what she wants to say in her head. "I think all this adoption talk has just stirred up a lot, you know?"

"Am I pushing?" I don't want to put too fine a point on it, but it is dawning on me that it's Tamara who is having the most trouble with the adoption. Dating hadn't been a problem. Marriage was never a problem. It's only when I came for her son that she grew tense.

"There's just some old memories popping up," she explains. "Shaking up a lot of dust."

"A few too many dust bunnies you didn't expect to find, huh?" I clear my throat, trying to figure out how to word what I want—*need*—to know. "Has Hank reached out lately?"

Tamara freezes. His name sucks the air out of the room. "What do you mean?"

"Nothing. I just . . . I suppose I was wondering how he might feel if he found out you married a guy who wants to adopt his child."

Tamara shakes her head. "I wouldn't worry about it. I gave him plenty of chances to be in this family and he never took a single one of them."

My eyes flick over to the adoption papers on the counter for reassurance. That's when I spot the envelope.

"What's this?"

It's resting on top of the adoption forms, the mound of papers on the table untouched since I printed them out. The ring of wine has dried into a deep purple.

"Somebody must have sent it to us by accident," Tamara says, filling her glass with tap water. She swirls the pinkish water and drinks. "Found it stuffed in the mail slot."

I must've stepped right over it when I was carrying Elijah to his room.

There is no address. All it says is:

SEAN.

I tear the envelope open. I can't control the tremors in my own hand.

"What are you doing?" Tamara asks, but I'm not listening anymore.

It's an old newspaper clipping, yellowed and brittle. It had been folded so long ago, the print has faded down the seam. The header is familiar enough.

Greenfield's ledger. The article was ripped from the front page of the smallest of small-town newspapers. Its circulation was so infinitesimal, in fact, they only printed an issue every other day. Strange for an obituary to make the front page.

The cheap newsprint rubs off on my fingers. I hadn't realized I was holding on to it that tightly. Whatever I touched will have my fingerprints smeared all over it.

The picture had misprinted. The four-tone ink is off by a millimeter, so the color of the man's skin drifts to the side of his face, all the color of his flesh spiriting away from him, as if his soul is separating from his body. Even with the printing error, I can still make out my kindergarten teacher wearing an oversized orange jumpsuit.

Mr. Woodhouse.

ACCUSED "SATANIC" TEACHER COMMITS SUICIDE

By Jonathan Salk

Former Greenfield Academy kindergarten teacher Thomas Woodhouse was found dead in his apartment early Monday morning. The cause of death is an apparent suicide by hanging. No note was found. Woodhouse had recently been acquitted of six counts of sexual assault after a year-long trial in which several of his students, some as young as five years old, accused him and five other faculty members of performing ritual sex abuse and satanic sacrifices in their classrooms and other parts of Greenfield. Woodhouse was seen as the leader of this group, who came to be known in the press as the Greenfield Six.

Federal investigators would later determine that these accusations were unfounded, but it would take another year for a jury in the Fairfax Circuit Court to declare Woodhouse not guilty. During that time, the trial quickly became a national sensation. Celia Jenkins, Woodhouse's defense attorney, blamed the length of the trial on a "quack cadre" of "traumatists," referring to psychotherapists who interrogated the child witnesses. Their methods, including hypnosis, were considered by psychological experts who testified for the defense to be coercive, leading to false memories. These child witnesses recounted midnight masses, grave robbings, orgies, and, in some truly bizarre accounts, fornication with Satan himself.

"I don't blame my kids," Woodhouse said following the court's decision. "I believe they were just scared. They got caught up in something they couldn't understand. It wasn't their fault."

When asked what was next for him, Woodhouse said, "now I can try to pick up the pieces of my own life. I want to get back to my family."

Woodhouse was thirty-six. He is survived by his estranged wife and daughter.

SEAN: 1983

The teachers came at night. They took the children from their beds and carried them out windows and back doors while their parents slept. The children were loaded onto a yellow school bus. When they woke, they were told they were going on a midnight field trip.

An adventure, the witness stated.

The children were brought to the cemetery of an abandoned church. They were escorted off the bus and told to hold hands. *Make sure you stick with your partner*, the witness recalled the defendant saying. The defendant wore a black robe, which made it hard to see his face, but the children recognized his voice.

The children were led to an open grave. A small coffin had been unearthed and pried apart. The students were shown the body of a little boy in a suit. His skin was gray. His face was wrinkled like a raisin. *A California Raisin*, the witness noted.

Five more teachers joined them and formed a ring around the coffin, including their headmaster. There were candles placed on the headstones, giving off just enough light for the witness to see each teacher's face as they pulled back their hoods.

Circle time, the defendant said. *Everyone hold hands.*

The gray boy was stiff. Like a G.I. Joe action figure. The teachers picked him up from his coffin and lifted him over their heads. They began to chant. The defendant had taught this chant to the children during school hours and instructed them to sing the words. The witness states that he and the other children did not understand these words. Nonsense words. Another language.

The teachers put the gray boy down and he began to move, like Pinocchio when Geppetto pulls his strings. *He's dancing. The gray boy is dancing!* the children said. The louder they sang, the faster he danced. The children were told to sing louder, watch him dance, *watch him dance!*

The gray boy danced up to each student and asked each of them, one by one, to open their mouths. He pinched at his own body. Pinched it hard enough to pull off a little bit of flesh. He held each sliver of skin up to the students and said, *Take and eat, for this is my body.*

These students did as they were told. They opened their mouths and let the gray boy place his flesh on their tongues.

The teachers all sang. Their voices lifted higher, *higher,* cheering the gray boy on. Their black robes opened to reveal their naked bodies. Their *boobies* and *wee-wees,* as the witness recalled. The accused Mr. Grantier. The accused Miss Macneill. The accused Mr. Sung. The accused Mrs. Haynes. The accused Mr. Jenkins. All of them naked.

The gray boy went down the row, pinching himself. *Take. Eat.* He was all bones before long. His arms, his chest. You could see through his ribs, all the way to his heart.

Now the teachers were touching each other. Touching their boobies. Their wee-wees. They put their lips all over each other's bodies, making kissy sounds, moaning sounds, as the kids continued to sing the song they had been taught to sing.

The gray boy finally reached the witness. He was the last to be fed. All the other boys and girls had eaten their fill. Now there was no flesh left. There was nothing left of his face even.

It looked like the gray boy was crying. *Why are you crying?* the witness asked.

I am crying because I have nothing . . . nothing left for you.

This made the witness very sad. He didn't want to be left out, so he began to cry, too.

Wait, the gray boy said. *For you, my brightest disciple, I have something special. For you, my star, I give all I have left . . .* The gray boy slipped his fingers through his ribs and tore out a piece of his heart and offered it to the witness. *Take and eat, for this is my body*, he said. The witness remarked that it tasted like Wonder Bread soaked in the juices of diced Del Monte vegetables with just a pinch of sugar. He never felt happier in all his life. Now he belonged.

J ust about everybody twisted in their seats as they listened to the prosecution share Sean's story. Some sighed. There was even sporadic laughter. Somebody sitting in the gallery muttered just under their breath, *Can you believe this shit?*

But it was quickly noted by the prosecution that this testimony was repeated by another witness. Key details of Jenny Cardiff's story overlapped with Sean's testimony.

Tommy Dennings's testimony also confirmed certain details. The bus. The cemetery.

Tommy's house had become the unofficial headquarters of the parents. *Just to keep everyone updated*, Mrs. Dennings said. She made Tommy go to his room during these meetings, but he perched at the top of the stairs, eavesdropping on the conversation in the living room.

Jenny's mother always left these meetings in tears. She would sit at the edge of Jenny's bed and share just enough of the story with her daughter to see if it could possibly be true. Jenny, always an obedient child, never liked to see her mother upset, so she would answer yes.

Now it wasn't merely one child's word but two. Then three. Soon it was half a dozen children. The specifics might have differed but the broad strokes, the gist, was the same. All the students who used to tease Sean were fusing the DNA of his story into their own personal accounts, whether they knew it or not. His narrative became the foundation for everyone else's. Kids who pushed Sean around were following his lead, changing their stories to sound like his.

Because Sean told it best.

As more classmates gave their statements, coming forward to speak, their testimonies coalesced into a single narrative. They spoke in one voice. No longer their own, but one.

Sean. His was the voice of a generation.

RICHARD: 2013

"**T**amara?"

"...yeah?" she manages, her eyelids fluttering open. "Don't forget to ..." she starts, but she's already gone. Tamara never has any problems passing out. I envy her ability to turn off at night. We'll lie on our backs and chat for the last few breaths before sleep takes her away.

Now I'm on my own. In bed. Alone.

Liar.

An arched window looks out onto the backyard where the tree swing had been. Our bedroom is a triangular converted attic space with sloping ceilings. It's like living in the tip of a pyramid. I've knocked my head on the wooden beams plenty of times. There's not much room for furniture up here. We've had to make do with a shared dresser that juts out a few inches from the wall, thanks to the slant of the eaves. There are only a handful of picture frames perched on top. A photo from our wedding. Another of her family. I don't have any photos.

"There's something I need to tell you." My voice is barely above a whisper. Tamara doesn't answer. "I need to come clean."

Isn't that what Miss Kinderman always said?

Don't you want to be clean?

Imagine a fib you told as a child. A little white lie. Now imagine that lie taking on a life of its own. Imagine having no control over it. If you ever did. Imagine it spreading. Growing. Imagine the consequences of that lie affecting everyone in your life. Imagine it consuming everything around you—your teachers, friends, family—until there's nobody left.

No one to love you. Imagine that lie haunting you for the rest of your life, following you no matter how far you run away from it.

Sean Crenshaw was five when he told his mother his kindergarten teacher abused him. She told the authorities, who roped in more adults. All these unfamiliar faces surrounding Sean wanted, *needed* his story to be true. Remember, this was 1983. Think about the country back then. Think of the Russians infiltrating our water systems. Think of the white van without windows rolling down the street at night, trawling for kids. Think about Dungeons & Dragons and the witchcraft it possessed. Think about the incantations backtracked on your Black Sabbath album. Think about the direct line to the devil and the new slew of 1-900 numbers kids could dial up. Think about *The Smurfs* and the other animated incubuses sneaking into your home through the cathode portal of your TV screen. Think of the wave of paranoia sweeping the nation, riding a tide of Coca-Cola and holy crusaders sobbing on the airwaves.

Everybody felt it. *The lies.* The deception of our pastors, our politicians. There was always this sense that someone you knew, or *thought* you knew, wasn't who they said they were.

Sean was never alone now. He had an audience. He had *believers*, followers hanging on his every word. He became a star witness. As more adults asked him different versions of the exact same question, feeding him key details, the boy repeated whatever he thought these adults wanted to hear. People's hearts went out to the boy as he spoke the truth. *From the mouths of babes.* When he spoke, the nation listened. Why would he lie? His story made its way into the newspapers. On the nightly news. The judge tried to put a lid on the press, but the trial spilled into the court of public opinion. Everyone was talking about these kids. What their teachers had done. It wasn't just one teacher that had abused him and his classmates anymore, but practically an entire faculty of devil worshippers. There was a cult hiding in plain sight, right here in their school, performing midnight rituals with its students . . . *and people believed.*

Six faculty members were charged with sexual assault. Never mind that there was no physical evidence, no hard-line proof to substantiate any of these stories. The students' claims were eventually debunked, but by then it was too late for the faculty at Greenfield. Sean couldn't keep the narrative from spreading. He didn't know how. Marriages were destroyed. Families were torn apart, children sent to foster homes.

All because of Sean. All because of me.

"That's not who I am," I whisper to Tamara. "I'm a different person."

Sean was just a little boy. Just a kid. He was scared.

Now his fear has become my fear. I'm scared because I don't remember everything that happened. I'm scared because I can't say for sure what's happening now. I'm scared because this emotion does not belong to me. It belongs to someone else.

Sean is dead.

And for all intents and purposes, he is. It was easy for me to bury him, especially after I became Richard. I'm a believer in fresh starts.

But lately I feel like I've been living on borrowed time. Like I sold my soul to the devil thirty years ago. Now he's coming to collect.

There were so many faces back then. Strangers emerged behind flash bulbs, bright and blinding, searing my eyes before fading. Nothing but shadows now. There are shapes within those shadows, silhouettes that take on the form of people Sean hurt. People who suffered.

I barely remember my mother. Even calling her *my* mother seems strange. She's the one piece of the past I continue to share with Sean. Adults whispered about her when they thought I wasn't listening. I was placed with a sympathetic foster family who went out of their way to hide me from the spotlight. Tim and Nancy already had their own family. Their kids were all grown up and out of the house. They read about my mother in the newspaper and made a decision to help rewrite my life. What I had done was unforgivable. The only hope I had at a normal life was to bury the past. Tim and Nancy made that decision for me. To hide me from myself.

To become someone else. To sacrifice Sean and become Richard.

Therapists helped me rebuild my life, piecing it together like I was Humpty Dumpty. *All the boy's foster parents and all the boy's therapists couldn't put Sean back together again . . .*

I've put Sean behind me. I consider his life a bad movie I watched years ago. Not something I remember, per se, but something I witnessed. When I think of my childhood, it begins with Tim and Nancy. *This* is my life. *This* is who I am.

Sean is dead.

I have to keep repeating it to myself. So . . . why is he back from the grave? What does he want from me now?

I've never lied to Tamara. She knows everything there is to know about Richard. But she doesn't know about Sean.

"Tamara?" I say her name out loud just to see if she's awake. Her body blends in with the dark. I can barely make out the contours of her body. Her arm rests on my stomach.

Still no sleep. I glance at the clock next to the bed. Three in the morning and I'm nowhere near drifting. There's a dull throb in my joints. My bones ache if I stay in one position for too long. I keep turning in bed. The sheets itch against my skin. The temperature's never quite right in our bedroom. The air is always stuffy. I notice a spot on the wall just above our bed. A shadow of mildew no larger than a quarter. Could be water damage from the roof. I've been staring at it for the last hour. It never blinks back. A master of the staring contest.

I count Tamara's tattoos like I'm counting sheep.

There's the thistle on her thigh.

A compass on her hip.

A star on her shoulder.

I remember the first time I saw Tamara undress. I gaped—gawped?—at the ink flowing across her body, just above the hemline of her summer dresses. I thought I knew everything about her—then, lo and behold, there was more. A secret self.

What's this? I asked, pointing to the thistle on her thigh.

That's milk thistle.

And why do you have a milk thistle tattooed on your leg?

It's a secret.

Oh, come on . . . You're really not going to tell me? That doesn't seem very fair.

It's supposed to break hexes. She leaned in to whisper, *and makes you a better lover.*

Once I made the mistake of murdering some metaphors in bed. *Your body is a picture book that I want to flip through.*

Did you just compare my body to a book? Tamara asked, sounding unimpressed. *Let's keep the de-personification out of our pillow talk, okay?*

Why didn't I tell her about Sean? There have been so many opportunities over the course of our relationship. There was our third date. You know the milestone: the confessional. This is the date where you begin to see—or don't—the potential for something more. Something substantial. Time to air out all the dirty laundry. It's a risk, definitely make-or-break, but you have to get everything off your chest before you can go any further. You have to confess.

That's when Tamara first told me about Elijah. Everything I assumed about her was suddenly recontextualized. I saw her in a totally new light. She hadn't even blinked, unafraid to reveal herself. She drew a line in the sand and waited for me to cross it. Daring me to.

I should have told her about Sean. That was my chance. *So, uh . . . I also have a kid in my life that you don't know about.*

I could've told her on the fourth date.

The fifth.

Why didn't I tell her leading up to our wedding? That final, prewedding confessional.

Speak now or forever hold your peace . . .

During the service, with all our friends and family—Tamara's family—surrounding us, as our officiant (not Mr. Stitch after all) asked if there was anyone who could show just cause why we couldn't lawfully be joined together, I swore I saw Mr. Woodhouse among our guests. I had to force myself to see that it wasn't actually him. That he wasn't really there.

Woodhouse is dead, I said to myself between vows. *He hung himself because of what Sean said.*

Now I'm too afraid to tell her. Afraid of what Tamara will think. Afraid that she'll leave.

"Sean."

I lift my head. Someone said my—

No, not my name.

His name.

The room is dark. Too dark to see clearly. Shadows within shadows within shadows—

There. On the other side of the dresser. Someone crouched in the corner.

Their eyes. Even in the dark, I can see they're staring right at me.

The gray boy.

He stands and slowly approaches our bed, his body swallowed in shadows. He himself is a shadow. The gray boy moves, suddenly standing over me. His hand reaches for my shoulder.

Take. Eat.

I can feel his cold fingers on my shoulder, feel the chill seep into my skin. I can hear the rasp from his throat as he leans in closer to whisper. *This is my body.*

I bring my arm up and in a single sweeping arc I swat the gray boy away. His body is so light, his limbs nothing but dry kindling. He makes the softest thud against the floor.

Crying.

The gray boy is crying. His voice lifts, wailing. The sound of it fills the room and wakes Tamara. As soon as she pulls herself out of her sleep, she turns on the nightstand lamp.

Light erupts throughout our bedroom. It takes a second for my eyes to adjust to the sudden burst. When they do, I find Elijah on the floor, face covered in tears.

Tamara is already out of bed and beside him, checking for bruises. "What happened?"

"Eli . . . ?" I sit up, bringing my feet to the floor.

The boy retreats into himself as soon as I reach out for him, as if he were—

As if I—

"What the hell's wrong with you?" Tamara hisses at me, shielding Elijah.

"I didn't . . ." I start to say, still stunned. "I didn't know . . ."

Tamara picks Elijah up from the floor before I can finish and rushes out. I hear her footsteps as she carries him to his bedroom, slamming the door.

I remain on the bed. I can see the weeping willow just outside. The severed rope from the tire swing sways in the breeze like a pendulum. *Ticktock*.

I spot my studio beyond the tree. I can't see much from this angle but when I slide up and lean forward, I notice the soft glow from the garage.

The light is on.

I stand in front of the television.

Someone turned on Tamara's old TV/VCR combo, the one I couldn't bring myself to throw away over the summer, resting dormant for months in the corner of my studio. Someone found it, plugged it in, and left it on in the middle of the night for me to find.

A flurry of gray static casts a dim glow across the garage walls. The paper wasp's nest glows dully from above, almost seething. Pulsing. The volume is cranked up, filling the small space with the crackle of static. It sounds like I'm stepping into a burning building.

There's a VHS cassette waiting for me in the deck.

I pull out the cassette to inspect it. There had been a label stuck to its spine at one point, but it's been torn away, leaving behind an adhesive residue. A single strip of masking tape remains on the top. In childlike scrawl, someone has written SEAN in Sharpie.

I slip the cassette back into the VCR.

And press PLAY.

The tape has been recorded over several times. There's no single image at first, but a distorted residue of several shows recorded on top of one another. Phantoms of programs that I can just barely glimpse before the image morphs into another. I hear the ghost of Alex P. Keaton for a moment before it overlaps with a jingle for low-calorie Coke.

Tracking lines drift over the screen, splitting the images. Michael J. Fox's melting face. A woman sipping from a soda can, smiling for the camera, her oversaturated lips bleeding red.

The recording finally settles. It cuts a few seconds into a program that's already commenced. Whoever recorded this didn't press RECORD until the opening credits reached the costume designer.

The credits are superimposed over a ring of candles. The pixelated image is dark, any detail lost on this degraded cassette, decades old by now, but I can still make out the flicker of flames set up in the shape of a pentagram. The soundtrack leans heavily on the synthesizers. The ominous drone intensifies the further into the credits we go, as the camera pulls back. That ring of candles grows smaller. Now I see several hooded figures standing behind each candle, holding them. Their eyes are hidden within the shadows of their black hoods while their mouths remain illuminated by candlelight. Their lips move. They're all chanting in unison. The electronic score suddenly strikes a higher note on the keyboard.

An anemic boy enters the circle. It's difficult to tell if he's really that pale or if it's the desaturation from the degraded recording, or the poor production value. Whatever it is, the boy's skin is sallow. All gray to me. He's guided into the center of the pentagram by a hooded man. The child glances up at the surrounding adults, fear all over his face. But he doesn't run. He simply sits and stares at them as the ring closes in.

We're on to the producers now, a long list of executives that require three separate title cards. As the credits rise and fade, I'm transfixed by the dimly lit scene behind them. The boy is handed a chalice to drink from. A bit spills down his chin. An accident. Just before he wipes the dribble away, we see that it's orange. *Hi-C.*

The digitized strings sting as the gray boy's eyes grow heavy. His chin dips. He's unable to hold his head up any longer. He's woozy. So sleepy. The hooded man guides him to the floor so that he's resting on his back now. The low drone of voices intensifies. Grows faster. They're repeating the same words over and over again. Nonsense words. Latin by way of Ozzy Osborne.

Executive produced by . . .

The hooded man now reaches into his robe and pulls out a warped dagger. At first I think it's the tracking on the VCR distorting the image—but no, the blade is shaped like a winding serpent, slithering to a sharp tip. It comes to me instantly: *Tamara's tattoo*. The chanting escalates as he lifts the dagger overhead, a breath away from bringing the blade down and stabbing the boy in the heart.

Directed by . . .

Just as the knife drops out of frame, the screen goes black. The chanting stops, halted in mid-hymn. We hear the boy scream in the darkness, his voice heavily reverbed to echo forever.

A final title card materializes: *What you are about to watch is inspired by true events. Though it is based upon real people, their names have been altered to protect the innocent.*

It's the made-for-TV movie based on the trial. I remember hearing about it, but I never saw it. I wasn't allowed to watch it as a kid and I certainly didn't seek it out as an adult.

I can't stop myself from watching it. Watching it all. That's what it's here for, isn't it? For me to witness. The woman playing Mom looks nothing like her. I recognize her from her guest role on *The Facts of Life*, but nobody would ever mistake her for my mother.

I feel like I'm looking into a funhouse mirror. My reflection warps and contorts into loose bands of oversaturated pixels across the screen.

Like watching a movie. Isn't that how I always explained Sean's life to myself?

But the story is all wrong. It's not the "movie" I remember watching. This is a remake by another storyteller. Someone with his own truth. His own message to share.

Who?

DAMNED IF YOU DO
SEAN: 1983

S ean's mother was having a difficult time reading the book. The words were barely there, slipping out half pronounced from her mouth. She lost her place on the page, her voice drifting away from the sentence. "Mom?" Sean gently nudged her with his elbow.

She blinked back to the bedroom, to the book between them. "Sorry . . . Where was I?"

But the story already lost its meaning. The words were just sounds. Before the trial, Mom didn't need to read from a book to tell a great story. The words were simply in her. She was a living tome. She would make up tales of dinosaurs battling knights and winged bats the size of station wagons saving unicorns and princesses with green skin and fairy wings. Just as she reached a cliff-hanger, she would slyly kiss him on the forehead and wish him goodnight.

"Don't stop there," Sean would plead. "Just a little more, please?"

"You know the rules," she'd say. "You'll just have to tune in tomorrow . . ."

Sure enough, Mom could pick up the thread right where she'd left off the night before, spinning the tale in a completely new direction.

Sean loved his mother's stories. Her capacity to create something out of nothing. Her imagination was always full of colors and textures and vivid sensations that seemed to manifest themselves right from the tip of her tongue. He wanted to live in his mother's world of words. The bare walls of his bedroom would recede, taking on the contours of whatever tale she told. They had yet to decorate their new home, but with Mom's stories, his room became a jungle or castle or spaceship blasting through the stratosphere. Sean could become anyone. His mother had granted him a potent form of magic, of casting spells with just the flick of his tongue. They were wizards and sorcerers, just like in Dungeons & Dragons, the game the older kids at school played. He wasn't allowed to play that game because a local boy had jumped off a bridge. But Sean didn't know that. He just knew that there was something evil about the game.

Sean didn't need D&D. He had her. But Mom's stories felt rotten lately. Her worlds shriveled, the words withering on her tongue, like berries dying on the vine. Had Mom lost her magic? Was she sick? That frightened Sean the most. Something was inside his mother, making her ill. Had his words somehow caused it? Had Sean made her ill?

For a moment, things had been better. The two of them were a team again. Sean's story had given them a new game to play. Mom joined in on the fun. They fit in. They were embraced by the families of Greenfield. People comforted her. Complete strangers. *We're so sorry for what happened*, they said. Finally, *finally*, people were nice to her. People were kind again.

This was her chance to breathe. Isn't that what she wanted? To belong to the crowd rather than be its target? What was a little white lie if it meant being a part of this community?

Eventually, Mom gave up on conjuring her own stories. She brought a book to bed now, reading aloud to him instead. Prefabricated fairy tales. Stories everybody knew. They were never as thrilling as her tales. Now Mom's mind seemed to wander when she read to him, never locking onto the words. Her attention drifted. Tonight, she just stopped reading altogether. She'd been in the middle of a sentence and then—nothing. It was as if her batteries ran out. Her mouth hung open slightly, her eyes locked onto some empty spot beyond the page. Out the bedroom window.

"Mommy?"

She closed the book, pressing it against her lap. "You know you can tell me anything? Whatever's on your mind or—or something you're feeling. No hiding from me, okay?"

"No hiding," he echoed.

This was Sean's chance. She had opened the door for him to tell her everything. The Truth. Take back the mean things he'd said about Mr. Woodhouse. He knew he had to do this, before it was too late. His stomach churned. *The truth hurts*, he remembered someone—an adult—saying. They were right. The truth was lodged in Sean's throat, choking him.

"It's okay, Sean," Mom started. "Whatever it is, you can—"

The window exploded. Shards of glass scattered across his bed. Mom rolled onto Sean to form a protective shield with her arms. His screams echoed through the tangle of her limbs.

"Stay in bed," she whispered fiercely to him. Mom's feet hit the floor.

After a few moments, Sean looked up and noticed her holding something.

A brick. Someone had thrown it through the window. He noticed the glass still intact in the window frame, a mouth full of jagged teeth breathing a cold wind into the room.

"Mommy..."

She stepped closer to the window, glass crunching under her feet. Her bare feet.

"Mom . . ."

She peered outside. A force field had been disrupted. The protective barrier that kept the outside world from seeping into their home was gone. Anything could crawl in now. Anyone.

What horrors she must've seen in the dark. Sean could only imagine.

DAMNED IF YOU DON'T
RICHARD: 2013

arent-teacher conferences are upon us. Moms and dads never
demand a progress report from their art teacher, but Condrey
insists we're all in this together. I open up my classroom for what
she calls walk-ins, just in case any parent wants to pop their head in and
say howdy.

"All ready?" Condrey asks behind me, peering through the classroom door.

I try not to show how startled I am and smile back. "The doctor is
in."

This is enough of an invitation for Condrey to step inside. "Everything all right?"

"Everything's great."

"How are your students? Any concerns?"

"None as far as I can tell."

Condrey takes me in. I have to stand there and let her look. I never
know how to handle myself when she does this, which is more often
than one might imagine. I simply submit to her silent inspection.

"Richard, I've been watching you lately . . . I know you've noticed."

Watching me?

"You've been great with the kids. They love you, that's clear. You bring such a . . . wonderful *energy* to Danvers."

". . . Thank you."

"We really have high hopes for you here, Richard. We want you to consider Danvers home. You and Tamara. The two of you can be a part of our family for a long time." There's something slithering underneath her words. I can feel it.

"That's great."

Condrey beams. "Good luck tonight." Then just like that, she leaves.

Do I want to be a part of this? This family? With a matriarch like Condrey?

Any parent can wander into my classroom and see what their child has been working on. I'll go through the same rigmarole all the teachers do—talking about the student's behavior, do they follow directions, do they turn their work in on time, do they work well with others, do they respect their classmates and adults, do they have a positive can-do attitude.

Nobody comes in. I could take a nap and no one would notice. I sit behind my desk and settle into the silence, marinating among the doodles and finger paintings. The macaroni portraits. All the squiggly lines like wriggling worms.

Penny for your thoughts, Tamara would say in a moment like this. *I'll throw in a nickel.*

Believe me, I'd say back, brushing it off, *you don't even wanna know . . .* Believe me.

Watching you, Condrey said. Why is Condrey always watching me? *Energy*, she said. *Wonderful energy.* She has *high hopes* for me. What does she want from me?

I pulled out our most recent projects for parents to pore over, ready to point out any artistic flourishes I might find. Moms and dads love to tell admission counselors their children have that magic touch. *Susie Q's art teacher sensed her talent from the get-go. Just look at her finger paintings. See the signs of Van Gogh?* Even in sleepy Danvers, parents are looking for that Ivy League angle as early as elementary school.

My adopted parents were retired alpha types. They'd already gone through it with their own kids by the time they scooped me up. I was Tim and Nancy's victory lap. Something they could brag about at their tennis socials. If there was an after-school club for artistic kids, they signed me up. Every minute of my life was accounted for. I never had a free moment to get lost in my thoughts. Which was the point. If I didn't stop to think back, maybe I'd forget who I was.

Forget Sean.

Tim and Nancy were in their fifties when I entered their lives. Tim was too old to play catch without feeling the creak in his shoulders. They were around but they weren't *there* for me. They didn't spin stories and surprise me with milkshakes and tell me I could always talk to them. Tim had a heart attack when I was in high school. Nancy's death was more drawn out. She suffered from dementia for the last few months of her life before passing away. I would visit her on holiday breaks from art school, but she would always look at me as if I were a stranger.

Who are you? she'd ask. I didn't blame her. Who had I been to her, really? I never felt like her son—more like someone passing through a witness protection program. It seems strange how adamant they had been about keeping me occupied, as if they meant to distract me. I should be thankful, how they bent over backward to provide me every opportunity to find myself, a new version of me, but it felt like they were burying me in extracurricular activities.

I snap back to my classroom. Someone is standing in the doorway.

Sandy's mother patiently waits for me to notice. "Mrs. Levin!" I hop up from my desk and greet her at the door, shaking her hand. She hasn't stepped inside. "Thanks for coming."

"Miss."

"Sorry. Miss Levin. Hi—I'm Richard. Richard Bellamy. Sandy's art teacher."

She winces at the sound of my name.

"Please. Have a seat. Sorry the desks are so little." I offer her the entirety of the classroom and all of its masterworks with a sweep of my hand. She takes in the room before entering, as if to search for a trap. She sits at one of the tiny desks, her eyes never settling.

"Is Sandy feeling at home?" I ask. "I know a big move can disrupt a kid's equilibrium."

"Yes," she says, though it doesn't sound like Miss Levin is answering in the affirmative.

"I was hoping you'd stop by," I say, "to say thanks again. For the other night."

"It's fine," she says, brushing it off. "I'm just glad your son is okay. Nothing bad happened?"

"Eli? No—he's already forgotten all about it." I pull out a few paintings of Sandy's and bring them to the desk. "Let's talk about Sandy! I don't say this lightly: she's one of my most talented students. Here are some watercolors we did this week. She's really got an eye for landscapes. I don't know if you're interested, but there are some summer programs that . . ."

Miss Levin isn't looking at her daughter's paintings. She's staring at me.

"Everything okay?" I ask.

"Sandy showed me."

"Showed you . . . what?" I have no idea what she's talking about. "Her piñata project?"

"The bruises."

Hold on.

Wait.

I hold out my hands in the gentlest, most placating gesture I can manage. This just went from zero to sixty—and way beyond my pay grade. How the hell am I supposed to handle this?

"On her legs. Her . . . upper thighs."

Jesus, this is too much.

"Okay. Wow. I'm so sorry to hear that. Do you think someone is hurting her?" I glance over Miss Levin's shoulder, toward the door, just to make sure it's open. Wide open. For some reason it feels safer to have it that way.

Sandy has always been shy. There have been times when she reminded me of myself when I was her age.

Not you. Of Sean, a voice whispers at the back of my mind. Right. Right right right.

Miss Levin doesn't answer.

"Sandy's never brought up any of this with me, Miss Levin. I haven't seen anything happen in my class—and if I had, believe me, I'd bring it to the principal's attention right away."

"You didn't know?" Her face darkens. "You didn't *notice*?"

I pause. "Miss Levin, I'm not sure what you mean."

I study her face. And that's when I realize she's afraid of me.

"Have you spoken with Mrs. Condrey?" I ask tentatively.

"Sandy said it's someone in your class."

"My class? *Who?*"

"Someone named Sean."

The classroom constricts. It won't settle. It won't stop spinning. Every picture on the wall comes to life, the finger paintings and stick figures turning their heads toward me, sucking the oxygen out of the room, until there's nothing to breathe.

"Sandy told me it all started when you taught them how to play that

. . . that game."

"Game? What game?" But I know her answer before she responds.

"Horsey."

INTERVIEW: April 7, 1983

KINDERMAN: Can I show you something, Sean? I don't know if I told you this, but I am an inventor. I can make all kinds of special machines and super cool devices that can do all kinds of neat things. Like this . . . I call it the Bad Snatcher. You ever make a cootie catcher?

CRENSHAW: (Nods.)

KINDERMAN: This is like that, but real. Kinda looks like a telephone, doesn't it?

CRENSHAW: Yeah.

KINDERMAN: See this part? That's where you talk into it. The difference with this kind of telephone, what makes it so special, is that when you call somebody with it, if there's something that makes you sad, it takes all that sad stuff and bad stuff and disappears it. *Poof.* All gone.

CRENSHAW: Really?

KINDERMAN: All you have to do is talk into this part—this part right here—and it'll take all that stuff you don't want inside of you and sucks it all out. Kinda like a vacuum, you know? Does your mom vacuum around the house a lot?

CRENSHAW: (Nods.)

KINDERMAN: Does your house get really dirty? All that dirt and all those dust bunnies hide under your bed? Your mom plugs in her vacuum and *sluuurps* all the dirty stuff away and the house is all clean again? That's exactly what the Bad Snatcher does. It slurps all the dirt and dust inside us. Because people are like houses, too. We want to be clean. Spotless. But sometimes, some things inside us, the secrets, they make us feel a little dirty . . . Do you ever feel dirty, Sean?

CRENSHAW: (. . .)

KINDERMAN: We all feel dirty sometimes. It's good to have a special device like the Bad Snatcher. The Bad Snatcher takes all the bad stuff away so that we can feel clean again. All you have to do is lean in and talk into the phone part here.

CRENSHAW: (. . .)

KINDERMAN: You can even whisper into it, if you want. You don't have to worry about anyone else listening in. Even me. It's just you and the Bad Snatcher.

CRENSHAW: (Leans in, examines the microphone.)

KINDERMAN: Have you ever talked into a tape recorder before? Maybe your mommy has one, or somebody at school has one, or maybe a friend?

CRENSHAW: Mark has a tape recorder.

KINDERMAN: Oh, good! What do you do with it?

CRENSHAW: We tape ourselves.

KINDERMAN: When you recorded yourself and played it back how did it sound?

CRENSHAW: Like somebody else.

KINDERMAN: It does, doesn't it? It's hard to recognize your own voice. Almost like someone else is saying it . . . That's what the Bad Snatcher does, too.

CRENSHAW: Your machine does that?

KINDERMAN: It does. All the secrets, all the dirt and dust inside you . . . it takes it away and it never comes back. Good as new. *Clean*. Wanna give it a try?

CRENSHAW: Okay.

KINDERMAN: Great! All right. Let's think of something that feels really stuck inside. Something that you might've thought you're not allowed to tell anybody . . .

CRENSHAW: I pushed Jason in the lunch line when he tried to cut.

KINDERMAN: Yeah, but I'm talking about *big* secrets, Sean.

That's just a crumb! What about the stuff you told the policeman? Do you remember that?

CRENSHAW: (Pauses. Nods.)

KINDERMAN: That was a pretty big secret! And I'm worried if you hold on to stuff like that for too long, you're gonna start feeling very dirty inside. Very, *very* dirty. You might never feel clean again. Because that's what happens when we hold onto a secret for too long, Sean. It changes the way we feel about ourselves forever. That dirty, grimy feeling never goes away. It'll be inside you for the rest of your life. Can you imagine living in a house that your mommy never vacuums? You have to clean yourself, Sean. You have to let those secrets out. All of them.

CRENSHAW: (. . .)

KINDERMAN: Tell me what happened in Mr. Woodhouse's classroom.

CRENSHAW: (. . .)

KINDERMAN: I don't think you understand the seriousness of this situation, Sean. People are getting hurt. Children like you . . . Do you want any more children to get hurt, Sean? Do you?

CRENSHAW: No . . .

KINDERMAN: Then you need to tell me everything that happened with Mr. Woodhouse. You need to stop him and his yucky friends from letting this continue. They're out there, Sean. Right now. More than we know. More than we can count. Hiding in plain sight. Do you want to help?

CRENSHAW: (Crying:) I want my mommy . . .

KINDERMAN: Stop crying.

CRENSHAW: I want my mommy!

KINDERMAN: No, Sean. You don't get to hide. You started this. You were a brave boy before, but now you're just being a little fraidy-cat. You can't be afraid now, Sean. It's too late. You need to be brave. You need to be clean. Come clean.

CRENSHAW: I . . . I want to be . . . I want to be clean.

KINDERMAN: How about this. I'm gonna give you the Bad Snatcher. I'll let you hold it, all by yourself. I'm gonna leave the room for a little while. No one else will be listening. You can tell it anything . . . and it'll be gone. Like it never happened.

CRENSHAW: Okay.

KINDERMAN: Okay. Good, Sean. So. Here you go. I want you to hold it like this, okay? Don't touch any of these buttons, all right? Just let it do what it's doing.

CRENSHAW: Okay.

KINDERMAN: Good. Now—remember what we said. Speak into the phone part right here. You don't have to get too, too close to it. It picks up everything. Even the teensiest whisper.

CRENSHAW: Okay.

KINDERMAN: I think you should tell the Bad Snatcher all about Mr. Woodhouse and his yucky friends. Think you can? That's the important stuff, Sean. That's the real dirty stuff.

CRENSHAW: Yeah.

KINDERMAN: Let's be clean again. Let's get rid of all the dust bunnies inside us.

CRENSHAW: The bunnies.

KINDERMAN: You can do it. I'll be right back.

(Interviewer leaves the room.)

CRENSHAW: (Whispers:) Can you hear me? Hello?

CRENSHAW: (. . .)

CRENSHAW: (Whispers:) Mr. Woodhouse cut the bunny. He cut it with a pencil. He took a pencil and poked it. The pencil went inside. And the bunny got all red. He pulled the pencil out and there was this wet

stuff and he pulled and the wet stuff came out with
it. He made me eat it. I didn't want to eat it but Mr.
Woodhouse said he'd hurt my mommy if I didn't. He
made me put my fingers inside the hole and take out
the stuff inside and eat it. He made us all eat some.

CRENSHAW: (Whispers:) Am I clean now? Am I clean?

KINDERMAN: (Returns:) How are we feeling, Sean? Do you
feel clean now?

CRENSHAW: I feel clean.

(END OF INTERVIEW.)

I told Miss Levin that her child was safe in my class. I told her I would find out who had hurt her daughter. I would find this *Sean* and bring him to Condrey right away.

I lied to this woman without blinking. She came for help, confiding in me, and I didn't even hesitate, simply letting the false promises slip out from my mouth without ever second-guessing myself. I told her what she wanted to hear so I could escape my own classroom.

Then I ran away.

A few teachers decided to go out after parent-teacher conferences wrapped up. *Wanna come?* Tamara asked. *We're going to try to get Mrs. Baugher tipsy again.*

Thanks for the invite but I'm pretty tuckered . . . All these parents really did me in.

Tamara couldn't help but snort. *Oh, really? All those conferences, huh?*

I made a show of it by stretching my weary bones. *Line 'em up, knock 'em all down.*

Okay, teach, she said. *Go get your beauty sleep.* Then, *Sure you're okay with Elijah?*

Of course.

Maybe give him a little space? she offered. *If he wants to talk, he'll come to you . . .*

Space, I echoed.

By the look on her face, I can tell Tamara is having second thoughts.

Go. Have fun. We'll be fine. I'll make it a boys night.

I won't be out too late, I promise. There's pesto in the freezer.

Green sauce, Elijah calls it. Never the red. The basil comes from Tamara's garden, along with all the various mystery herbs I can't keep straight. That corner of the yard is off-limits to me, she says. Now I can't help but wonder what secret ingredients she's growing back there to cast her spells.

It took a while before Tamara felt comfortable leaving Elijah at home with me. But once she did, I sensed a certain relief sweep over her. She didn't have to do this all by herself anymore. Three years on her own was enough. She welcomed the help now. Depended on it.

Now I just had to master making Elijah his favorite meal. I'd spent most of my bachelor days straining spaghetti, dumping in a jar of Prego, and eating straight from the pot.

Surely I am capable of making angel hair pesto pasta. Surely.

The water boils on the stove, ready for the angel hair. No other pasta will suffice for Eli. I have a surplus of pasta left over from class. For our macaroni self-portrait projects, my students glue cheeks of lasagna onto a sheet of construction paper. Wagon wheel eyes. Rigatoni, penne, linguine. I always buy more pasta than we end up using. *To the victors, the spoils of spaghetti . . .*

Elijah colors at the kitchen table while I man the pot.

"Whatcha drawing?"

"Nothing."

I spot a lot of red on the paper, whatever it is. "How was school today, bud?"

"Fine." Elijah keeps coloring, not looking up from his paper.

"Anything happen?"

"No."

Ah—the monosyllabic conversation. Wonderful. I am still in the doghouse with Eli. He presses the crayon hard against the paper, long red slashes branching across the page.

I glance back at the boiling pot on the stove. The roiling water.

What's your first firm memory?

Psychologists say most children's recollections kick in as early as two, but some cerebral phenomenon known as childhood amnesia eventually takes those memories away. But unique events—trauma— will leave their indelible imprint on a child's mind. Trauma will linger forever.

I remember our station wagon.

I see Mom's hair swirl just below the surface of the simmering water. Her head sinks deeper. If I can just reach her, grab her, I can pull her out of the water before she drowns. Pull her onto the side of the river and force the air back into her lungs. Let her breathe. She wanted me in the car. That had been her plan. She meant for us to be together. Our road trip.

Jesus Christ. I back away from the pot. Was I really just about to reach my hand into boiling water? *What the fuck's happening to me?*

"Dinner's ready, Eli," I manage to say. "Wash your hands." No response. "Let's go. Clean the table. Now."

Eli lets out a groan, clearly unhappy at the interruption. *"Okay, okay."*

Dinner is stilted. Without Tamara around to run interference between us, there aren't many topics for the two of us to choose from. He's still mad at me, I get that. He hasn't made eye contact with me all night, pretending to look elsewhere whenever I turn to him. I have to hope that he'll forgive me at some point.

Forgive and forget.

It's impossible to drag information out from a five-year-old. The direct approach never works. You have to sidle up to the truth. If you ask specifically for the thing you want, they'll shut down. Repeating the question never works. Kids go on lockdown. You have to be creative with your interrogation technique. Learn the gentle art of kindergarten cross-examinations.

"So the piñata project was pretty fun, huh?"

I get the slightest nod from Eli as he struggles to spin his angel hair with his plastic fork.

"Sandy should play baseball, don't you think?"

Elijah glances up and wrinkles his nose as if to say, *What a stupid question.*

"It's hard at a new school. All those new faces. Must be tough for Sandy to make pals."

"Sandy's got friends," Elijah says, just to prove me wrong. That I'm an idiot.

"Oh yeah? Who?"

He shrugs.

"You don't know?" I ask, mock incredulously. "You know everybody in school!"

"Nobody knows who he is."

He.

"Oh?" I keep my tone conversationally curious. "A boy, huh? You don't know him?"

Another shrug.

"He must be invisible." It's always good to posit the thought that this is all make-believe. An imaginary friend is easier to discredit. "Did Sandy say if this friend has a name? Lafcadio?"

"Noooo." Elijah thinks this is hilarious. Sometimes I forget that he's still a *little* little kid.

"No? Then I bet it's, um . . . Skeletor?"

"No!"

"Then what is it, huh?"

"Sean."

Elijah grins. His first smile all night. His lips are stained green, flecks of basil stuck between his teeth. He dives back into his meal. He must have assumed our chat is over. *Case closed.*

The pesto clings to the pasta and all I see is blonde hair covered in algae, fanned on a bed of kelp. Elijah twists my mother's locks into the tines of his fork before forcing her hair into his mouth. I don't know how long I stare, watching him eat. I haven't spoken, haven't cogitated a single thought beyond the name.

Sean. This is spreading somehow. Infecting others. Who here knows about my past?

Who I am?

Could this be me? The question pops into my head. It's so abrupt, it almost doesn't feel like I thought it. Somebody else must have asked it. *Am I the one doing this?*

I can't see myself doing these things. It doesn't sound like me. Feel like me.

The devil made me do it. Isn't that what they always say?

This isn't me. I have to keep repeating it to myself: *This isn't me.*

What if . . . ? Gnawing thoughts. I can hear them, like rats crawling through the walls. *What if I'm responsible and don't realize it? Is that even possible?*

I have to get my memories straight. I need to begin at the beginning and work my way through everything I remember and try to understand what the hell's happening.

Elijah returns to his coloring between bites, running red crayon over a fresh sheet.

The paper. Elijah is drawing on a sheet of paper he found on the kitchen table.

The adoption forms.

"*Don't.*" I lunge and grab the paper from under Elijah's crayon, accidentally sending an errant slash of red across the page. Eli's shoulders bunch up to his ears, slipping into his shell.

Weegee. The drawing is unmistakable. It's his cat, torn open. Crayola intestines spill out from its abdomen. The green grass swirls with so much red.

"Elijah." I try to keep my voice as steady as I can. "Did you do this? To Weegee?"

Eli shakes his head. "You did."

"That's not true. I would never . . ." I'm unable to finish the thought the moment I notice the stack of adoption forms. I let go of the paper in my hand to pick up the next sheet.

A ring of children. A lanky stick figure towers over the rest, his arms extending beyond their normal proportions, as if he has four elbows. A daddy longlegs. A teacher.

Circle time.

"How did you . . ." I pick up the next sheet. A group of children stand in a ring. Crooked teeth colored in black sprout all around them. Not teeth. Headstones. They're in a cemetery. In the center of the children's circle is a boy dressed in his Sunday best. His skin is gray.

I flip through each sheet, grabbing the top page and glancing at the hand-drawn image. A tangle of stick figures knot into one another. An orgy of adults, teachers, a mass of spiders, their limbs intertwined and tugging. So many drawings. The entire stack has been colored.

There's paper all over the floor. All from Sean's childhood. My childhood. *My* lies.

"How . . ."

"Sean told me," Eli says, staring back.

"Who's Sean?" I demand. "Tell me."

Eli won't answer. He's breathing deeply through his nose, afraid but holding his ground.

"Who's Sean?"

Nothing. The fear is all over his face. I can see it but I can't stop myself from yelling.

"WHO'S SEAN?"

My cell phone rings. Eli uses the distraction to escape, running out from the kitchen. The sound of his feet carries through the house as I scramble for my phone.

The area code seizes my attention. Someone is calling from Greenfield. Again.

Don't answer.

I let the call go directly to voicemail. Not that they'll leave a message. They haven't before.

My phone rings again, the high-pitched trill working its way up my spine.

Don't answer.

I bring my phone to my ear and listen. I don't know what to say. I can hear breathing on the other end of the line.

"Sean? Is that you?" I haven't heard her voice since I was a boy. I'm suddenly five all over again, just a scared boy, as if the last thirty years never happened.

"Mom?"

"There you are. I've been looking everywhere for—"

My fingers slide across the screen to power down my phone before she can call again.

Turn it off turn it off turn it—

The same number pops up again as the phone trills in my hands, like a baby bird. I could crush it, simply squeeze my fist until its fragile bones snap, and I'd never hear her voice again.

Don't answer just turn it off TURN IT OFF.

But it won't stop, will it? This will never end. She'll find me. She already has. Swiping my phone, I open the channel between us again.

"Sean." It's no longer a question. "You changed your name . . . why would you do that?"

"Mom . . ." My voice sounds so small. It feels weak, her name quickly dissipating. I'm trembling. There isn't a bone in my body that can hold the rest of me up. Hold me together.

"Did you think I wouldn't find you? That you could hide from me?"

Eli is in his bedroom. Tamara is still out, so it's just me. Me and my mother on the phone. I can see her, imagine her after all these years, still as young as the last time I laid eyes on her. Still as beautiful. Sunk in the murk. The water all around us. Swallowing us whole.

"Why?" she asks. "Why are you hiding? Why did you run away from me?"

"Because . . ." Because I'm afraid. Because I'm ashamed of what I've done.

To her. To Mr. Woodhouse.

This is all my fault.

"Don't worry, hon," she says, her warm voice offering up some semblance of security. She's trying to comfort me. "Of course you'd run. Who wouldn't? After what you did?"

I look around the kitchen. The house has settled into its stillness. Her voice feels like footsteps on the floor, the warp of the wood bending with each step. She's coming closer.

Closer now . . .

Closer . . .

"All those lives you destroyed. The families you tore apart . . . You did that, Sean. *You.*"

"I . . . I'm sorry."

"That's very considerate of you, Sean. Should I call you Sean? Or do you prefer Richard?"

She's mocking me. *Taunting* me. Is Mom laughing? *This can't be happening*, I think. *It's not possible.*

"It's not you," I say.

"Then who is it, Sean? Who am I?"

Kinderman. Her face pops right into my head. Could she have found me? Tim and Nancy had severed ties with her immediately following the trial. They'd gone out of their way to distance me from anyone associated with the case, no matter what they said to the press.

"My mother is dead."

"Does that mean you won't talk to me?"

"This is sick," I hiss into the phone. "Whoever this is, *you're sick*."

"I believed you, Sean . . . Every word."

"I'm calling the police!"

"What are you going to tell them? Will you tell them about me? About *you*, Sean?"

I need to hang up. Turn off the phone. But it clings to my skin. Everything feels like it's covered in a glistening film, like I'm caught in a cobweb. It's too late. Too late to run.

"I see you're drawing again, Sean. I love it when you draw. I always have."

"I'm not."

"Don't lie to me," she says. "I saw you. Saw your picture of me."

She's here. She's seen me in the studio. Seen the sketch. Where is she calling from? Could she be here now? Outside our house? Is she in our yard, peering through a window?

"Go out to the studio. I have a gift for you."

"No," I protest. But it's weak. My voice is so small. A boy's voice.

I'm powerless against her. I do as I'm told.

"There's something I want you to see . . . See for yourself." She continues to talk as I leave the kitchen. "I've found someone new for you to sketch." Her voice follows me as I step outside, crossing the yard to the garage. "To *inspire* you . . ." The cold air crystalizes in my lungs, each breath scraping my throat. "It makes me happy to see you expressing yourself again."

A harsh odor washes over me as soon as I open the garage door. Sweet meat. Spoiled fruit. The grease of it coats my throat the moment I breathe in, unable to spit it out. I suddenly remember that it's Wee-gee. I left him in my studio last night and forgot to dispose his body after the Eli incident. Now the smell of him has permeated the space, clinging to the beams. Wood has a memory for scent, absorbing decay. Now it'll never forget. My studio will smell like death forever.

Before I enter, I know someone has been inside. There are small white squares scattered everywhere.

Polaroids.

My studio is *filled* with them. Dozens of photographs taped to the walls, arranged on the floor, attached to the easel.

And they're all of the same person.

A girl.

Sandy Levin.

Some are out of focus, her form fuzzy around the edges. The camera came too close to her, the flash blanching her pale skin. She's wrapped her arms around her shins, shielding herself from the probing lens, as if to protect her against its intruding gaze. In some pictures, she glances off, trying to hide from the camera. In most, though, she stares directly at the lens, looking out at me with empty eyes.

My stomach clenches. She's everywhere. "I . . ."

"Yes, Sean? What is it?"

I forgot I was even holding the phone. My mother's voice startles me. "I didn't do this."

"Do what, son?"

"This wasn't me."

"If it wasn't you, then . . . *who?*" She answers her own question. "Was it *Richard?*"

I buckle forward and vomit across the floor. Angel hair pasta fans over my feet. Her hair. The swell of bile from my stomach came so quick I didn't have time to run for the door.

This wasn't me. *This wasn't me.* It's all I can think, can say, repeating it to myself over and over, echoing through the studio. "It wasn't me. It wasn't me. It wasn't—"

"You're married now," Mom whispers into my ear. "You have a son. You must be so happy. To have this new life. But it can all go away, Sean. Families can be so fragile, can't they?"

What if . . . ? the gnawing thoughts whisper. *What if you're talking to yourself?*

I glance at the phone in my hand, suddenly wondering if I'm even talking to my mother—or not. Am I doing this to myself? Who else but me knows what happened?

Mom did.

Bringing the phone back to my ear, I ask, "What do you want from me?"

"You've made other people very, very angry, Sean. Stirring the pot, like you have. *Double, double toil and trouble.* They're watching you right now. They want to finish what you started. *Full circle.* Unless . . ."

Silence from the other end. "Unless *what?*"

"You can end this, son. It's the only way. Do it for me, Sean. For your mother."

History must repeat itself.

Must come full circle.

The line goes dead. The garage window is before me. The world on the other side is black. Obsidian. The longer I stare through it, the more my eyes can make out shadows.

Shadows within shadows taking shape. Silhouettes of strangers staring in. Of *others*.

This is not me, I say. But I can't hear myself say it. The words have no voice. I have to force myself to say it again, louder this time, nearly shouting, "This isn't me."

I pick up the Polaroids from the floor. I scour the garage, checking under every chair and box until I'm convinced I've collected them all. Now I have a deck of cards. I shuffle them, feeling the flick of each picture against my fingertips before tossing them into the fire pit Tamara and I set up for those cold nights together. I only have a little bit of time left before she returns home, so I douse the scattered stack and light the match right away, watching every last image of Sandy warp and bubble, listening to them hiss and crackle.

Other people, Mom said. *Other people.*

This isn't me, I keep repeating to myself. My own incantation around the fire. Rather than invoke some spirit, summoning them from the flames, my own personal sacrifice, I wanted to do away with this demon. Whoever he was. He wasn't me. This wasn't me.

This isn't me. This isn't me. This isn't me.

I almost believe myself by the time the last Polaroid curls into ash. Glancing back at the house, I spot the gray silhouette of a boy at the kitchen window. He steps away from the glass, knowing he's been caught spying, disappearing from sight. I watch Elijah run back to his bedroom.

DAMNED IF YOU DO
SEAN: 1983

- -

Officially speaking, nobody knew who started the fire.

But everyone knew who started the fire.

A window in the cafeteria had been smashed during the night. An *unknown assailant* crept into the building, wandering down its darkened halls. There were no alarms, no night guards. Each empty classroom sat in perfect stillness. The desks were lined up in even rows, chairs pushed in, like skeletons hunched over in the shadows.

Mr. Woodhouse's classroom was at the far end of the northern hall. Its walls were covered in charcoal self-portraits drawn by the students. The assignment for the students was to draw themselves how they wanted the world to see them: As a superhero. President. Even a cat, if they wished. Mr. Woodhouse didn't give his children any restrictions. He merely wanted them to imagine their future. The possibilities. *Be whoever you want to be.* Their scribbled eyes stared blankly back at this *unknown assailant*.

One charge brought against Mr. Woodhouse that received the most media attention was his usage of rituals in class, such as *circle time*.

Circle time was usually at the end of the day, just before the final bell. Mr. Woodhouse would have his kids sit on the carpet in a perfect circle. He didn't like using the term *Indian style,* though most teachers still called it that. He preferred *criss-cross applesauce.* His kids formed a ring on the floor, knees touching.

Mr. Woodhouse would ask his students to talk about their favorite part of the day and least favorite part of the day. *What's your rose and what's your thorn?*

He would have them close their eyes. *Can you see it?* he would ask. *Is it clear in your inner eye now?* He would then ask his children to imagine themselves putting that knowledge in a box. It could be as simple as a cardboard box—*skrch-skrch*—but it was their own special, secret receptacle hidden within their head where only they could access that knowledge.

You'll hold onto this knowledge for the rest of your lives, Mr. Woodhouse insisted, pressing his index finger against his temple, *where it can be called upon whenever you need it. Even as adults, it'll be here. Right here. Just waiting for you to open it . . . so fill it up.*

Mr. Woodhouse would then have them all sing *special* songs with words nobody had heard before, lyrics that Mr. Woodhouse himself had written, just for his children. The students were told not to share the words with anyone outside the circle. Not their parents or their friends.

The songs themselves could only be sung when it was circle time, when the students' eyes were closed, so that they couldn't see what Mr. Woodhouse was doing.

Sean said he peeped. He hadn't meant to. He knew Mr. Woodhouse would be very mad if he found out Sean had opened his eyes during circle time. But Sean couldn't help himself. He had to look. Just once. The students' voices were climbing higher and higher. It was impossible not to sway as they sang. A steady rhythm manifested itself naturally as they rocked left to right, like kelp along a river bottom. The higher their voices climbed, the faster their bodies swayed, which was strange, because Sean wasn't aware of the students' movements when he'd had his eyes closed. In the dark, there was nothing but the music. It was only when he peeked that he was even aware of this strange, rhythmic motion.

Mr. Woodhouse was in the middle of the circle. He had no clothes on. He had selected a boy from the ring—*duck, duck, GOOSE!*—and ushered him into the center and set him down on his back and, *oh it's Tommy, it's Tommy Dennings,* and just as the circle's swaying reached its peak, the students' voices no longer their voices but the ululations of something far more carnal, necks bent back, eyes rolling up into their skulls—

Mr. Woodhouse was staring directly at Sean.

No peeking, he whispered.

When Sean shared a version of this with the kind policeman, and then later with the kind Miss Kinderman, and then with the not-so-kind district attorney, he said he was scared of Mr. Woodhouse because now his teacher knew that he peeked when he wasn't supposed to. He was afraid, very afraid for his life, and his mom's life, because Sean knew Mr. Woodhouse's secret.

The jury heard bits and pieces of Sean's recorded interviews, but the story now belonged to the prosecutor and Miss Kinderman. Each added their own narrative flourish—making sure that Sean's words were heard—spinning his story further and further out. Perhaps this *unknown assailant* heard the prosecutor tell Sean's story in the courtroom; or heard snippets of it on the six o'clock news from their local anchor; or read about it in the newspaper. At a certain point it didn't matter who was telling the story. The story belonged to everyone now.

This *unknown assailant* must have pictured these ritualistic sex acts committed right there on the floor during circle time, as he—or she—poured an accelerant over the carpet. Kerosene splashed across the blackboards. Over the desks. Along the walls with all their hand-drawn pictures. The Crayola stick figures. Their spiraling eyes.

This *unknown assailant* backed out of the room, using the last of the kerosene to draw a highly flammable tail across the hallway floor.

The fire woke closer to the cafeteria. A slithering snake of flame wound all the way back to Mr. Woodhouse's classroom and made its hissing presence known.

The self-portraits turned to kindling. The desks collapsed. The fiberglass tiles along the ceiling blistered and fell, exposing heating ducts and wires.

The glass within the framed photograph on Mr. Woodhouse's desk cracked, then burned. The picture of his wife and daughter, smiling for the camera, curled into flame.

Shortly before two a.m., a truck delivering the local newspaper noticed the smoke. The driver phoned the fire in from the closest gas station.

By the time the fire department arrived, the blaze had spread through most of the school's northern hall, where the kindergarten and Head Start classrooms were located.

Sean woke to the sound of sirens tearing through the street. The rumble of a fire truck passed his window, the flimsy sheet of cardboard taped to the frame losing its grip and slipping to the floor. He lifted his head just in time to see the truck zoom by their house.

Greenfield only had a volunteer fire service, necessitating the usage of the neighboring county's department, twenty miles away. By the time their trucks pulled up, most of the building was on fire. The families were already there. They stood before the blaze, faces bathed in its glow. The Gilmores. The Cardiffs. The Dellacorts and Denningses. The Blackmers. The Evanses.

They came to watch the school burn.

RICHARD: 2013

You've made other people very, very angry. Mom's words keep echoing through my head. *Others.* She said there are others. Others watching me.

But it wasn't Mom. It couldn't be.

"Good morning, Richard," someone says as I pass them in the hall. I don't see their face. I don't even know who said it. I couldn't sleep last night. I can't focus on who's in front of me.

"Morning," I respond automatically. Was it a teacher? Do they even work here?

Nod. Smile. Repeat: *Good morning, good morning, good morning . . .*

"Morning, Rich."

"Morning."

You're talking to yourself again, Tamara would say if she were here with me, slipping her head into my field of vision and finding my eyes, snapping me back into focus.

Was I? I'd usually ask, trying to play it off. *Sorry . . . Just got a lot on my mind, I guess.*

Talking to myself. Talking in my sleep. Talking to someone who's not even there.

Kinderman. It has to be Miss Kinderman. The more I think about it, the more the notion takes root. There's no one else. Who else knew all these pieces of my past? Memories I can't even remember. She's the only one. Now she's pretending to be my mother.

It has to be her. I can't shake it now, the certainty of it. *But why?*

When winter hits and it's too cold for me to bike, Tamara, Elijah, and I drive to school together in the family Jeep. But this morning I was out the door before Tamara had even crawled out of bed. I didn't say goodbye to either of them. I needed to leave before Eli woke. I had to think about how I was going to handle this. The kid thought I killed his cat, for Christ's sake. There was something he knew. Something he wasn't telling me.

Did you think I wouldn't find you? she'd said. *That you could hide from me?*

Kinderman is the only person who makes sense. Has to be her. Had she gotten to Eli somehow? Asked him to play along?

The Polaroids. How the hell could Kinderman have taken all those photos of Sandy? Five-year-old's aren't alone for even a second these days.

Is Sandy in danger? Why isn't she saying anything?

"Morning, Richard."

"Morning, Hallie." Was that Hallie?

"Morning, Rich."

Miss Castevet is no longer the first to arrive at school. Ever since Professor Howdy passed, she's drifted. She doesn't say a word when we walk by one another. Her face is downright sour. Jesus, can that biddy scowl. What did I do to her? Why is she looking at me like that?

Others. The word echoes in my mind.

Teachers shuffle to the faculty lounge for a top-up, filling their travel mugs to the hilt with coffee before heading to class and beginning their day.

I should go straight to my room. I should avoid everyone. But my body is locked on autopilot, letting my feet lead me wherever they want, where they always go at this hour.

Welcome to the teachers' lounge. Our Alamo. The lounge holds all the essentials for our survival: a fridge full of milk containers and Tupperware lunches. A coffeepot simmers throughout the day, the odor of burnt Folgers filling the room.

Mr. Dunstan hums to himself on the couch. His face is hidden behind a newspaper, but I know it's him.

Miss Castevet sits at the round table by the kitchen area nursing a mug of tea. She's staring off into space. Her eyes hold on to nothing. Lost.

Hadn't I just passed her in the hall? How'd she get here before I did?

"Good morning, Richard," a voice speaks behind me.

I spin around too fast.

Condrey steps back. "Sorry. Didn't mean to startle you . . ."

"No, sorry, my fault." How can I play this off? "Didn't get much sleep last night."

"Everything all right?"

"Just fine." I never envied Condrey's job. Always juggling the expectations of the progressive parental pack, keeping the school's numbers up to maintain its reformist status. She serves so many masters. The board of education. The parents.

Others.

"Can I talk to you for a quick sec?" she asks.

Mr. Dunstan lowers his newspaper long enough to clock Condrey and me, then quickly lifts the paper back up to continue humming. What's that song? It's really nagging at me now.

"I just wanted to check in. See how everything went last night." She leans in and whispers, "With Sandy's mom?"

I can't meet Condrey's eyes. I glance off to the side.

Miss Castevet is staring straight at me now. Something has snapped her back into focus.

"Miss Levin called my office a couple of times," Condrey says. "She won't leave a message. I haven't had a chance to call her back, but she's clearly wound up about something."

Just tell her . . .

This is my chance. I can tell Condrey everything. She's opened the door for me.

Tell her!

Mr. Dustan's humming has intensified. It's like he's conducting a fucking one-man symphony. The drone is so loud, it's all I can hear. How can Condrey stand it?

"I'm talking to all her teachers," she says. "Just in case they've noticed anything."

"Anything," I echo. If I were a bit more shrewd, I would have picked up the context without her having to spell it out. But I'm far too tired for that now. Too numb.

"Have you seen any signs of trouble?" she asks, rather diplomatically.

I focus on Miss Castevet. She hasn't blinked. Her eyes sharpen themselves against me. I notice the corner of her mouth lift into the slightest smirk. She's grinning at me.

I can tell Condrey is losing her patience. "Have you?"

Mr. Dunstan's song drills into my head. The drone of bees. A whole hive. I can see them pushing against the insides of his cheeks, his face bulging, pulsing, alive with writhing insects, his mouth full of them, struggling to break free, break free and sing, sing, sing their song for all to hear.

"I haven't."

"Nothing?" Condrey sounds doubtful. "Nothing at all?"

"Nothing at all." I turn to the coffeepot. I open the cabinet above the sink and grab a mug, any mug. This one reads: DON'T TALK TO ME UNTIL THIS MUG IS EMPTY.

"Miss Levin has been a handful all year," Condrey says behind my shoulder. "Don't worry, I'm dealing with her."

I turn toward her. There must be a puzzled look on my face because she winks right at me, as if to suggest that we're in this together. Or is it something else?

Why would Condrey wink at me? Why is she smiling like that? "It would help if you could keep an eye on Sandy for me. Make sure she's okay. We need to stay on top of this."

"Of course," I say, pouring coffee.

"Has Sandy . . . talked to you at all? Said anything that might lead you to believe there's something going on at home? Anything?"

This coffee is going to eat a hole through my intestinal lining. I can already taste the acid building up in my stomach. But I have to occupy my hands with something. Focus on something, *anything*, other than this conversation. Other than Miss Castevet—her eyes following me across the room. Other than Mr. Dunstan's insectal sonata. I have to keep myself from humming along. It's in me now. I can't get the earworm out of my head.

"She hasn't said anything to me," I say, just to fill the air with the sound of my voice and block out everything else. I pull the half-gallon cardboard carton of milk from the fridge. There's a black-and-white photograph of a face on the carton's side. A boy smiles back at me. His pixelated face is blurry due to a misprint, his features smeared away from where they're supposed to be.

HAVE YOU SEEN THIS CHILD?

It's Eli. His face is on the carton. The milk slips out of my fingers. Condrey and I both leap back as it crashes to the floor.

Mr. Dunstan finally—*finally*—stops humming as he lowers the newspaper. The room sounds so quiet now. The silence is worse. It's somehow even louder now than when he was chanting. He was chanting, wasn't he?

Condrey says something, but I can't hear anything other than the reverberations from Mr. Dunstan's song. I thought he stopped. Did he pick up the chant again, or is it in my head?

The song. What is that song?

Milk gushes over the floor, pulsing out from the carton. I lean over to pick it up and then turn back to the other teachers in the lounge. "Which one of you did this?"

Miss Castanet doesn't say a word. Dunstan shakes his head a bit too quickly.

"Richard?" Condrey asks. "Are you okay?"

I have to pinch my eyes shut for a moment, squeezing them tight before opening them again and discovering the face of another child, some other boy, not Elijah, smiling at me.

I nod to Condrey. Even approximate something like a smile. *All good.*

"Just let me know if anything comes up." Condrey keeps at me. She's choosing to pretend nothing happened. "If we miss something, we could really be in trouble."

Dunstan's humming again. I almost yell at him to shut up *shut the fuck up* but I have to keep it together.

The song. Now I remember where I heard it. I *knew* I recognized it. It's from the made-for-TV movie, during the opening credits sequence.

I leave the spilled milk behind and rush out of the teachers' lounge and into the hall.

"Richard—" someone calls out.

Get to class, I think. *Just get to class.* I'll be safe there. In my room. I pull out my keys, rattling in my hand as I fumble through them before finding the right one and bring it up to—

The door to my classroom is open.

I notice the glow first. The slightest flicker of firelight in the otherwise dark room.

Someone broke into my classroom. *My room.* I feel the sting of it, the very violation of this intrusion. I should turn on the lights. There are no windows in my room since it's located in the middle of the building. With the lights off it's truly pitch-black. But something tells me not to hit the switch. I want to see what's laid out before me. Take it all in the way it's meant to be.

By candlelight.

The desks have been rearranged into a circle. A ring of red and black votive candles are positioned on the desktops, drawing me in but not quite illuminating the center of the circle.

I step inside, even though I know I shouldn't. I shouldn't be entering this space.

Run, Sean says. *RUN.*

But I can't. I can't turn back. Not now. Not ever. Someone has done this for me and me alone. They want me to see this.

To bear witness.

The flames flicker when I step in, my very presence in the room disturbing the air. My eyes roam, adjusting to the darkness, seeing what I couldn't before. All the pictures on the walls, all my students' drawings, have been defiled, each one crossed out with frenzied *X*s. Pictures of families slashed in magic marker. Ceramic pinch pots shattered. Our papier-mâché projects have been torn open and thrown to the floor. But the center of the room is clear. Clean.

I want to be clean.

There are markings on the floor. Even before I can see it completely, I know what it is.

A pentagram.

Just like the opening scene from the movie. Like the ritual I described to Kinderman. To all those adults who lapped up my story like so much spilled milk.

I feel eyes on me. The shadows in the room shift. Something is moving. Behind me. Over my shoulders. In the corners. Something hiding inside the dark. I turn and see them. All of them.

Dolls. A ring of puppets stripped of clothing. They're the same kind of anatomically correct puppets you'd find in a therapist's office. *Point to where the bad man touched you* . . . There have to be dozens of them, too many to count, all of them left in various sexual positions around the room. A fucking orgy in the toy shop. I can almost hear them moaning—no, singing.

I walk toward the pentagram.

This is for me.

All for me.

That's when I see it. A severed hand. Perched upright, palm facing the entrance. Facing me. The fingers are so small. Even from a safe distance, I can tell it's a child's.

The gray boy. He's come back for me.

His fingernails shine like the sun, the tips on fire, burning toward heaven.

Waving at me.

Hungry, Sean? Take. Eat. For this is my body . . .

Someone shrieks behind me, pulling me out of my reverie. Miss Gordon screams in the doorway.

SEAN: 1983

"If you're just now tuning in, you're watching *Satan's Playground: Devil Worship in America*," Manuel Cassavetes soberly intoned, speaking directly to the camera. "I'd like to encourage parents to please make sure your children are not watching this unsupervised."

The glare of the studio lights was too bright for Sean. He couldn't help but wince and squirm in his seat. His hair clung to his sweaty brow. His suit was itchy. His collar only grew tighter at his neck, his tie constricting around his throat.

"What you are about to hear is shocking," Mr. Cassavetes continued. "It is heinous. But above all else . . . it is very, very real."

Sean kept his attention on his host.

"Though we may never know what the exact number is," he said with scripted precision, "as of this live broadcast, it is estimated that there are over a million practicing Satanists in the United States. *One million*. The mind can only reel at such a staggering figure."

A woman from the studio audience gasped, using her hand to fan herself with Pentecostal furor. She reminded Sean of Miss Betty. How long had it been since he'd seen her?

This felt more like church services to Sean. Mr. Cassavetes preached his own televised form of fire and brimstone. The producers populated their pews with a motley assortment of audience members—churchgoers, self-professed devil worshippers, heavy-metal fans, and schoolmarms. A few waved homemade signs.

KEEP SATAN AWAY FROM OUR BABIES.

MCDONALDS DONATES 2 THE DEVIL! RAY KROC GIVES 20% TO SATAN.

THE DEVIL DOESN'T BELONG IN OUR SCHOOLS.

From where Sean sat, they were a shapeless mass of silhouettes. He hardly understood why he was here. He only knew that grown-ups had become very interested in his story.

"These devil worshippers are a highly organized, well-funded operation wholly unknown to those around them," Cassavetes said. "They can be members of your church, your school, your own family. They can be the parents of your children's classmates, politicians, or even police officers. The people we trust with our safety, our lives. They . . . are . . . *everywhere*."

The moment the man with the headset announced they were taking a commercial break, Mr. Cassavetes seemed like a completely different person. His body relaxed. All that fury faded.

He was nothing but smiles now.

"On fire tonight," he said to no one in particular as a cluster of fussy assistants swarmed around him, powdering his temples and touching up his subtle eye shadow. His unnaturally tan skin seemed incapable of perspiring. One assistant took a small, fine-toothed comb and groomed his mustache. That mustache—full-bodied, perfectly coiffed—was clearly Mr. Cassavetes's most distinguishing feature, Sean thought.

"Better pace yourself," the man with the headset said. "Eighty-four minutes to go."

"You ain't seen nothing yet . . ."

Mr. Cassavetes glanced over at Sean as his team continued to primp. When they made eye contact, Mr. Cassavetes gave Sean a wink. Just a little something between the two of them.

Don't worry, kid, that glint in Mr. Cassavetes's eye said. *We got this . . .*

Sean and his mother had originally been in the live studio audience in the front row. At one point during the broadcast, Mr. Cassavetes had stepped down from the stage and addressed Sean directly. He placed a comforting hand on the boy's shoulder and squeezed, letting him know that the cameras were on both of them. That all the world was watching. Watching him.

It was also their cue that their segment was coming up. Shortly after that, the man with the headset had ushered them onstage. "Remember to breathe," he whispered to Sean just before leaving him alone with his mom. Good advice. Sean nodded, repeating his sage words.

Remember to breathe . . .

Remember to breathe . . .

Breathe . . .

People swarmed around them until—just like that—they scurried backstage. Sean glanced out at the audience.

All their eyes, staring, waiting for him to—

"And we're back in five!" the man wearing the headset announced.

Licking their lips.

"Four . . ."

Their glistening lips.

The man with the headset silently brought up three fingers.

Their forked tongues.

Two fingers.

So wet under the spotlight, so red.

One.

Mr. Cassavetes gave Sean another wink and then turned to the camera. "Hello and welcome back to our show," he said. "We have some very special guests joining us tonight . . ."

Mom hadn't let go of Sean's hand through the whole show. Her palms were sweating. She must have been nervous, too. Maybe even more nervous than Sean. Anytime someone approached from behind, she'd startle. It was happening more and more lately.

Mom was afraid of everybody now. And who could blame her? Her son was the target of a secret network of Satan worshippers. The devil was everywhere, waiting for her to slip.

Turn her back.

Let him go.

That's when the devil would pounce. That's when his devotees would take Sean away from her. She couldn't tell for sure who they were or how many, but she was positive they were among them right now, hiding in the studio audience. Perhaps even on the television crew.

They look just like us, was how Mr. Cassavetes put it. *They are everywhere.*

They were here, watching her at that very moment. Waiting.

The "special news broadcast" was on live television. Sean hadn't understood at first. Wasn't all TV live? Except for Saturday morning cartoons, like *The Smurfs*? He'd overheard the woman in the row behind him whispering about how Smurfs taught kids witchcraft. Not to mention communism. There's a reason why Papa Smurf resembles Karl Marx, she said. Her church successfully petitioned their local affiliate to take that carnal cartoon off the air, a victory that brought this particular row of audience members much pleasure. Satan lost his syndication.

Was He-Man really dangerous? How could Papa Smurf serve Satan? Did adults actually believe this stuff? It seemed silly to Sean . . .

Didn't they know it was all pretend?

This was still a game, wasn't it? Was everyone playing along now? Who was in on it?

Mr. Cassavetes explained to Sean that while, yes, his favorite TV shows featured living, breathing human beings, this was happening in real time. Nothing staged or phony about it. What Sean said would be seen by millions of people across the country the moment he said it. Sean didn't understand "broadcast" and "on air" and "prime time," but Cassavetes sure took it seriously. It had to be important, then, whatever it meant.

"We have a brave boy with us tonight," Mr. Cassavetes announced to the people watching at home. "You may recognize Sean Crenshaw from the Greenfield Six trial that has transfixed the nation. Sean is one of the innocent children who suffered at the hands of his kindergarten teacher and five other faculty members who have been charged with satanic ritual abuse."

Why did everybody keep calling him brave? He didn't feel brave. What had he done to deserve all this attention?

He wanted to take it all back. Everything he said to Mr. Yucky and the Bad Snatcher. It felt wrong now, having all these eyes on him.

He glanced at his mother. She kept staring off into the audience. The sea of people. Her eyes never settled on one spot. Always moving. Never focusing. She hadn't eaten recently. She was looking thin. Her cheek bones poked through but her eyes sank back.

Just her and him.

Against the world.

Just her and him.

Against the devil.

Just her and him . . . and Miss Kinderman, who sat on the other side of Sean in a smart light-purple pantsuit. Her hair looked different. Shinier. She was wearing more makeup than usual, even more than she wore during their sessions. Her shoulders looked bigger some-how. Puffier, almost. Sean slowly brought his hand up and tapped her shoulder. It was squishy.

Miss Kinderman belonged on TV. On *Dallas* with the other beauti-ful women. She smiled the widest smile whenever the cameras were pointed at her, or put on a thoughtful expression when Mr. Cassavetes asked a question that seemed to merit deep consideration.

Mom and Miss Kinderman had been talking less and less to each other. When Mom came to pick Sean up from his sessions, she would wait in the station wagon. He felt as if he was stuck between them now, as if this were a game of tug-of-war and he was the rope.

They were going to pull him to pieces.

The segment before had been a prerecorded tour of Greenfield Academy, now nothing but a gutted shell of burnt timber. Sean barely recognized it. Was that Mr. Woodhouse's classroom? He didn't even realize his school had burned down. Mom had pulled him out months ago. Maybe longer? It was so hard to tell, being stuck at home all day. *You'll go back next year*, Mom promised. *We'll find you an even better school, with new friends. And better teachers, and . . .*

Sean didn't want to go to a new school. All the kids at Greenfield wanted to be his friend now. Always asking him what happened. Always wanting to hear his side of the story.

"Thank you again for agreeing to be here tonight, Sean," Mr. Cassa-vetes said as he leaned in. "Do you mind if I call you Sean? Speaking out like this takes courage. Courage a child your age should never have to show . . ." Cassavetes turned away from Sean and faced the camera. "But the world is never just, is it? *Out of the mouths of babes*, as it says in scripture."

So many eyes. The eyes in the audience.

The camera. That glass eye.

Staring.

"How are you feeling, Sean? Are you scared? It's okay to be scared. I would be if I were in your shoes . . . But I want you to know you're safe here. With me."

Sean nodded.

"Now, Sean," Mr. Cassavetes started, just as he told him he would when they prepped backstage earlier that afternoon. "In your own words, as best as you can, can you describe how your teacher brought Satan into your classroom?"

Sean nodded again. "He made us sit in a circle and close our eyes. He made us sing a song he taught us with funny words . . ."

It was so easy. Saying these words. He'd said them so many times before. The more he spoke, the more he noticed how the audience reacted. A woman brought her hand to her mouth, stifling a gasp. Another woman's eyes glistened with tears. So many distraught faces. All of them saying, *poor you.*

How brave.

"I want to remind our viewers that there have been multiple reports of grave desecrations, graffiti of occult symbols." Cassavetes had to keep the pace building without going too far. He quickly pivoted, crossing his arms and pinching his chin, as if to summon a question from somewhere deep within his valiant heart. "Sean, if you can . . . I'm curious: What made you take part in these terrible things? Why didn't you speak up? Tell your mother?"

"Because . . ." What was Sean supposed to say again? "He was my teacher."

Someone from the audience let out a shout, like a balloon popping.

"*My teacher,*" Mr. Cassavetes repeated. "Someone you have been told to trust. To depend on. To learn from. A teacher is supposed to show you the ways of the world . . . What hope do our children have if their own teachers are indoctrinating them into the ways of Satan?"

Mr. Cassavetes let this question hang in the air for a moment.

"Mrs. Crenshaw, I have to imagine this has been particularly diffi-cult on you ..."

Mom nodded. Her mouth made a funny shape. To Sean, it looked like she was sucking on a hard, sour candy.

"What is it like to hear your son say these things?"

"It's ..." she started, then halted. Her eyes darted to her hand, still gripping onto Sean. Squeezing. "It's terrifying."

"Now I understand that your husband is no longer a part of your family."

"That's correct ..."

"What were the warning signs that you missed?"

Mom's pinched expression turned into something that was harder for Sean to read. "Excuse me?"

"You're going to have to forgive me, ma'am ... but a part of tonight's program is to help show *other* parents how they might be able to stop this from happening in their family. Looking at your own personal experiences, your son's molestation, will help those watching at home—"

"I protected my son," Mom called out. Her voice was higher than before.

"Of course you—"

"I love my son." Her lips tightened. "I did everything I could to—to keep him safe."

Sean didn't like the way Mr. Cassavetes was talking to his mom. It sounded like he was saying it was all her fault. That she was a bad mother. That wasn't a part of their deal. Mr. Cassavetes never said any-thing about that before the show started. He was changing the rules.

He was playing a different game. All by himself. With rules only he knew.

Mr. Cassavetes was cheating.

"And how do you react to claims your son made about cannibalism?"

Sean's mother opened her mouth but couldn't speak.

Cannibalism? Sean was suddenly stuck in the stickiness of the word. *What's that?*

"Allegedly, students were forced to eat the flesh of aborted fetuses," Cassavetes said without a hint of doubt. "We've had reports that young women—kids themselves—were impregnated by these devil worshippers, forced to abort their babies on an altar."

Sean was confused. Mr. Cassavetes was saying things that Sean had never said before.

"Students like Sean were allegedly forced to eat the flesh of these babies, and I can't help but ask *how* in the world we, as a nation, have come to this? How can we make this stop?"

Sean looked at his mother, whose face was practically on fire. Mr. Cassavetes noticed too and turned to the camera. "Joining us now is a trained specialist and child psychologist, Dr. Mia Kinderman. Dr. Kinderman has been working exclusively with Sean and other victims of the Greenfield Six. Her findings have been revelatory."

"Thank you for having me, Manuel."

Could a man with a leathery tan like Mr. Cassavetes blush? Not under that much makeup, but his smile took on a sheepish quality, as if he were being bashful.

"Dr. Kinderman," Mr. Cassavetes continued, "what can you tell us about your research?"

"Well, Manuel, given that this is an ongoing case and I'm working with children, the lion's share of my findings must remain private. But, that said, from what I'm able to discuss with the public, I must say . . . this epidemic is far worse than anyone can imagine."

"Worse? How so?"

"Ritualistic abuse is a cancer. It is spreading throughout our communities, small town after small town. It has made its way into our schools and it has infected our children."

"But *how*? Why children, Dr. Kinderman? Why target our most innocent?"

"*Because* of their innocence. Because Satanism has one goal and one goal only. To make people despair. If they can corrupt our most impressionable citizens . . . what hope do we have?"

"How could such atrocious acts go unnoticed for so long? How did we get to this point?"

"Simple," she said. "Because nobody wants to believe something so evil as this is possible. And yet . . . here we are. It's only when someone brave, like Sean, steps forward and shines a light on this type of moral corruption that the rest of the world is willing to listen."

Miss Kinderman turned to Sean and smiled.

That's when it struck him. Miss Kinderman was looking more and more like his mother every day. Or the way she *used* to look. Healthier, happier. More beautiful. How much longer would it be until there was nothing left of his mother and Miss Kinderman took her place?

Sean wanted to run. Run right off the stage. He wanted to grab his mother's hand and pull her away from this strange and scary place.

"Do you believe Sean's testimony? These heinous claims of devil worship?"

Miss Kinderman considered this. "I think, as a culture, we must believe our children. No matter what."

Now Mr. Cassavetes looked directly at Sean. "It's possible that there are people watching our show tonight who may have been involved in the same secret organization of Satan worshippers as your teacher. Is there something you might want to say to them, Sean?"

Sean considered this as best he could. What could he say?

"Stop hurting me. Stop hurting my mom," he said directly to Mr. Cassavetes, looking him right in the eye. "Get away from me."

Mr. Cassavetes smiled a knowing smile. "*Stop hurting me,*" he repeated. "Such a simple plea. And yet . . . look at how low we've gone, to where the innocent cries of our most vulnerable go unanswered. Our country is in the midst of a holy war right now, ladies and gentlemen. I want to follow Sean's courageous lead and speak directly to those disciples of the devil who are watching tonight. I know you are." He looked into the camera, taking on a stern, puffed-up stance. He pointed at the lens and jabbed at the air with his index finger. "You may hide in the shadows, you may creep in the corners of our country, but you'll be brought into light, under the eyes of God, and you'll not—I repeat, *you will not*—win. Not in my America. Evil will not prevail. Thank you for watching."

The studio audience jumped to their feet and cheered. Most of them. Some pushed against their neighbors. Some yanked the posterboard signs from the hands of their fellow audience members and ripped them in half. A fight broke out in the back. A pair of linebacker security guards rushed in to break it up.

But all Sean heard was the applause. They were cheering for him. Worshipping him.

He was a star. A bright, shining star.

He looked up into his mother's face. *I did what you wanted, Mom. Are you proud of me?*

But Mom wasn't there. Not really. Her body, yes, but the rest of her was gone. Even if he was only five, Sean knew when his mother was there and when she was not.

He turned back to the crowd. Tucked into the audience, two rows back, was a little valley of shadow. Sean had to squint to be sure, but he saw someone he recognized.

A child staring back at him, unaffected by the chaos around him.

Sean waved.

The gray boy waved back.

RICHARD: 2013

I remember the parents. How they gathered outside the courthouse every morning during the trial. The police set up barricades around the main entrance. Blue-painted roadblocks flanked the sidewalk, creating a narrow egress for officers to escort Mr. Woodhouse inside without being attacked by a stray mother. Protestors pressed against the blockade, brandishing their homemade signs over their heads.

RIDE THE LIGHTNING, WOODHOUSE (along with a crude sketch of an electric chair).

THE DEVIL YOU KNOW (with a photocopy of Mr. Woodhouse's mugshot).

SEE YOU IN HELL (a caricature of Mr. Woodhouse bent over, ready to receive a pitchfork up his rear end delivered by the devil).

Mothers spat at Mr. Woodhouse as he walked by. He kept his head low, an officer at either side, shoulder to shoulder with him. I barely recognized him in his orange jumpsuit. That couldn't be my kindergarten teacher. Who was this man?

I saw Tommy Dennings's mom lean over the wooden stanchion

and spit a wad of phlegm directly at Mr. Woodhouse's right cheek. A riled-up dad leaned forward and grabbed his arm, dragging Mr. Woodhouse closer. More parents took hold, seizing him, until Mr. Woodhouse's slight body was swallowed up by a knot of parents. The police couldn't yank him back, couldn't pry him out.

These parents were going to rip Mr. Woodhouse apart. They wanted blood. His blood. They called out his name, shouting it over and over, until it sounded like an invocation.

Woodhouse, Woodhouse, Woodhouse . . .

"You okay?" Tamara whispers into my ear. "Where did you go just now?"

"I'm right here."

"No . . . You went off somewhere again. In your head. Can you tell me?"

"It's nothing," I say. "I just want to get—"

Far, far away from here.

"—this over with."

That hand. I keep seeing the child's hand in my head. Its flaming fingers waving at me. It looked so real. I could've sworn it was flesh and bone—but it was just the severed appendage from a department-store mannequin, lopped off at the wrist. Its fingers had been dipped in some sort of combustible substance. Sterno, maybe. What looked like blood before was just more tempera, pilfered from my own art supply closet.

This isn't happening, I keep repeating to myself.

Sail a-way.

Sail a-way.

Sail a-way.

"I'm here, okay?" Tamara squeezes my hand. "You don't have to go through this alone."

Condrey called an emergency PTA meeting that evening. There's no getting around this. She can only get out in front of it. She has to craft her own narrative of the incident in hopes of steering the conversation away from the rattled parents now demanding answers. A paranoid din has overtaken the auditorium. Every last seat is filled with distraught parents.

I don't recognize any of these faces. The demographics of Danvers keep shifting. Fewer suits and ties, more beards and vintage dresses. Hipster parents. Condrey kowtows to nearly every demand these eco-moms and -dads have. Composting. A community garden. Solar panels. A gluten-free lunch menu. Now they want answers for what happened in their school.

The Friends of Danvers want blood.

"If I could have everyone quiet down, please," Condrey announces into the microphone onstage. "Let's begin, everybody, thanks."

I spot Sandy in the audience. Miss Levin brought her along, which seems strange. Parents don't usually drag their kids to these meetings. They'd be bored out of their minds. Hell—I'm usually bored out of my fucking skull. But Sandy's mother won't let her out of her sight. Not anymore.

Sandy's head is in its standard lowered position. She doesn't look happy to be here. Pretty safe to say nobody is. *I'm right there with you, Sandy,* I think. *Let's sail a-way, sail a-way, sail a-way.*

Tamara and I sit in the rear. Teachers steer clear of these meetings, but we're parents too. Or, at least, Tamara is. I'm an imposter, a cuckoo who lays its eggs in the nest of another bird to nurture and raise. *Brood parasites,* they're called. Maybe I'm a parental parasite. A cuckoo dad.

Tamara leans over and whispers, "How long did you talk to the police?"

"Three or four hours. They wouldn't let me go."

"What did they ask you?"

"Nothing."

"Nothing?"

"*Nothing*. Just routine questions."

"Jesus. You don't have to snap at me."

Detective Merrin had put me under the microscope, like I was the one who had done this, as if I were the guilty party here. Like he didn't believe me.

Mr. Bellamy, he started. It was impossible to make eye contact with him. Merrin was closing in on his sixties. He'd probably attended the ritualistic crime seminars thirty years ago. Most police departments had to sit through the FBI slideshows on how to handle cases like mine that had been cropping up around the country. Had he learned about the warning signs? The telltale graffiti? The black candles and desecrated graves? Did he recognize me specifically?

That's when I notice a father staring at me.

He's four rows ahead of us. His head is completely turned around, looking straight at me. *Glaring.* He's wearing a wool cashmere topcoat. Slate gray. The lights have been left up in the auditorium so there's no hiding in the dark. I glance over my shoulder, just to make sure he's not looking at someone behind me—but no, there's no denying that he's staring right at me.

"The administration is more than happy to provide parents a voice for their concerns," Condrey announces before giving the school's official version of the events.

Yes, the school immediately notified the authorities after this morning's incident.

Yes, of course, the matter was dealt with in the safest and most efficient manner possible.

No minor laid eyes on the scene. Only the teacher whose classroom this unfortunate episode occurred in.

Yes—it's true that one of the school's pets was found disemboweled on the soccer field a few days ago, but there is no evidence to suggest that these two incidents are related.

Mrs. Condrey was calm and cool, like she'd been all day. She handled the whole fiasco rather efficiently when I showed up to her office, distraught and babbling. Come to think of it, she wasn't shocked at all. *Like she already knew . . .*

The other teachers were quick to clamor around the door to my classroom. Everybody wanted to sneak a peek. See the burning fingers for themselves. The gray boy's hand.

Don't call him that, I admonish myself. *It's not him.*

"Let's dispel any rumors here and now," Condrey says. "The authorities have assured me that they will find who is responsible for this and bring him to justice."

Bring him to justice. Everyone demands justice, but what they're really after is—

Blood, I say into the microphone. *Mr. Woodhouse made us drink blood.*

I'm sitting in a room and speaking into a microphone in front of other grown-ups.

I'm telling the microphone about how Mr. Woodhouse would dig up graves of children and chop off their hands. A virgin's hands, apparently, were very powerful tools of black magic. A satanic priest could curse anyone they wished with it. I knew this because a police officer told me all about it. I heard him talking about how he'd read about black masses and what kind of rituals they perform in cemeteries. This seemed like a reasonable thing to share. Like *the right thing.* Isn't that why the officer told me in the first place? To share with the microphone?

"You wanna go?" Tamara whispers. "We can sneak out if you want to . . ."

"Can we?"

Too late. Condrey opens the floor for questions.

"What's the administration doing?" one dad in a navy-blue cotton crewneck sweater asks. "Are you just going to let our kids come to school and hope it doesn't happen again?"

"We'll open our doors as soon as the police department says it's okay," Condrey offers. "Hopefully tomorrow."

Hopefully sends a wave of ire rippling through the audience. School closings meant a mad dash for childcare, which meant missing work, which meant time and money.

"What are the police doing?" a mother calls out from the rear, decked out in a glen plaid blazer. "Do they have any leads?"

"That's for the police to say," Condrey replies. "I don't have any more information."

"I'm sorry, but this all sounds like bullshit to me."

Condrey, our *princiPAL*, our friend till the end, leans into the microphone and takes a quieter tone. "Please. I'm just as stunned by all of this as you are . . . But let's try to keep calm. There's no need to resort to profanity."

My mind wanders back to the interview with Merrin.

What did you see first?

(The open door.)

What was different about the classroom?

(The flickering. The pulse from the candles.)

Who else has keys to your room?

(The custodian. The principal. Miss Kinderman.)

When did you leave school the night before?

(After parent-teacher conferences.)

Can anyone verify where you were last night?

(Eli. Tamara. Mom. Kinderman.)

At what time did you arrive at school this morning?

(Early. One of the first, if not the very first.)

Why do you think someone would do this?

(They know who I am. What I've done.)

Do you think it's something personal?

(Mom told me things must come full circle.)

Are there any parents or teachers who you've had any disagreements with recently?

(Others. There are others.)

Why you, Mr. Bellamy?

I couldn't tell Detective Merrin who I was. Who I am. If he knew about Sean, then he would think that I was the one—

That I had—

"I don't know about you," another father says. He's wearing a charcoal wool herringbone half-zip sweater. "But I'm not bringing my kid back until whoever did this is behind bars."

An echo of consent rises. *Pull out yer pitchforks, parents.* I thought we were better than this. We couldn't fall for this type of hysteria now. But here it is. History repeating itself.

Full circle.

"People, *please.*" Condrey has to fight hard to keep things on track. Conversations break off. Separate pockets of upset parents speak among themselves, whispering around me. "Let me assure you, this school, *our school*, is a safe space. Your children are safe here at Danvers."

"How?" another parent asks. I couldn't see who. All I have is their voice, brimming with indignation. "How could you let something like this happen?" More shouts of self-righteous consent sound off. The anger is rising. An anger that echoes through history.

The circle completing itself.

Circle time, the birthday card read, nestled within Professor Howdy's open chest cavity. Written just for me—for Sean—on our birthday.

Mr. Woodhouse was thirty-six when the trial started. When he killed himself.

Happy birthday, Sean, I think, since nobody else will say it. *Just like Woodhouse.*

After the interview with Merrin, I looked up Kinderman and found out she's still alive—no surprise there—and has a listed number. She's been waiting for me to find her. To give her a call. I programmed her number into my cell but I couldn't muster the courage to dial. Not yet. What would she even say to me? *Hello, Sean, I've been waiting for you* . . . She followed me to Danvers. She entered my new life and now she's exacting some sort of—I don't know, some sort of twisted counternarrative that replicates my testimony from when I was a child? To what end?

Another woman in the auditorium is staring at me. Who is she?

Others. I hear Mom's voice in the back of my head. *What if . . . What if there really is a cult?* What if I accidentally tapped into something as a boy? That's what Mr. Cassavetes claimed on his TV special. What if my stories were true? What if there is a secret organization of devil worshippers? It sounds absurd. I should be laughing my ass off for even thinking it. But . . .

What if . . . ? What if they're here? What if they're sitting around me right now? What if they're in this auditorium, hiding among all the mothers and fathers? What if they're parents?

The faculty. The admin. Jesus, even the police. Who knows how far this network goes?

An image of my mother comes back to me. Her face. Her paranoia. Her *delusions.* That's what they were. The people she passed on the street. The strangers she saw wandering outside our window. At the peak of her paranoia, Mom believed, actually *believed.* She never realized her own son, her angel, her own flesh and blood, had lied to her. To the press. To everyone.

Miss Levin stands up from her seat. I can see she's clearly working up the nerve to speak.

"My daughter," she starts, waiting for the room to quiet down. Nobody hears her.

Nobody but me. I'm all ears. I am bearing witness.

"My daughter was in that art class," she calls out. She's scanning the room, looking for a sympathetic face. "My daughter told me that he—"

My entire body tenses.

Miss Levin starts again, "My daughter told me that Mr. Bellamy—"

I can't breathe.

"He . . ." Miss Levin continues, her voice filling the vast expanse of the auditorium. "He told their class how to play these games. To do *these things* to each other. While he watched."

I turn to Tamara. Even if she's sitting right next to me, I can't see her. The distance feels too far, as if the space between us is expanding. Her eyes widen, and I feel her slipping away.

She looks frightened. Of me.

I try to say something. I know I try. But the words aren't there. The air isn't there.

Sandy stands next to her mother, like she's being presented. With her mother's encouragement, Sandy looks around and finds me in the audience. When she does, she lifts her arm and points at me. "Mr. Bellamy did it."

INTERVIEW: October 27, 2013

MERRIN: The time is . . . nine thirty-four p.m. Interview
    with Richard Bellamy is now commencing. Detective
    Merrin and Detective Burstyn are present.
BURSTYN: Thanks for coming in.
MERRIN: For the record, you are here of your own voli-
    tion. Is that correct?
BELLAMY: Yes.
MERRIN: To be clear, you are not under arrest. No charges
    have been filed. You can stop this interview at any
    time. Is that understood?
BELLAMY: I understand.
MERRIN: Anything you say can be used later. It's not a
    confession, but it is still admissible in court. Is
    that understood?
BELLAMY: Yes.
BURSTYN: You sure you don't want a lawyer present?
BELLAMY: No. Do I—do I need one?
BURSTYN: Not if you've got nothing to hide . . .
BELLAMY: Then yes—I mean, no, I do not want a lawyer
    present.
BURSTYN: You mind if we get down to brass tacks? Why
    come in?
BELLAMY: Because it's not true.
BURSTYN: What's not true?
BELLAMY: What Sandy's mom—what—what Miss Levin said.
    It's not true.
BURSTYN: Why do you think she'd say something like
    that?
BELLAMY: I—I have no fucking clue. I don't know her.
    I've only seen her twice. At school functions. She's
    always struck me as, I don't know . . . a little
    intense.
BURSTYN: Intense?

BELLAMY: High-strung.

BURSTYN: I've known a few high-strung ladies in my day.

BELLAMY: It's not like that. Don't—please don't bend my words.

BURSTYN: Sorry. I take it back. She's not high-strung. She's . . . "intense."

BELLAMY: All these parents are anxious. The only time they ever come to talk to me is when they want to get their kids into an expensive school and they want proof that their son or daughter is the next Picasso or something.

MERRIN: My kid's enrolled in this school. Fucking tuition kills me. Every month, I wanna shoot myself. One year's enough to send me to the poorhouse.

BURSTYN: It's public school for my boys all the way. Worked just fine for me.

MERRIN: Miss Levin wanted to enroll her daughter into another school?

BELLAMY: No. The other night when we had parent-teacher conferences—

MERRIN: Which night?

BELLAMY: Thursday. Miss Levin came in. To speak to me about Sandy.

MERRIN: She came to you?

BELLAMY: Yes.

MERRIN: To talk about how her daughter was doing in your class?

BELLAMY: Correct.

BURSTYN: How's she doing?

BELLAMY: Excuse me?

BURSTYN: Sandy. How's she doing in your class?

BELLAMY: Great. She's one of my best students.

MERRIN: Good for her.

BELLAMY: I mean, it's finger painting and macaroni art. I'm not teaching them rocket science. I'm trying to get them to tap into their creativity.

BURSTYN: Tap in?

BELLAMY: How do you want me to put it?

BURSTYN: These are your words, not mine. I'm just repeating them.

BELLAMY: No, you're taking my words and—you're taking
my words and making them sound different. Sound
wrong.

MERRIN: Did Miss Levin strike you as being intense or
high-strung that night? The night of parent-teacher
conferences? Was she acting differently?

BELLAMY: High-strung isn't the right word. I—I want to
take that back. Can I?

BURSTYN: You can do whatever you want, man. It's your
time.

BELLAMY: She just seemed like, she looked like she was
under duress. Stressed.

MERRIN: How so?

BELLAMY: Miss Levin suggested someone—a student was—
was hurting Sandy.

MERRIN: Which student?

BELLAMY: (. . .)

MERRIN: Mr. Bellamy? Richard?

BURSTYN: You think she was making it up?

BELLAMY: No. I—I don't know. Maybe Sandy was afraid?
She could've been hiding the truth. Whoever the real
student was. So she wouldn't get hurt again.

MERRIN: What was the name of the student?

BELLAMY: I already told you.

BURSTYN: No, you didn't.

MERRIN: You don't remember the student's name?

BELLAMY: No.

MERRIN: Mr. Bellamy, if you're protecting one of your
students—or if you believe not telling us this student's name will help in some way, I just want you

to know, for your own personal sake, that we'll be
able to find out who it is. We can ask other people.
We can ask Sandy. Or her mom. Or even other people
in the—

BELLAMY: Sean.

BURSTYN: Sean what?

BELLAMY: She didn't give a last name.

BURSTYN: You don't know your own student's last name?

BELLAMY: There's no Sean in my class. There are plenty
of Seans in our school.

MERRIN: It's possible it could've been someone else? Someone outside of class?

BELLAMY: Maybe. Sandy's mom—Miss Levin said it was
someone in our class.

MERRIN: You agree? Disagree?

BELLAMY: There's no Sean in our class.

BURSTYN: Yeah, but . . . what do you think? About it being
some other student?

BELLAMY: I don't know.

MERRIN: Why didn't you bring it up with the principal?

BELLAMY: I did.

BURSTYN: You did?

BELLAMY: We had a conversation about Miss Levin this
morning.

BURSTYN: And that's it? Case closed?

BELLAMY: There wasn't time to follow up.

BURSTYN: Rich. I know it's been a pretty shitty day
for you. We get that. But here's the thing . . . It's
starting to feel like there's a lot of crap circling
around you. You notice that? You got one hell of a
storm cloud hanging over your head right now . . .
and it's fucking raining down on you. Real hard. Why
do you think that is?

BELLAMY: I'm here because I want to be. I came in because
I wanted to set—

BURSTYN: You did, that's true—

BELLAMY: —to set the record straight. That's all I want to do.

MERRIN: That's what we want, too. We want to hear your side of the story.

BELLAMY: I need to—I want to just make sure that this isn't—

BURSTYN: Tell us your story, Rich. That's all we're after here.

BELLAMY: I could lose my job. Christ, I could lose my job over this.

MERRIN: Why'd she lie? Why would Miss Levin lie about something like this?

BELLAMY: I think there's—there's something wrong with her.

BURSTYN: That's your medical opinion?

BELLAMY: You want me to answer the question or not?

BURSTYN: Go ahead.

BELLAMY: Sandy is—I don't know. Anxious. Something's going on with her.

MERRIN: How so? How do you know?

BELLAMY: She keeps to herself. Timid. You can tell with certain students that there's, there might be something, I don't know, something going on at home. With their parents. With Sandy, it just seemed like, like her mom was a handful.

BURSTYN: Miss Levin's a handful?

BELLAMY: You asked. I'm telling you what I—what I—what I've witnessed.

MERRIN: How is Sandy in the classroom?

BELLAMY: Fine. Just . . . on her own a lot of the time. In her shell.

MERRIN: Does she have any friends?

BELLAMY: Yeah. Well—no. No, none that I can think of off the top of my head.

MERRIN: You ever see any bruises? Any marks?

BELLAMY: No. None.

MERRIN: Did you look? You'd notice something like that, right? Bruises?

BELLAMY: I mean, if they were visible . . . Yes. And if I had seen them, I would've reported them directly to the principal. To Mrs. Condrey.

BURSTYN: Sure you would've.

BELLAMY: What's that supposed to mean?

BURSTYN: Nothing.

BELLAMY: No—what did you mean by that?

MERRIN: You're tired. Maybe we should do this another time? When you're—

BELLAMY: I know how this looks. But it's not true. It's not. I need—need to—

BURSTYN: We get it.

BELLAMY: Then why are you looking at me like that?

BURSTYN: Like what?

BELLAMY: Like I'm—like I'm . . .

MERRIN: Nothing's come up in class before? No other complaints? No fights?

BELLAMY: Why don't you ask Mrs. Condrey?

BURSTYN: We're asking you.

BELLAMY: No, no complaints.

MERRIN: No problems with any other students? Their parents?

BELLAMY: No.

BURSTYN: You ever done anything to anybody that, I don't know, they'd be angry over? Ever get in a disagreement with somebody or an altercation?

BELLAMY: No. Absolutely not.

BURSTYN: Nobody's ever got any reason to get back at you for anything?

BELLAMY: (. . .)

MERRIN: Nobody would have it out for you, Richard?

BELLAMY: (. . .)

MERRIN: Richard?

BELLAMY: . . . No.

BURSTYN: Come again? Lost you there for a second.

BELLAMY: No.

BURSTYN: So. Let's put it this way. Yeah, you came in. Yeah, you're here of your own volition. And that's all good. That makes our job a lot easier.

BELLAMY: I didn't do anything, I swear . . .

MERRIN: You sure you're not misremembering anything? Maybe there's something you're forgetting? Something you're not telling us?

BELLAMY: I didn't do anything. How many times do I have to say it?

BURSTYN: It's all right. We're all friends here. You can tell us.

BELLAMY: Tell you what? What is there to tell? I didn't do—

BURSTYN: You got to see this as an opportunity, Rich. This is your one and only chance to get out in front of the story, you know? Before it takes on a life of its own.

MERRIN: All we want to hear is the truth.

BELLAMY: I *have* been telling you the truth!

BURSTYN: Feels like you might be hiding something. Or forgetting something? How about that? People forget things all the time—and then, one day, oh, there it is, right outta the blue. "How could I ever forget that?" Know what I'm saying?

BELLAMY: I have nothing to hide.

BURSTYN: See . . . Richard, when you say stuff like that . . . Hate to break it to you . . .

BELLAMY: What? What?

MERRIN: It makes you sound like you have something to hide.

BELLAMY: But I don't—

BURSTYN: Maybe you don't want to remember. Maybe you've done something and you're trying to hide it from yourself. Shit like that happens all the time.

BELLAMY: You can't be serious. Are—are you serious right now?

BURSTYN: You'd be surprised what people lie to themselves about. People lie to themselves all the time. You just gotta be honest with yourself, Rich. Come clean.

BELLAMY: I haven't done any—

BURSTYN: Only a matter of time, Richard.

BELLAMY: Whoa, wait . . . Hold on. Just—just hold on. What's going on here?

MERRIN: Get it off your chest.

BELLAMY: You—you don't think I—think I actually did this?

BURSTYN: Come on, Richie . . . You don't have to deny it. Not with us.

BELLAMY: I'm not denying anything!

MERRIN: We're going to find out what we want to find out, sooner or later. And if we find out you've been lying to us, well, then, you're in a whole heap of trouble.

BELLAMY: There's nothing to—

BURSTYN: You came in here . . . all on your own. That says a lot, don't you think?

MERRIN: Speaks volumes.

BURSTYN: The truth shall set you free, as they say.

BELLAMY: But I—I didn't . . . I . . .

BURSTYN: You'll feel better if you do. Get it off your chest. All of this goes away.

MERRIN: Like a dam breaking.

BELLAMY: Jesus Christ, what the fuck is this? What are you doing?

BURSTYN: Let it go, Rich. Tell us the truth.

BELLAMY: I think—I think I've said enough.

BURSTYN: Oh, now you've had enough? You're done now?

BELLAMY: I want to go home now.

MERRIN: In a little bit.

BELLAMY: I want to go home.

BURSTYN: What if we want to keep you a little longer?

BELLAMY: You . . . You can't do that. Can you? You said so. I'm here of my own—of my own volition.

BURSTYN: Yeah, that was before. This is now.

MERRIN: You're a person of interest. Your story is really interesting to us.

BURSTYN: We're just getting to the good part. Don't hold back on us now, Richie. Stick around. Just a little longer. Just to chat. That's all we want. Hand to God.

MERRIN: You'll feel better. Getting all this out of your system.

BELLAMY: Would you stop saying that? There's nothing to—

BURSTYN: You think that, maybe, there was one day? In class? Just you and—

BELLAMY: No—

BURSTYN: Maybe, just maybe, Sandy is looking for some help . . .

BELLAMY: Oh, Jesus—

BURSTYN: You're her teacher. She looks up to you . . .

BELLAMY: No.

BURSTYN: No?

BELLAMY: I—I can't see myself doing this. Any of this. I—I just can't . . .

BURSTYN: Nobody ever does, believe me. See it.

MERRIN: That doesn't mean they didn't do it.

BURSTYN: Seeing is believing. So it's better to just . . . flip the blinders on.

MERRIN: Maybe even imagine it's someone else doing it? "It doesn't even feel like I'm doing it, somebody else is." "It's just like watching a movie."

BELLAMY: No. No. No no no . . .

MERRIN: Just tell us. Tell us what you did.

BURSTYN: Think of it as a flick. "It didn't feel real. It was like watching a movie . . ." Something like that. So tell us what happened in the movie of your life.

BELLAMY: I—I think I'm—I'm going to be sick. I need to go to the bathroom . . .

BURSTYN: Keep it together, Richie. Just for a little while longer.

BELLAMY: Can I get a—a trashcan? A bucket?

BURSTYN: Quit playing around, man. Buck the fuck up.

MERRIN: Breathe, Richard. Just breathe. In, out . . . In, out . . .

BURSTYN: Better now? Got something on your mind that you wanna get out?

BELLAMY: No . . .

MERRIN: It's for the better. You'll remember. Sooner or later.

BURSTYN: They always do.

BELLAMY: But—why? Why don't I remember? Why wouldn't I remember?

MERRIN: Would you? Would you really want to remember something like this?

BURSTYN: Better to bury it. Stuff it in a box. Lock it up in the back of the brain.

MERRIN: And toss away the key.

BURSTYN: You never know what else is back there. Maybe something that happened to you when you were a kid, with a family member. An uncle, maybe a neighbor, something you've tried to forget for a long time now . . .

MERRIN: History's repeating itself.

BURSTYN: That's where we need to go, Rich. That's what you need to remember.

MERRIN: Crack it open. Key or no key.

BURSTYN: Get it off your chest. Relieve yourself.

MERRIN: Unburden thyself, son.

BURSTYN: Let it all come flooding out.

BELLAMY: I . . . I'm not . . .

BURSTYN: This victim shit isn't doing you any favors. Coming in here and claiming you're all innocent isn't helping. Fuck that noise. What would help you now, the only thing that's gonna save your ass, is you starting to tell the truth.

BELLAMY: If this is true then—then it's a part of me I don't even know about.

BURSTYN: That's understandable. Wall it off, right? Hell, I would. But now you need to take a sledgehammer to that wall and break through. Bust it down.

BELLAMY: I—I can't—I don't want to remember . . .

BURSTYN: But it's there, isn't it? Somewhere in the way, way back?

BELLAMY: I . . . oh God . . .

BURSTYN: There it is. You can see it, can't you?

BELLAMY: Oh God . . .

BURSTYN: Almost there . . . Almost got it . . . Just a little bit further . . .

BELLAMY: No. Please, stop.

MERRIN: We're trying to help you, Richard.

BURSTYN: We want to help. Make it easy for yourself. Do the right thing here.

MERRIN: It's not what you remember, it's about what you *don't* remember.

BELLAMY: I don't want to . . . want to remember any of it.

MERRIN: See? Your brain is working overtime to keep you from remembering. It's trying to protect you by forgetting. Instead of you racking your brain over what you remember, start with what you don't . . .

BURSTYN: Think of Sandy . . .

MERRIN: Yes—think of Sandy. Do it for her.

BELLAMY: For Sandy . . .

BURSTYN: That's it. For Sandy.

BELLAMY: For Sean.

MERRIN: . . . Richard?

BELLAMY: (. . .)

BURSTYN: Hey. Richie? Where'd you go?

BELLAMY: I want a lawyer.

BURSTYN: Ah, come on . . . Don't do that. Not now. Not while the getting's good. We were just getting somewhere! You go that way, you lawyer up on us, Richie, I swear to fucking Christ, on my mother's fucking grave . . . We will come after you. We will come after you so fucking hard, you won't know what hit you. You'll get down on your knees and beg for forgiveness. Do you understand that this is your one and only chance to do something right? To make this right and make it all go away? You get this shot once in a fucking lifetime, my friend, and it's right here, right fuck-ing now. You lawyer up, so help me, you'll never get this chance again.

MERRIN: This is your chance to atone. To confess.

BURSTYN: You know what they do to fucks like you in prison, Richie? Do you know what they will do to you when they find out why you're there? You won't last a fucking night, Richie. You won't live to see your first fucking sunset.

MERRIN: Richard. Please. This is your last chance. Don't do this to yourself. Don't do this to the people you love. Your family. Talk to us. Before it's too late.

BELLAMY: (. . .)

MERRIN: Richard?

BELLAMY: I want my lawyer.

(INTERVIEW TERMINATED.)

DAMNED IF YOU DON'T
RICHARD: 2013

There's an elderly woman in the police station parking lot who won't stop staring at me. I've never seen her before in my life. She's not a part of the influx of young homeowners. Definitely old Danvers. Born, and born again, right here. Her shoulders sag forward, her spine drooping like a question mark that lost its lower bulb. She pushes an empty cart through the lot, halting long enough to take me in.

She's wearing a T-shirt two sizes too big for her frame. Printed on the front, it reads: JESUS SAVES. On the back: BECAUSE HE SHOPS AT WALMART.

She's looking at me like we know each other. Have always known each other. Her eyes trail after me as I leave the station. The woman won't stop staring, even after I open the passenger door to Tamara's Cherokee and duck in. We lock eyes once more through the window.

Miss Betty. She looks exactly like Miss Betty. I haven't thought about her in years. She smiles at me, as if she's just recognized me, and waves. The moment her hand fans through the air, it blurs. Her fingers distort into a hazy smudge. Her lips pull back to expose a row of dried corn kernels. Diced vegetables spill from her mouth, green beans and cubed carrots tumbling down her chin. I pinch my eyes shut and push the image away as Tamara pulls out from the lot.

I spent eight hours at the precinct. Whenever I insisted on leaving, Detective Merrin found an excuse to keep me. *Just one more question,* he kept saying. *Hold on a minute . . .*

One more thing . . .

Almost done . . .

This was a game to them. There were no formal charges. Not yet. Merrin considered me *permissible to be at large*, which meant I was free to go. I wasn't considered a *flight risk*.

We'll be keeping an eye on you, Merrin said. *Don't go too far, okay?*

Where would I even go? Where could I run to now? They had already found me.

The *Others*.

I haven't slept for days. I'm losing track of time. I can't think straight. There's a persistent buzz in my head that only I can hear, like a paper wasp's nest, like Dunstan's humming, throwing me off balance. I can't keep my equilibrium. Everything feels fuzzy around the edges. The sharp corners of the building look like carpet fibers to me. As soon as I stepped out of the station, the sunlight jabbed their beams directly into my eyes, fueling a slow-mounting migraine that's only grown worse in the Jeep. The cars, all the surrounding people, everything around me is out of focus. I can't see people's faces. Their features look gauzy. I can't help but think they're all staring. Smiling at me.

"I just want to go home," I say—I think I say—out loud. Tamara doesn't respond. I don't know if I said it loud enough. But I need to go home. Crawl into bed. Sleep. Never wake up.

Tamara hasn't said a word since she arrived at the station. Her eyes remain on the road, never meeting mine. I've tried talking to her, thanking her for—

Rescuing me.

—picking me up but she doesn't answer. I wonder if she heard me, if I'm even talking. I keep quiet, keep to myself, my focus drifting out the window to all the people on the street.

Others.

Turning their heads.

Others.

Staring back.

Others.

Smiling.

"Is it true?" Tamara asks the windshield.

I turn to her, grateful to hear her voice. I wish she would look at me. *Please, just look at me. See me.* But she won't make eye contact. Won't acknowledge that I'm right next to her.

"It's not what you think it is . . ." My voice is hoarse, my throat feels like sandpaper.

"Just tell me it isn't true. What they're saying."

"Tamara, please—let me explain." I realize how hollow it sounds. There are so many things that aren't true, it's impossible to list them all. Even I can't make the words sound right. Not when I'm this exhausted. This *empty*.

"I can't let you back into our house—anywhere near Elijah."

"I would never hurt Eli. *Never.*"

"Then . . . *how*?" She shakes her head, searching for the right rendition of *how*. There are so many versions to pick from. Which *how* fits here? "He showed me, Richard."

"Showed you what?"

"The bruises. On his arm. I saw them this morning."

"I—" My train of thought snaps like a bone. "Did he say how he got them?"

Where did these bruises come from? Such a simple question.

"He wouldn't tell me. But his arm is black-and-blue." Tamara's foot presses on the gas, reflexively revving the engine.

Who did this to you?

"All I can think about is that woman, *that mother*, and her little girl. What they said about you."

Was it your teacher?

"They're lying, Tamara—"

"That girl pointed at you. She looked right at you."

"It's not true—"

"She said your name. And then I—I see Eli's bruises and he told me about how you shouted at him and—"

"I never laid a hand on Eli!"

"What about Weegee?"

"What do you mean?"

"Do you know what happened to him?"

  I don't respond.

"Did you do something to him?"

"No! I . . ."

"I went into your studio. Jesus, Rich, *I found him.*"

"That—that wasn't me! The night we came back from the fair, I found him hanging from the—from the tire swing. I didn't say anything because you were so worked up over—"

We miss the turn that takes us back to our house.

I crane my neck to watch our road slip off into the surrounding tree line, swallowed by pines. "Where are we going?"

Tamara doesn't say a word. She still hasn't looked at me.

"Tamara . . . Where are you taking me?"

"To a hotel." She doesn't need to say why. A level of trust has been breached and I won't be allowed back into the house until . . . when, exactly? I make things right? Clean this mess up?

"I'll explain everything. I swear. I just—*please*. I need you to believe me."

"I don't know what to believe anymore."

Elijah is slipping away.

Tell her about me, Sean whispers.

Tamara is slipping away.

Tell her now!

My family, slipping through my fingers.

TELL HER.

"Pull over," I say. Too forcefully. "Please."

Tamara pulls onto the shoulder. The Jeep's parked just a few paces away from the farmers market. It must be Saturday. The weekend market is up and running. A Danvers tradition. A half dozen open-air tents are set up in a gravel parking lot just off the highway selling everything from corn to kale to fresh milk and venison. There's a crowd of J. Crew catalogue models wandering from tent to tent. Stepford parents. The Friends of Danvers. Tamara and I could've easily been among them. That would've been us on any other day, in any other life than this one.

Tamara cuts the engine. The keys remain in the ignition. She sits back in her seat, still gripping the steering wheel, elbows locked, bracing herself for what I'm about to say.

"I can explain this. I can explain everything."

The muscles in her neck tighten, the tendons like two steel cables clamping down on her throat. She still can't bring herself to look—to see me. "I want to believe you. I do. I'm trying, but . . . I can't stop seeing that girl. That poor girl. I'd never forgive myself if I . . . if I brought something, someone like that into . . . into our house. If anyone ever hurt Elijah . . ."

"No one's going to hurt him, I swear. Just hear me out. Please? *Please*."

Say my name, Sean whispers.

"We've talked about my childhood before. About . . . me. But there are certain things I haven't told you, because . . . because . . ."

Say it.

"This was—what, 1983? There was a rumor going around about my teacher, and I . . . So many parents were getting paranoid about predators at school . . . so when my mom saw these bruises on my body, she panicked. I made up a story, and she believed me and called the police, and they got involved and one thing led to another . . . Before I knew it, before I could stop it . . ."

Tamara's lips part. I can see her panic mounting.

"It got out of hand so quickly. I couldn't take it back. Couldn't make it go away. More people got involved. People I didn't know. Lawyers and the FBI and . . . and it became this tidal wave that swept up so many people. No matter what I said, there was no stopping it. My mother, she—she couldn't take care of me anymore. Couldn't take care of herself . . ."

This is all coming out wrong. I can't make the story sound the way it is in my head. I'm losing Tamara, but I have to keep talking, keep telling her my story, the only story I've ever had, in hopes that—if I can just reach the end—she might understand. That's all I want in this world.

I need Tamara to believe me.

"My adopted parents put as much distance between me and what happened as possible. They wanted to protect me from myself. I took their name and they pushed away the press. We created this new narrative for myself. A story for everybody to believe. Something that fit the new me and buried the old. We moved on. It was like we forgot it even happened."

Forgot me, I want to say. "I forgot, too."

Please, just look at me, I want to say. *It's me! It's Richard.*

No it's not, Sean whispers.

"I was five. Most of it I can't remember anymore. That part of me, that part of my life . . . it feels like a bad dream now. It doesn't exist. This is who I am now. This is me."

I take Tamara's hand. She lets me. Her arm merely hangs there, limply suspended from her shoulder. A rag doll. "Please," I say. "It's me."

Tamara looks at her hand in mine, as if it belongs to somebody else. She follows the length of my arm until she finds my face. Her eyes are wide, weltering. "Who are you?"

Say my name. Say it.

"My name is . . . was . . . Sean."

Hearing myself say my own name, out loud, for the first time in years sounds like a death rattle to my ears. That last exhalation before passing away. It releases Sean. The presence of my childhood self fills the car with a pungent odor. Something decaying. A dead child.

A gray boy.

For the longest time, I wondered, even fantasized, that *coming clean* and saying his name would somehow unburden myself. A weight lifting off the shoulders. But there's no relief. No divestment, no shedding of skin. I'm still me. Whoever that is.

"Who *are* you," she repeats. It's not a question this time. Not anymore.

"Tamara. Please. I need your help. Someone, I don't know who, is using my past to—"

She yanks her arm away and brings both hands to her face, rubbing her eyes. Her sleeve tugs at her elbow, exposing the lower coil of her tattoo. I stare at the snake wrapped around her arm, the serpent conjured from her scars. It looks like a dagger to me. A winding knife.

I lose myself in Tamara's tattoo. All her tattoos. All the images on her body represent something significant in her life. She imbued her body with deeper meaning, like an open book.

A book of spells. Tamara, my witch.

What had she said about the thistle on her thigh? *It's supposed to break hexes.*

What did the compass symbolize? What about the star on her shoulder?

She keeps asking me who I am, but what about *her?*

Who was *she?*

What if . . . ? What if Tamara was one of them?

One of the *Others?*

I just got into the car with a complete stranger, forgetting every warning we were told as children. All this time, for our entire relationship, what if she always knew I was Sean? Asking that one simple question opens a floodgate of others. They begin with a trickle, the queries dribbling from my head. But more questions come rushing in. They won't stop now.

What if Sean is the reason Tamara was with me in the first place? What if she was tending to me? Holding onto me until the *others* were ready? How else could she have fallen in love with me? All this time, *all this time*, she knew, *she knew* I was Sean because . . . how else?

How else could she have ever loved someone like me?

The scar along her arm. The story she told me. What if that's not really how she got it? What if she received the burn? What if she was branded? Marked? Isn't that what they do? I know it's not true, that it couldn't possibly be true, but—*what if?* That's all I have now. This nagging sense of doubt echoes through my head, *Whatifwhatifwhatifwhatif . . .*

What about the cardboard box? The remnants of Hank left out in the garage? Tamara must've known I'd go through his belongings. She wanted me to find them.

What if she wanted me to become him?

The two of us stare at each other like we've never known each other at all.

"What do you want from me?"

Tamara's face tightens. *"Excuse me?"*

"How did you find me?"

"What the fuck are you *talking* about?"

"How long have you known? What are you going to do—"

She slams her fist against my shoulder. *"Get out.* Get out of my fucking car!" She reels her fist back and starts punching. Aiming for my face. My ear. My chest. She won't stop shouting. Her fists hit whatever part of me she can find. Clawing at me now. Scraping my neck. I can't help but feel the slightest sense of relief, like I'm standing in a rainstorm after languishing in the sun for hours, the steady shower rinsing the sweat from my skin. I could have sat there and let her crush me. Obliterate me into a million pieces of flesh and bone. Until there's nothing left.

I want it. Need her to destroy me.

"Get out get out GET OUT!"

I finally open the door and spill onto the shoulder. I hit the ground. Gravel digs into my arm, cutting me. Picking myself up, I stare back at Tamara as she turns the ignition.

"Tamara—"

"Don't come near my son ever again!"

My son. Not two days ago he had been so close to becoming *our son.* Gone now.

Tamara speeds off without shutting the door. The tires kick up loose gravel before the Jeep reaches the pavement and screeches away. I stand at the side of the road, watching her go.

I'm not alone.

Across the street, a couple is just leaving the farmers market. They're dressed to match—him in a slate-gray cashmere cardigan and her in a mock turtleneck sweater of the same hue. She's carrying a tote bag full of freshly shucked corn. Strands of silk still cling to the ears. At this distance, it looks like hair. Blonde hair. Wisps spill over the brim and flutter in the wind.

When the road is clear, the man releases the woman's hand and runs across the street. "Everything okay?"

"I'm fine." I feel my knees buckle, my legs weakening, unable to hold the rest of myself up. I start to list. The man grabs my arm before I fall. "I just need to . . . need to . . ."

A sob escapes my mouth. It comes from deep within my chest.

"Hey—it's okay. I got you. You're not alone."

Not alone. He says it calmly, so reassuringly. He wants me to feel safe. I lose myself in his clean-shaven face. Not a nick on his chin. His skin still has the remnants of a summer tan. But somehow I can't put his features together. His face is a puzzle to me, scattered about.

"It's Richard, right?"

I pull out from his grip and stumble back. "How do you know my name?"

"Whoa. Easy now." He holds his hands up in placating gesture, as if to assure me that *everything's just fine*, that *this is all just a big misunderstanding*. That I'm not alone.

"This is, uh . . . weird. But . . ." He lets out an awkward chuckle. "Sorry. This isn't how I expected this to go, but . . . I'm Hank."

He holds out his hand for me.

"I'm Elijah's father," he offers. His hand remains open for me to take. "Or . . . I was. I've been . . . I've been thinking about reaching out to Tamara lately but could never figure out the timing."

My stomach turns over. I knew I'd seen him at the fair. *I knew it.* "What do you want from us?"

Hank's expression hitches. "Look, this isn't how I thought this would all go down. My girlfriend and I—" He turns to the woman across the street, watching us. She switches her tote from one hand to the next. The decapitated head inside must be getting heavy. "—live in Mechanicsville. I didn't know Tamara and Eli were living here—or, hell, that she even got remarried. I just filled in the gaps with Facebook after I saw you two together."

He offers up a reassuring smile, as if to say, *Trust me*.

"I don't know what Tamara's told you," he continues. "I'm sure it's not pretty. But I've cleaned up since we were together. Did a solid stint in rehab. Now I'm in the program. Been spending the last year or so trying to make amends and just . . . I feel like it can't be an accident that I'm here in the same town as her and Eli."

Can't be an accident.

"Look, I can tell this is a bad time. Why don't we just exchange numbers and maybe I—"

"Stay away." None of this is coincidence. None of this is by chance. He's a part of this. He's been following me. *Can't be an accident.*

"I'm sorry if I—"

"*Stay away from me!*" I rush off, leaving him by the side of the highway. I glance over my shoulder to make sure he's not following. He stands there, struck. His girlfriend has crossed the street now, the two of them standing together, staring at me as I pick up my pace.

"That's him?" I swear I hear her whisper.

"That's him."

The farmers market. The customers are watching. Staring. Now they're all whispering. "That's him," they say. "The art teacher." They know who I am. How do they all know?

What if . . .

People are watching. On the street. From the other side of windows. They have the same look in their eyes. I see them speaking to each other, discussing me under their breath, their hushed tones just out of earshot. What if they've always been here, hiding among us?

HAVE YOU SEEN ME? The telephone poles all ask the same question. Now I can. I see them all.

MISSING. HELP. It's too late. The animals go first. That's a part of their ritual. Now they're ready for me. They don't think I see them. I have to pretend. Pretend that I don't notice.

It's impossible not to sense their eyes following me down the street, wherever I go.

There are eyes everywhere.

They are here. Right now. Hiding in plain sight. They look like you or me or anyone else.

But they are watching. Always watching.

I never believed. Never thought it was true.

What if . . . ? What if Mom was right? What if she saw them and I didn't believe her?

What if the stories are true?

Mr. Cassavetes's closing thought was practically a sermon. He stood before the studio audience as if they were his congregation. *The devil is here,* he said, *in our backyard, in our homes, as we speak. His followers, his disciples, are hidden among us at this very moment. There is a widespread network of Satan worshippers operating throughout our great nation,* he proclaimed. *This secret society exists in the open daylight, right under the sun for all to see. They are engaged in child pornography. Sex trafficking. The torture of children. They brainwash our boys and girls into becoming devil worshippers, continuing their profane legacy . . .*

These devil worshippers have infiltrated the highest levels of our society. They are embedded within the very institutions that hold our nation up and maintain its laws, in order to subvert our society, subvert our institutions, subvert our very laws. They want to create chaos. They want to let this world burn. Its houses of worship, its schools. They want the world to descend into darkness and let their master rise, rise up and bask in the flames of our nation.

How did Mr. Cassavetes know?

Because our children told us so, he said. *From the mouths of babes, we've been told that this threat is here. That evil is here. Evil walks amongst us and we have to heed the warning.*

I never believed. I never believed because I was the one who made it up. The stories were mine. The lies. I never believed—until now. Until the devil began believing in me.

In Richard.

I thought I could run away from myself. Hide. But there's no hiding. Not from them.

What if the people living here have known about me this whole time? What if they followed me? They've known all along. They've just been waiting for the right moment.

Full circle.

These people have always been too perfect. Too clean. All the cookie-cutter residents, wearing crisp catalogue-brand clothes, the refurbished stores for a revamped Danvers brought back from the dead, the prefab antiquity of this entire gentrified hamlet . . . it's all a façade.

A mask.

I've been in their box this whole time, an animal imprisoned in their cardboard container, trying to claw my way out . . . but the walls are too high. I'm trapped in this town.

I'm their sacrifice. All this time they've been prodding me along, pushing me in whatever direction they needed me to go. Leading me to this. This has been their plan all along. I never wanted to be an art teacher. I never planned to have a wife and kid. They made me this way. They turned me into *him.*

Now I see them everywhere. You have to know what to look for.

The devil's in the details.

They look like us. Talk like us.

They *are* us.

There. That woman. *There*. That man. This whole fucking fake town. Danvers is just an elaborate cage to keep me in until they're ready. Finish what they started all those years ago.

To sacrifice me.

I'm trapped. A rabbit in a cardboard box. I rub my eyes, kneading the sleeplessness from them. The sheer weight of exhaustion. Everything's blurring. The sun stings.

A bird in my pocket begins to trill.

My phone.

I don't want to answer—but how can't I? This is never going to end. They know where I am. They've always known. I answer without saying a word, bringing the phone to my ear.

"It's time, Sean," Mom whispers. Her voice sounds so compassionate. There's a tenderness to her words, I can hear it. "Put an end to all this. It's for your own good, son."

"Why are you doing this to me?" I sound pitiful. Such a frightened little boy.

"Come home, Sean. Come back to me. I'm waiting for you, honey."

The line goes dead.

I need to run. Hide. Get as far away from these people as humanly possible. I sense them following. They're right behind me, just at my back, keeping a safe distance so I won't notice. But there's more of them now. More eyes. All of them saying my name. Whispering it.

They know my name. They all know my name.

Sean.

Sean.

Sean.

School. I can hide in my classroom. It's the only place. There's nowhere else for me now.

Nowhere safe.

DAMNED IF YOU DO
SEAN: 1983

- -

"**W**ake up, Sean."

First he felt fingernails. Then shaking. He couldn't wake up. He was tired. So very tired.

"Sean, wake up . . . *Sean!*"

His eyes snapped open. The room was dark, but he could just barely make out his mother kneeling right next to him, her hands clinging to his Star Wars sheets. It almost seemed like she'd never left his side after they said their bedtime prayers. "What time is—"

"*Ssh,*" she hissed. Sean felt her fingernails dig into his skin, leaving their mark. She glanced around the room as if to make sure no one heard. "Don't say a word. *They're here.*"

She took his hand. Her breathing was erratic, chest rising and falling. "I woke up when I heard something outside my window. Scratching. *Claws.* I peeked out and I—I saw them."

Mom's grip tightened, crushing his birdlike bones.

"Mom, you're *hurting* me."

This seemed to bring her back to the room. To Sean. She blinked once, twice, looking at him, almost as if she had forgotten who she was talking to. "They're trying to find a way in."

Sean had a nightlight next to his bed—a plastic mold of Papa Smurf that glowed a dull blue. There wasn't nearly enough light to illuminate his whole room, but it was adequate at keeping the shadows at bay around the headboard of his bed. *To protect you from monsters*, Mom had promised when she first plugged it in. Bathed in this blue light, Mom looked a little like a monster herself. Her skin was drained of blood. Her eyes were sunken, her cheekbones hollow.

"We have to get out of here," she whispered. "We have to go. *Now.*"

She leapt to her feet and yanked Sean out of bed, almost dislocating his arm.

"Ow!"

"*Quiet,*" she hissed again. They made their way into the hall. Pressing her back against the wall, Mom slowly slid down the darkened corridor. She kept one hand against Sean's chest, shielding him from whatever danger might be hiding a step or two ahead, a mother bear protecting her cub.

They passed the kitchen. Mom had stopped doing the dishes weeks ago. Stacks of dirty plates and bowls rose up from the sink, spilling onto the counter. Sean could just make out the faint buzz of flies. The lingering smell had a greasy sting to it. Rotten fruit and spaghetti sauce. When did they last eat spaghetti? Wasn't that a week ago?

The days blended together by now. When was the last time he'd left the house? Sean didn't want to tell Mom she'd missed his sixth birthday. He was pretty positive it was a month ago by now, but maybe he was wrong. The last time he mentioned it to her, she merely stared off into space, not focusing on him but drifting into a thought that she didn't want to share.

The curtains in the living room were always closed now. If Sean ever went near them, Mom slapped his wrist. Even during the day, she insisted they stay down. Sunlight never made its way into their house anymore. The family remained sealed behind the blinds for fear that one of the lingering news crews might be right outside their window, ready to capture them on camera. They wouldn't leave Sean alone. Whenever the two of them stepped out for an appointment with Miss Kinderman, the reporters swarmed. The women in their pencil skirts, mics in hand, shouting their questions. The probing lens of their cameras, zooming in on Sean's face.

The longer the trial dragged on, the more interest there was in Sean. There were always a half dozen roving eyewitness-news vans stationed on the block, barricading their driveway. The network call letters seemed like complicated math equations Sean wasn't equipped to calculate. K12 TV. UH89 NEWS. KBCW-TV + WGBO-4. But once the sun went down, the reporters left.

So who was Mom so afraid of now? Who was outside?

"Stay away from the windows," she said. "If they see you, they'll know we're here."

"Mom, I'm scared . . ."

Mom knelt before Sean. "I know, baby. I know . . . I'm scared, too." She tried to put on a brave face for him, but it looked so flimsy. A maternal mask that didn't quite fit. Even in the dark, he could tell she was pretending. She held her hand up but hesitated to touch him, struggling to find the most consoling spot on Sean's body. She settled on combing the hair out of his eyes with her fingers, just the gentlest brushing back of his bangs from his brow. It had been so long since he'd gotten a haircut. Mom used to do it, tried to, at least, but the last time she had taken a pair of scissors to his hair his bangs came out completely lopsided. *He can't look like a weedwhacker attacked him,* the prosecutor scolded her. *Here's five bucks. Take him to the barber and fix it.* That had been months ago.

"I need you to be brave for me, okay?" Mom said, snapping Sean from his thoughts and back to their living room. "I need for you to stay here while I go get a few things, okay?"

"Don't leave me."

"It'll just be for a little while, okay? Less than a minute."

"Where are we going?"

"It's not safe here anymore," she said. "They know we're here. We need to get out of the house. Just stay here, sit on the couch, and stay very, very still. I'll be right back."

"No!" He grabbed her this time, wrapping his arms around her and holding on. She pried free from his grip, holding him at an arm's length.

"Just don't make a sound. Do you understand? Be brave for me."

Sean nodded.

"Good, baby. That's good." She wrapped her arms around him and squeezed, forcing the air from his lungs in a little puff. "I promise I won't let anything happen to you. Not this time."

This time.

Sean didn't understand what she meant by this, not at first, but after she left him on the living room couch and he was all alone, all by himself, with nothing but the silence of the room and his own wandering thoughts, it dawned on him, slowly but surely . . . *This time* meant Mr. Woodhouse. The other teachers. She meant Sean's story. About them hurting him.

She believed him. Always believed him. Believed every word.

His words.

Sean slowly turned his head toward the window. Just on the other side of the curtain was . . . what, exactly? More teachers? More of these bad people?

That's what his mother believed. Did he believe it, too?

All the bad people from his testimony were closing in. Mom heard them, she said.

Right now. Outside. Trying to get in.

Was Miss Kinderman outside? Was she one of them? Had she been helping them all along? Perhaps this was part of her plan. First, she would replace his mother. Swap bodies with her. Then she'd have Sean all to herself. She could do whatever she wanted with him.

Sean slid across the couch until he could reach the curtain with his fingers. He slowly lifted his hand. Pinched the fabric. He peered outside and didn't see anyone.

The street was empty.

Nobody was there.

Mom seized Sean by the wrist, wrenching his hand back from the curtain. *"Don't,"* she yelled, trying to keep her voice low but failing. "Don't let them see you!" She yanked him into the center of the living room. On one knee, she leaned into his face and whispered, "Listen to me, Sean. *Listen.* I need you to be brave for me, okay? I have to get the car out of the garage. But as soon as I start the engine, they'll know we're trying to run."

Even when she couldn't focus on him, jumping at every stray sound, Sean gave his mother his undivided attention. Whatever game she was playing, it felt safer to play along.

"I need you to hide in the back seat, okay?" she said. "Don't make a sound."

How could he tell her none of this was real? How could he make her believe him now? If he told her The Truth, what would she say? Would she believe it? Believe him?

"Once we're out of the house, there's no coming back. Never again."

"But what about—"

"Ssh." She brought her finger up—but instead of pressing it to her own lips, she forced it against his. He felt her index finger settle into the divot of his upper lip. "They're listening!"

This was wrong. He knew that. This felt *all wrong.* But he couldn't stop it. Stop her.

"I'm going to protect you this time," she said. "I promise. We're going somewhere where they'll never, *ever* find you. Never again." She wrapped her arms around him and hugged him so tight, it almost hurt. Her breath was warm against the side of his face, the heat of her exhales seeping into his ear. "Don't let them see you."

For the first time in all of Sean's life, he was suddenly afraid. Truly afraid.

Afraid of his mother.

"Let's go, baby." She kissed his temple. "My brave boy."

RICHARD: 2013

Condrey welcomes students back with a sunny-sounding announcement over the intercom. Her voice reverberates through each classroom, swearing everything is all right.

Nothing to fear here, kiddies . . .

Most parents have kept their kids at home today, even if school has reopened. That makes it easy for me to slip through the cafeteria loading dock. I just have to wait until first period starts before entering the hall, hiding until the bell rings.

The door to my classroom is sealed with police tape. I tear it away like a child unwrapping a Christmas gift. I close the door behind me before flipping on the lights.

When my eyes settle on the mess, I feel my knees soften. My body finds the floor, slowly lowering itself until my legs fold into a heap. *Criss-cross applesauce.* A sound escapes my mouth, rooted deep in my chest, a moan rising up from my lungs, but I can't recognize it.

The Museum of Modern Masterpieces is gone.

The pictures have been torn down, scattered across the floor. Only their ripped corners remain taped to the wall.

My classroom was supposed to be a safe space. Now there's nowhere else to run.

Kinderman won.

I have no choice but to call her. There's nothing left. I have no one else to talk to. I can imagine her waiting for me to call, knowing this moment is coming.

Full circle.

I reach up to the light switch and flip it off, sitting in the dark. I don't want to see my room, what the police have done. They've desecrated this space.

Kinderman picks up on the fourth ring. "Hello?" I recognize her voice. It doesn't sound like the woman who's been calling me, doesn't sound like my mother at all. "Who is this?"

"It's—" Not Richard. "Sean."

". . . Sean?" It's a question not born out of concern but confusion. She has no idea who I am. It hasn't hit her yet. The memory of me. She's still in the dark.

"Sean Crenshaw." When she doesn't respond, I say, "You tried to replace my mother."

"How did you get this number?" Whatever congenial warmth she once offered evaporates through the receiver.

"Why are you doing this to me?" I didn't mean to shout, but something about the tone of her voice, the confusion and contempt, makes me furious. "I trusted you. My mother trusted you. You made me say these things. You made me see them. Believe in them . . ."

"Sean, I don't know what you—"

"*Stop trying to be my mother!*"

"I'm sorry, Sean. There's nothing I can do for you." She's choosing her words carefully, speaking in an even tone. "Everything I did was to protect the children. To protect *you*."

"You're lying."

"Nobody else was willing to listen. To let you all tell your side of the story. I listened. I listened to all the children. We were doing good work. We were protecting you. All of you."

"Then why hasn't it stopped?" My voice rises again. "Why is it happening again?"

"Now?" She's pretending. Pretending not to understand.

"Don't lie to me!"

"I believed *you*, Sean. Trusted *you*. But you lied to *me*. To all of us." Kinderman's voice rises. "I had to close my practice because of you. I lost everything! And all I did was give you a voice. I helped you tell your side of the story when nobody else was willing to listen."

I refuse to believe her. I can't. *She's lying.* She has to be. "How did you find me?"

Silence. Then, coldly, "Don't call this number again."

"Why are you doing this to me?"

"If you call, I'll notify the police."

"Why—"

The line goes dead.

I dial again. It rings before going to voicemail. *"You have reached the . . ."*

I hang up. Dial again. This time it goes straight to voicemail. *"You have reached . . ."*

I dial again. *"You have . . ."*

Again. *"You . . ."*

I leave my classroom and walk swiftly down the hall. Most rooms are only half full. The students turn and notice me peering in. Eyes wide at the sight of me. Something in the way they look at me tells me how I must appear to them. A ghost haunting their halls.

"Richard?"

At first, I don't recognize my name. That name. Responding to

Richard feels strange now, like a costume. A disguise. Don't they know I'm Sean? Or are we still playing a game?

Condrey stands at a safe distance. We're alone in the hall. Her blazer for the day is red. Bloody tempera. "Richard," she says, her tone even. Calm. "What are you doing here?"

My throat is too dry to manifest the words clearly. "Going to class," I manage. Even smile. *I can pretend, too*, I think. *See? I can play these silly games just like the rest of you.*

"I'm sorry, Richard, but . . . you can't be here." She takes the slightest step forward.

"I just want to go to my class . . ."

"Richard. Please—"

"Stop calling me that!" I don't mean to shout. I don't mean to scare her. But hearing that name, hearing the tone of her voice, the soothing quality of it, feels false to me. A trap.

Condrey blanches. That's when I know for sure it's all been a performance. All this time, she's wanted me to believe that she's on my side, that she's my princiPAL, friends till the end.

But of course it's a lie, like all the others.

"Hey, Rich . . ."

I spin around to see Mr. Dunstan. He's holding out his hands. Was he trying to sneak up on me? "Let's go outside, okay?"

"Stay away." I take a step back.

I look at the walls. The pictures taped to them. Stick figures. Crooked Crayola smiles. Distorted eyes. Warped bodies. It's all right there, out in the open, hiding in plain sight.

This school has been teaching its students the same ceremonies all along.

Miss Castevet peers out from her classroom doorway. I swear I see her lick her lips. Her tongue is much too long.

The teachers. It's always been the teachers. Mrs. Gordon. Mme.

Choule. Mr. Costanza. They're surrounding me now. They're all staring, waiting for me to turn my back.

"Rich, please." Dunstan steps toward me. I hear the hum from
behind his lips, the song, the song is there, buzzing behind his teeth.
"Don't do this . . . Not in front of the children."

"Stay away from me!"

The bell rings just then, startling everyone. It could've been a gun-
shot, the way it makes the teachers jump. Before Condrey can turn
the tide and keep the kids inside their classrooms, a flood of students
fills the hall. They pass us, unaware of what's happening. They head to
their next class. Their next lesson. Their ritual.

"Stop," I shout. Several students freeze, like it's a game. *Red light,
green light.* They're all looking at me. Staring. "You need to run before
they—"

Mr. Dunstan threads his arms through my own from behind, wrapping his hands around my neck and forcing me over. I never knew he
was that agile. *That strong.* I try to bring my arms around to push back
but I can't reach him. He's dragging me down the hallway. Away from
the kids. I yank my head forward, hoping the weight of my body will
throw him off-balance. His grip around my neck slips, giving me just
enough leverage to pry free.

I stumble out of his arms and start running. Pushing through the
children. All the children. None of them move. They stand stock-still.
Some are crying. Eyes wide. Mouths open.

It's too late for them. Too late to save them. I have to keep running.
I push past the last of the students, sending one falling to the ground
before I burst through the doors.

The sun is too bright. It stings. I have to shield my eyes.

A black pillar of smoke snakes into the sky, winding its way over
town. The column is close enough to see it roil and contort from the
tree line. It looks as if it's coming from behind the school. Along the

bike path. Toward the houses just on the other side.

Our house.

DAMNED IF YOU DON'T
RICHARD: 2013

I hear Tamara before I see the fire. All other sound is drowned out by her sobbing, no matter how loud. Not the sirens from the fire trucks. The roar of the blaze. Not the low murmur from the onlookers standing at a safe distance. These sounds mean nothing to me.

All I hear is Tamara, her throat raw from wailing.

"Where is he where is he where is he . . ." It's meant to be a question—and at one point I imagine it had been. But not anymore. Not with the answer burning before her.

Tamara keeps repeating the words anyhow until they lose their shape.

A fireman wraps his arms around her waist, holding her back from breaking the perimeter. Tamara gives in and leans back against the fireman's chest as they stare at the flames, the soft orange glow playing across their cheeks.

There isn't much of the house left by the time I reach our street. The hipped roof has collapsed. The pillars along the front porch have buckled. Sheets of flame lap at the windows.

The garage is gone. It must've burned down first. The walls of the studio are cindered ribs, a few boards stubbornly standing up like the chest cavity of some prehistoric beast.

The volunteer fire department does what they can, but there's no containing the blaze.

Let the fire burn itself out. Let the flames eat their fill.

I stop before Tamara. She won't look away from the house, searching for her son.

I say her name. Quietly at first. I try again, but there's no tearing Tamara's attention away from the fire. The flames have her undivided attention. She won't let them go.

I grip her arms. The fireman releases his hold and her legs buckle. She's free-falling through her own nightmare now. Nothing will ever be the same.

"Tamara," I say again, louder. Squeezing her arms. Her eyes break away from the fire. She doesn't recognize me. I'm just another stranger standing between her and her son.

"They won't let me." Her voice crumbles. "Won't let me . . ."

"Tamara, please . . ."

"He's in there. I have to . . . have to get him back."

All at once, her muscles snap taut. She pulls out from my grip, suddenly seeing me for the first time. "What did you do?"

"Tamara, I didn't. This wasn't—"

"Get away from me." Tamara turns and marches toward the embers of her house.

"Tamara!" I race after her, catching her before she walks into the fire. She would have climbed those melting steps if she could.

"I have to get him back."

"Tamara, stop—"

As soon as I get my hands around her, pulling her away from the fire, she screams and starts digging her fingernails into my skin, clawing at me.

It takes two firefighters to pull her back. She nearly overpowers us all, her sheer determination to save her son filling her with adrenaline. But it's too late.

"He's still in there! He's still in there! Please, someone, save my son my boy please . . ."

I let her go, watching as the firefighters drag Tamara away from the flames. Her voice carries. There's no escaping it.

A group of onlookers stands at a safe distance. They gather together to watch the fire devour our house. These are our neighbors. But I don't recognize them. Not anymore.

They want this. This is what they want to see.

What if . . . ? The gnawing thoughts whisper. *What if they had wanted Elijah all along?*

In order to make mothers and fathers despair, they need a child. Someone innocent. To make the world weep.

This is all my fault. If I hadn't come into their lives, if I hadn't led them right to Elijah, none of this would have happened. He would still be alive.

Look at them, I think. The flames reflect in their obsidian eyes, like marbles. Doll's eyes. They're basking in the flames. *Rejoicing.* It won't be long before they'll be dancing, all of them locking arms and circling the blaze, their voices lifting higher, higher as they all sing. They'll rip their clothes off and dance around the inferno, naked, their wrinkled bodies writhing.

The world is burning. The devil has won.

"Is this what you want?" I shout.

Everyone's attention turns to me, snapping away from the fire.

"Is this what you're after?" My legs give out and I find myself on the ground. My mouth opens to sob, but there's nothing there. No sound. I'm empty. Completely empty.

Eli's gone. The thought echoes through my head. *Eli's gone.*

The devil has won.

My eyes settle upon a hand in front of me. A woman's hand, palm facing the sky.

I look up to see Sandy's mother reaching for me. She smiles warmly, like Mom once did.

"Time for a road trip."

DAMNED IF YOU DON'T
RICHARD: 2013

E lijah is fast asleep in the back seat of Miss Levin's Honda Accord, completely lost to the world and all the chaos conjured up by his absence. He knows he's not supposed to talk to strangers. Then again, Miss Levin isn't exactly a stranger—is she? Not with Sandy at her side. There she is, too, fast asleep in the back seat, buckled in right beside him.

The car is parked a few blocks away, hidden within the shade of a paper birch. How long have they been asleep? How could the sirens not wake them? How could Elijah not hear his mother shrieking?

"Get in," Miss Levin says.

"Fuck you," I say, summoning my last iota of defiance.

"Get in, Sean." She slides into the driver's seat. The engine turns, humming to life. Her hands rest on the wheel, glaring at me through the passenger window.

I'm not letting her drive away with Elijah. I open the passenger door and climb in beside her.

Miss Levin pulls out a thermos from the footwell. There's a chipped picture of Papa Smurf on its side. Most of the paint has faded, leaving behind a blue phantom. I had a thermos just like it when I was a kid. "Hi-C," she answers before I ask. "Hope you like cherry. I couldn't find orange."

I turn to the back seat, taking in Eli, I notice his lips are stained a deep pink. So are Sandy's. "No."

"We're not leaving until you drink," Miss Levin says.

"I won't."

"If you don't, you'll never know what happened to your mother."

"I know what happened."

"Do you? I'm sure you've told yourself all kinds of things so you can sleep at night. No matter who it hurts . . . Everyone around you is nothing but collateral damage to your lies."

She's relying on my sense of curiosity to see this through. To understand.

Of course she's right. I've come this far. Can't stop now. I have to know. Have to see this through to the bitter end. She doesn't need to put a gun to my head. She knows I'll follow her.

We're playing a game.

Simon says . . . drink.

I take a deep pull directly from the thermos. A flood of artificial flavoring spreads through my empty stomach, much too sweet. I haven't had Hi-C since I was a kid.

"That's not so bad, is it? Drink it up." She's treating me like a child. I notice a chalky undertaste on my tongue, a hidden bitterness lingering in the juice.

"Why burn down our house?"

"You think I did that?" She almost laughs. "Talk to your neighbors, not me."

"I didn't do anything. None of this—none of this is true. This—this isn't—"

Isn't me.

"Sounds familiar," she says. "People will believe anything when they're afraid. Especially when it's their own children at risk. And when you put a face to their fear? Give it a name of someone they know? Someone from their own community, maybe? Well . . . that person becomes a monster in everyone else's eyes. It doesn't matter if he's innocent or not. Not anymore. Because all anyone will ever see when they look at that person again is a monster."

She offers this up so casually, so matter-of-factly, as if we were merely having a conversation between friends and she's giving me some sage advice. A helping hand.

"Who *are* you?"

She looks over at me and smiles. It's not threatening in any way. Just hurt. It stings her somehow. "You don't remember me, do you? You don't remember anything at all . . ."

I know her. That's what she's insinuating. I know her from somewhere. Where? *When?*

"Jenna."

Jenna. Had I known Miss Levin's first name was Jenna?

"Jenna Woodhouse. You knew my father. Levin was my mother's maiden name. I took it when she changed it back, but . . . Levin never fit. *Jenna Levin.* It never felt quite right to my ear."

He is survived by his estranged wife and daughter . . .

Had she gone to Greenfield, too? Was she in my class? Had she always been there and I never realized it? Never remembered?

Jenna shifts the car into drive. Before I can protest, we're heading down the road.

Away from Tamara.

Shadows start to take shape in my mind. I'm beginning to see.

See her.

Jenna Woodhouse.

The girl in the background . . .

Jenna Woodhouse.

The little girl in the pictures on my teacher's desk, smiling between her mom and dad . . .

Jenna.

The girl staring back at me . . .

I see her now. See her everywhere. In Mr. Woodhouse's classroom. The courtroom. The studio audience. Wherever my memory takes me, I spot Jenna Woodhouse hiding in the crowd.

"You took my father away from me," she says.

"I didn't . . . I didn't know. I didn't know it was—"

"He couldn't stop people from believing. Even after he was exonerated, after everybody knew it was all just a hoax, people never stopped whispering about him. They still believed."

"I—I was just a kid."

"Just a *kid*? I'm sorry, but why does that matter? *Just a kid.*"

"Kids—kids make things up for no reason."

Liar.

"They believed you. They listened to you. You could've stopped everything, if you'd just spoken up and taken it all back. *You could have saved him.*"

"Take me," I say. "We'll go wherever you want, but—please. Leave Eli out—"

"It's my turn to talk!" The outburst sets both children shifting in the back seat, but neither wakes. "Nobody took pity on me. Nobody tried to protect me like they protected *you*. Everywhere I went, everyone made sure I knew who my father *really* was."

A daughter. I keep repeating it to myself. *Mr. Woodhouse had a daughter.*

"I didn't . . ." My words fade away. The car accelerates, pushing us toward the county line.

Over the river and through the woods . . .

Danvers disappears. There's nothing but a canopy of trees wrapping around Route 3.

"My life wasn't like yours," she says. "I wasn't allowed to forget who I was. Even after my dad killed himself, people wouldn't let him go. Wouldn't let him be at peace. They needed someone to take his blame . . . so they blamed me. I became the scapegoat for all of your lies."

Scapegoat: a person blamed for something someone else did.

A sacrifice.

I study Jenna's face. When I look in her eyes, Mr. Woodhouse stares back.

"I knew you'd need help remembering . . . We have to finish what you started."

I can't focus on her words. Something roils in my stomach.

"The devil doesn't exist, Sean. But I got you to believe, didn't I? Believe your own lies."

My head grows heavier. My chin dips to my chest. My neck snaps back up. The world outside my window spins—the trees, their branches, the leaves won't stop spiraling.

"You were so willing to believe. Believe everything. I barely had to do a thing."

"I was just . . ." I have to dig deep and shovel the words out. "Just . . . kid . . ."

"What about me?" Jenna shouts. "I was a child, too. What did I do to deserve this? What did any of us do to deserve the hell you put us all through?"

The trees thin down to my right. I peer out my window and see the crystalline sheen of the Rappahannock. The sun hits the water's surface, striking my eyes. I wince at its brightness.

We're about to cross the bridge.

"How many families did you tear apart? How many lives did you demolish?"

I fumble for my door's handle. My fingers wrap around it and pull, but my hand slips. The door won't open. Child safety locks.

"You were never punished for what you did. You never had to say you were sorry. You just got to move on with your life and start over! A clean slate! Like nothing ever happened . . ."

A fresh start.

My skull rolls over the headrest. My eyes skim across the blur of water outside. We're coming up on the bridge too quickly. Two narrow lanes suspended over the water.

"I saw you. I saw you following in my father's footsteps . . . *and you didn't even realize it!*"

The past is never through with us. The stories I created as a child took on a life of their own. I lied—and those lies reverberated into the lives of everyone surrounding me. My stories devoured entire families. They destroyed my family, they destroyed hers.

"Look at me, Sean. *Look.*" She slaps me across the face, waking me up. "Remember me. Remember what you've done. You have to live with your lies. I am your lie. Sandy is your lie."

Sandy? What about her? What did I do to her?

The river swells around the car. I see blue on both sides now. The Rappahannock's glassy sheen shimmers with the sun's reflection. The bridge's rusted abutments undulate, warping outside the windshield as they wrap around the car, as if the metal is embracing us.

"Do you remember now, Sean? Do you remember me?"

Yes—yes, I remember now. I remember everything.

"Do you believe?"

I believe.

I'm five years old again. I'm back in Mom's station wagon, barreling down the highway. The world blurs beyond our windshield, nothing but speed, as Mom tries to escape the clutches of that invisible presence always at our backs, always in the rearview mirror, always closing in.

I grab the wheel. I have to make her stop. Stop the car. Before we—

Before—

"What are you doing?" Jenna pulls the wheel in the other direction. The two of us struggle for control over the car. Her foot presses on the accelerator. The engine heaves from the sudden thrust. The speedometer quickly climbs to sixty-five miles an hour, seventy.

Someone screams. The sound of it fills the car, singing along with the screeching tires.

A boy.

It sounds like Sean, like me, but it's coming from over my shoulder. From the back seat. Eli has woken up. He lets out a single cry before the car smashes into the bridge abutment.

To bear witness to the water.

DAMNED IF YOU DO
SEAN: 1983

"Keep your seatbelt on," Mom instructed. "No matter what happens, don't take it off."

Taking his head in her hands, she firmly pressed her lips against his brow. She examined him closely, combing his hair with her fingers. She took him in, all of him. She patted his head. Fussed with his clothes one last time. Making him look perfect. She had packed his Sunday best before they abandoned their home in the middle of the night, a lifetime ago. He had his fancy shoes on, polished until they shimmered, even in the dark. Obsidian black. Just like the gray boy from Miss Betty's picture.

"There. That's good. That's good. Now, how about some music?"

Before Sean could answer, Mom flipped the stereo on. Static seeped through the speakers as she surfed from station to station, sonic waves crashing against their car. She eventually settled on the pulsing chords of The Police's "Every Breath You Take."

"I love this song." She bobbed her head along, searching for the rhythm with her neck. She turned the volume up until it was difficult for Sean to talk over the music. "This is nice. Isn't this nice? You can sing along, even if you don't know the words."

She shifted the car into drive, humming along to the song. Her rhythm was off. Mom couldn't keep up, distracted by some more prominent thought. She was struggling to avoid it, whatever it was. Pretend it wasn't there. That it didn't exist.

The song was meant to distract them but it wasn't working. Mom was lost. Lost in her thoughts, that expansive cloud forming in her head. No one, not even Sean, could reach her.

"Mom?"

Nothing. No answer. Mom continued to hum along to the song, nodding.

Sean tried again. "Mommy?"

Her focus was on every chord, every lyric, every breath, *dut-dut, dut-dut, dut-dut*, every move, every vow, *dut-dut, dut-dut-dut*, while turning the car onto the highway.

"*Mom!*"

Mom cranked the volume even higher. The song stung Sean's ears. Something about how she was acting behind the wheel compelled him to unbuckle his seatbelt—even though Mom always told him not to— sliding quietly across the sticky leatherette.

Mom was talking to herself now. Even when she spoke, it was as if she were talking to someone else. Not Sean, but some other version of him.

"Almost there," she said into the rearview mirror. "Everything's going to be okay now."

Every time he asked his mother where they were going, she avoided the question. Pretending she didn't hear him, humming along to the radio instead. She was playing her own game. Without him. Acting as if everything was perfectly normal when nothing was normal at all. As if driving in the middle of the night was normal. As if wearing his

Sunday clothes on a Tuesday—it was a Tuesday, right?—was normal. As if leaving everything behind, their house, Miss Kinderman, school, was perfectly normal. But it wasn't. None of this was normal.

Mom wasn't normal. Not anymore. She had been getting worse and worse. She shielded her son from every passing stranger. Shouted at people who stood too close in line at the rest area. Always grabbing Sean by the arm and tugging him away from anyone who said hello.

Always driving. Sleeping in the back seat. Waking up somewhere else. A different back road. A different town.

The engine heaved. Sean could hear the strain just under the music, pushing the car further along. It pushed him deeper into his seat.

Sean wanted to take it back. Take it all back. He wanted to tell his mom he had lied. That it wasn't Mr. Woodhouse. It was never Mr. Woodhouse or any of the other teachers at school.

A game. It was just a game. Just for the two of them to play together. *All for you, Mom*, he thought. *I did it all for you.*

"It's not true," he managed. The words were barely there, but he'd said it. He had been so scared of the truth. What would happen if it were to finally come out that he'd been lying all along? They would take him away, wouldn't they? Just like Mom said? The adults in their neckties would finally swoop in and separate their family? "I made it all up, Mommy . . ."

The car was moving faster. He couldn't tell for sure, but he sensed the momentum all around him, thrusting him against the door as the station wagon propelled itself forward.

"I made it up . . ." He said it louder now, fighting the music. "I lied, Mommy . . ."

Mom's head turned slightly to her right shoulder, as if she'd just heard something in the car. But the moment passed, and her focus drifted back to the windshield and the darkness ahead. Nothing Sean said seemed to penetrate that dense shield of music, so he told her he loved her. It was all he could say anymore, all he could think to do. To help save them.

But she never heard him.

"I love you, Mommy," he said again from the back seat of the car, trying it once more. Just in case. That these magic words might break the spell his mother was under and bring her back, let her foot off the accelerator, slow the car down to a stop and come back to him.

Mom merely nodded to herself, smiling her pained smile, her eyes focused on the darkened road outside the windshield, humming even louder to the song. Blocking Sean out.

The road disappeared.

The headlights brushed over a black sheet of glass. It was so smooth at first. It seemed to reach into the horizon, that glass, farther than the car's high beams could ever reach.

The station wagon dipped. It felt like they were on a roller coaster, suddenly plunging forward. The front fender pushed through that blackened glass. The impact thrust Sean forward. He folded over, his head tapping his knees. Without his seatbelt on, Sean tumbled into the footwell, his body slamming against the back of his mother's seat. He scrambled back up, grabbing hold of her headrest and pulling himself into his seat again. When he looked out the windshield, at the churning shadows surrounding them, they looked like wraiths drifting by the car, swallowing it in a cloud of muck. Sean gasped.

Water. That was water outside the car, he realized. The headlights branched out into the brackish expanse, swirling around the hood.

A boat ramp. The station wagon continued to roll down the concrete slope, forcing its way into the vast expanse of black surrounding them.

The hood was gone. Water lapped at the windshield, slapping against the glass.

The radio was still on.

Every breath you take . . .

Sean could hear the thin trickle of water reaching inside.

Every move you make . . .

The water was now in the car. Pooling at his feet.

Rising to his ankles.

Filling up the footwell until he pulled his legs away.

Reaching for his seat.

Mom merely kept her hands gripped on the steering wheel, holding on so tight her knuckles turned white. She pressed her foot down on the accelerator. The car heaved. The engine bay filled with water, muting the motor's rev.

We're going to drown, Sean thought. *We're going to drown!*

"It's going to be okay," Mom said, never looking back. She was still driving through the night, on a highway that led their family to safety. Soon. They would be there soon.

Sean glanced out his window. There was nothing to see but a whirling blackness enveloping the car. Glancing into the spacious rear compartment of the station wagon, he saw the last of the night sky disappear beneath the river's surface as the water lapped at the glass.

They were underwater now, the entire car submerged. Mom hadn't moved. She kept on driving, humming along to the song. That was the worst part. The scariest part to Sean.

Hearing her hum.

Sean gripped his window's handle and started to roll it down. A fresh rush of water smashed against his temple. It smacked his cheek, his ear. The water wanted to come inside.

Coughing, Sean rolled down the window until there was enough of a gap to slip through. Water filled the back seat. The leatherette was slippery, like eel skin.

His body lifted from where he sat, levitating.

When he screamed, water rushed into his mouth. He choked on the cold.

Sean took a deep breath, bringing in as much air as his lungs would allow, and slipped under the water's surface. It was far too dark in the car to see anything. He had to run his hands over his mother until his fingers eventually brushed against her seatbelt and found the buckle.

Sean pushed the button and—

It wouldn't unlock. Wouldn't release her.

Sean pushed harder. *Harder*. But nothing seemed to work. The seatbelt wouldn't open.

Mom remained behind the wheel, still driving. Her hair fanned through the water like spaghetti radiating around her head.

Sean's lungs felt as if they were filled with broken glass. He needed air.

Needed to escape.

His mother never looked back, never turned her head to see her son swim through the cracked window and rise to the surface. She kept driving, driving, running away from those invisible forces closing in. The evil presence that had been chasing them for months. Hunting them down wherever they ran. They would be safe here. They could hide down here. Hide all the way at the bottom of the river with the kelp.

His last image of his mother was of her humming underwater, the thinnest ribbon of bubbles issuing from her mouth. When the song ended in her head, she parted her lips and let the water in.

DAMNED IF YOU DON'T
RICHARD: 2013

Sean is screaming in the back seat. I wake to his voice, shrieking from the rear of the car.

That's Sean, isn't it? It has to be.

Everything inside the station wagon has gone dark. The world beyond the windows has disappeared, lost in churning water.

Mom drove straight into the river. I remember seeing the bridge's embankment, a rusted guardrail separating the road from the water below. The car smashed through the feeble partition, free-falling through the air before plunging under the water's surface.

Wait—that's not how it happened. I can't fight off the fog enveloping my head. Everything in my body has slowed down. I can feel my blood thrumming through my veins, thickened to a sludge. I can't lift my arms without straining. It's all too heavy.

Mom's head smashed against the windshield. A halo of cracks radiated around her skull, a sunburst, bright and blinding. It stung my eyes to look at her. I watched her skull ricochet off the windshield before my own head met the glove compartment and then—

Then everything went black.

Wait—that's not how it happened at all.

What's going on here?

There's water at my feet. The car is filling fast. The sun is gone, barely reaching through the murky sheen of the enveloping river. The slightest hint of green branches out around us, a forest of stained glass. Light. That has to be sunlight.

I don't know how long I've been unconscious. My forehead stings. I can't see. I bring my fingers to my temple and touch something wet. Blood. There's blood running down my face.

Is this really happening? Is history repeating itself? Am I watching the movie of my life?

Mom is slung over the steering wheel. Her body is limp, a puppet without a hand to animate her. Her eyes remain open, unblinking, staring at me. She's not moving. Her breathing is so shallow, if there's breath at all.

This isn't how it happened. Someone's rewriting the past, revising the way I remember it. I can't get my bearings. A searing pain slices through my neck when I turn to the back seat.

There I am.

I see Sean next to the gray boy. They're clinging to each other, kicking their feet at the rising water. They're screaming. The water laps at their feet. They can't kick it away. Can't stop the rising tide. The blackness fills their laps, swallowing their legs. They won't let go of each other. Sean embraces the gray boy as the hungry river closes in. It's going to swallow them whole if they don't escape.

I try to fast-forward the VHS tape a bit in my mind. Try to remember what happens next.

How does this end? I can't recall. It's all black to me. My skull is throbbing. Cracked open. I feel my memories bleeding out and pouring into my eyes, stinging me. Blinding me.

I can't remember how this story ends. It's my story—I should know, but I can't trace it.

"Dad," Sean cries. "Daddy, please!"

But it's not Sean.

Not me.

Those who don't learn history are doomed to repeat it.

My brain clicks in just in time. *It's Eli.*

Eli is in the back seat. I struggle to unbuckle my seatbelt and climb into the back. I fall into a lopsided bathtub. The cold water cuts through the fog, helping me focus.

"Hold on to me," I manage to say as I try to unbuckle their belts. The gray boy—no, not a boy—Sandy, it's Sandy—immediately levitates from her seat as soon as she's free. Her arms flail about, unsure how to stay afloat. She never learned to swim. Didn't her mother teach her?

There's no handle for the window. Last time this happened, there was a handle. It's gone. This window is controlled by a button. I press down and—

Nothing happens. I reach over to the other door and try that window. Nothing.

The windshield. I have to slither back to the front seat. I can't tell if the vehicle is leaning forward or backward. There's nothing to orient my sense of direction. There's no light. It's all black outside the windows and now it's seeping in, ready to swallow us all.

Mom's head—

Jenna.

That's Mom, isn't it?

No, it's Jenna.

Jenna's head made impact with the windshield, fracturing the glass into a cobweb. I have to embed myself into the seat next to her, inches away from her limp body. Her arms are tangled in the steering wheel, neck bent.

I bring my legs up until my feet press against the cracked windshield and push as hard as I can. The windshield bulges, fracturing further under my heels, but it doesn't break.

I have to kick. Each time my heels strike the glass, I feel a pang ring up the bones in my legs, like a tuning fork striking a hard surface. The pain reverberates through the rest of my body.

I have to keep kicking.

Harder.

Water finally begins to dribble through the cracks.

Harder.

I kick again.

And again.

Again.

The windshield folds open under my heels and swallows my feet. Glass digs into my ankles, sinking its fangs in. This fresh sensation sends a surge of pain through my body.

The car is alive. It's going to eat me. Devour us all.

The river forces its way in. The sheer pressure of water forces open the glass until it shatters completely. A flood smashes against my chest, rushing inside and swallowing us.

"Breathe," I shout through the surging water. "Breathe now—"

But it's too late. There's no air anymore. It's all gone. Any trapped oxygen drifts off in these tiny pockets along the car's ceiling, rolling toward the windshield and escaping.

Whatever breath is left in our lungs is all we have.

I spin around, trying to find Elijah and Sandy in the dark. Their bodies have been forced back by the rush of water, pushing them deeper into the car. I falter through the water, grabbing them both. I hold on to them, each tucked under an arm and pressed to my side, as I kick up—or down—through the windshield. Jagged teeth slice at my back. The glass rakes across my skin, opening fresh channels along my flesh, but I push harder.

I have to pull us from the mouth of this leviathan. All I want to do is scream from the stinging pain, but I know the water is waiting to come in, just like it had waited for my mother. It wants me to part my lips and give in.

Elijah and Sandy writhe about in my arms. I pray they have more air than I do.

Once we're free from the car, I can't figure which way is up. There's a burning in my chest, the oxygen already dissolving from my lungs. There's no more air. Nothing to breathe.

All I can do is kick . . .

Kick . . .

Kick . . .

The water darkens. Not from the lack of sunlight, but within my head. Shadows percolate in the corner of my eyes, eclipsing everything, until there's nothing else to see.

It's all going black.

I keep kicking. The surface has to be close. Has to be just on the other side of one last kick. Just one more . . . But I can't see. Can't feel anything other than the singe in my lungs. My throat. Everything within my chest feels like it's on fire, while my skin is now pleasantly numb.

Where is the surface? Where is the air?

Where is . . .

I'm sorry, Eli. I brought this darkness with me, inside our home. I brought it straight to you. It's always been in me, hiding. I never would have entered your life if I'd known. I wouldn't wish this upon anyone, I swear. Believe me. Everything else is lies. Most of them mine.

There's no hiding from this. Who I am. These shadows have always been behind me. No—not following me, but inside. I've always been the gray boy. An indefinable shape. An absence of light, hollow and

278 CLAY McLEOD CHAPMAN

featureless. I have nothing to call my own. I am nothing. No one.

I lied. I lied to you. Your mother. I lied even when I didn't realize I was lying.

I lied to myself.

What happens if you believe in a lie, believe it with every fiber of your body? Does it become real, somehow? Does the lie become the truth? Your truth?

I was born from my own lies. Richard Bellamy never existed.

I'm not even real.

DAMNED IF YOU DO, DAMNED IF YOU DON'T

This is the version of the story that fits best.

Miss Levin had come to our house, luring Eli outside with promises of a game.

We're going on a road trip, she'd told him.

She gave Eli something sweet to drink. *Too sweet*, he said. His head felt fuzzy and he quickly drifted off.

Jenna had drugged her daughter as well. We were all meant to be in that car together, our road trip to the river bottom.

Because she was trying to kill us, wasn't she? That had been her plan all along. The puzzle pieces fit.

This is the truth that makes sense to me. You just have to look at it from my point of view.

You have to believe.

The authorities didn't believe me at first. Detective Merrin thought I had kidnapped Elijah and Sandy. He speculated I had "done something" to Miss Levin.

But Elijah backed up my story. He said when he woke up, the car was already underwater. The river would have taken us all had it not been for me. I couldn't save Miss Levin, but I saved him and Sandy. I was the hero.

It sounds good, doesn't it? Who would believe that it was actually Eli who pulled me and Sandy from the car? That doesn't sound right. Those pieces don't fit. The story doesn't fit.

I should be dead right now.

In some ways I am.

I like to believe Richard Bellamy drowned and Sean Crenshaw emerged from the water, crawling back into this life.

That's my story. The death and rebirth of Sean can now finally come to a close.

Full circle.

It took a hydraulic crane to haul Jenna Woodhouse's car from the Rappahannock. A regular tow truck couldn't reach it, so the police had to bring in a telescoping boom truck, positioning it on the bridge where the car had rammed through the rusted abutment. Divers tethered the crane's hook to the rear bumper and slowly hauled it up.

Sandy stood at the water's edge, watching her mother's car twirl in the air. A paramedic draped a wool blanket over her shoulders, but she wouldn't move, transfixed by the sight of the suspended car. She was waiting for her mother.

Jenna's body dislodged itself, slipping through the windshield and washing downstream. Sandy didn't see the divers carry her mother out of the water. There must have been a part of her that believed she had escaped somehow. It's easier to believe things like that.

I would, if I were her.

When Tamara arrived at the riverbank, she pulled Eli's mud-covered body into her arms. His hair was matted down, that mop top covering his eyes. She couldn't stop gripping him. She needed to touch everything, take inventory of his limbs to confirm nothing was missing.

Tamara and I saw each other. Her eyes found mine and immediately turned away. It would take time to get everybody's story straight. I just had to be patient. To regain her trust.

Every day is a step toward understanding who I was and moving toward who I can be.

I am looking for forgiveness.

I am looking for myself.

The last thing Tamara said to me was that she didn't know who I was anymore, if she ever knew me to begin with. *Are you Sean or are you Richard?*

That had been months ago. I respected her need for space, for distance, leaving them be. Then, out of the blue, the most miraculous thing happened . . .

Elijah asked to see me.

See *me.*

Tamara supervised our hangouts. She refused to leave us alone. We'd meet at the park or a playground of Tamara's choosing. After a few successful outings, we went to Elijah's favorite restaurant.

Is Eli sleeping through the night? I asked while he was in the restroom.

No, she replied, giving as little of herself to me as possible.

He'll get there. Just give it time.

Time, she echoed.

Guess what? Condrey's considering giving me my job back. Not my old job, exactly. There's a summer program that she's trying to start—

Richard, stop.

Sean, I corrected her. *It's . . . Sean.*

I have to believe we'll find each other again. That I can find my way back to my family.

Time. That's all I have. Healing takes time.

Sandy is on her own. No extended family, no relatives. Apparently, she screams her head off whenever social services tries splitting her and Eli apart. They found a foster family willing to house her temporarily, but that only lasted a few sleepless nights before they gave up.

Tamara will foster Sandy for the short term until the state figures out what to do. She has an apartment near downtown that's big enough for the three of them. Sandy apparently crawls into Eli's bed at night. Tamara often finds them nestled together in the morning.

Me—my new digs are farther off the interstate. I don't know if I'm technically still in the county limits or not, but I'm close enough. I'm staying in a drab complex where everyone is content minding their own business, keeping their heads low, which is fine for the time being.

Tonight is Eli's first sleepover. It's a big step and I'm not taking it lightly. Months of rebuilding trust have led to this. Tamara can call or text anytime she wants, just to check in. I know it's hard, but she understands this is something he wants, and she's at a point where she's willing to give him just about whatever he asks for, as long as it brings him back to how he was.

Who he was.

I've already mapped out the itinerary for Boys Night: Pizza. A movie. Painting.

I've been getting Eli's room ready for him. The apartment isn't much to look at. I haven't decorated the place and I doubt I ever will. The eggshell suits me just fine. As far as furniture is concerned, I only picked up the essentials. A couch. A TV/DVD player. A set of cutlery for two.

I also got my hands on some art supplies, just for tonight. The Big Night.

When he finally arrives, he takes in the empty canvas surrounding him, four walls waiting for him to attack. "Go to town," I say. "Paint it however you want."

"Really? Won't we get in trouble?"

"So what if I lose the deposit? You better go full-on Jackson Pollock in this joint."

Eli splashes the bedroom walls with all kinds of color. No need to stay in the lines. Just get it out, all that pent-up emotion. Release whatever might be trapped inside since the car accident. I don't want him to hold onto his emotions, to bury them—like I did when I was his age.

History will not repeat itself.

There are moments when I see her—Jenna—standing in a crowd. I'll pass her on the street. Spot her from the corner of my eye. I'll stop and turn. Wait and see. But she's never really there.

If it hadn't been for her, I never would've found myself again.

Found Sean.

Jenna helped me rediscover whom I've been hiding from. Had I known who she was before she died, I wonder if I would've been capable of asking her for forgiveness.

I wonder if she would have been capable of giving it to me.

I guess we'll never know, will we?

What I put her family through was unforgivable. What she put my family through was unforgivable too, but I hope we would've forgiven each other.

I keep asking for forgiveness from ghosts. I need to ask myself the same thing...

Can I begin to forgive myself? For all the things that I've done?

How can I atone?

Eli, I think. He's my second chance.

His bedtime is nine p.m. on weekends. Tamara wanted him in bed no later than nine thirty, but this is his first night here. It's a special occasion. What's an extra hour going to hurt? I tell him we can keep it between him and me. Our little secret.

I tuck him in. A splatter pattern of paint still speckles our skin, illuminated by the nightstand lamp. I turn it off and the two of us are left in the dark. The bespattered paint on the walls looks like cobwebs in the shadows.

"Do you think . . ." Eli hesitates, struggling to find the right words. Once he thinks he's finally got them, he starts again. "Do you think Sandy's mom really meant to drown us?"

I choose my words carefully. "We can ask ourselves over and over, racking our brains for some explanation, but . . . there never will be an answer. Sometimes it's best to just let it go."

Forgive and forget, I want to say, even if I'm not sure I believe it. I think about the moment in the car. On the bridge. Jenna started to accelerate, steering for the abutment.

I heard Eli scream from the back seat. That's when I grabbed the steering wheel.

That's how it happened. How I remember it happening.

"Do you think you'll ever come back home?" he asks. "With Mom?"

"I hope so."

"Me, too."

"Put in a good word for me. She'll listen to you."

He laughs. "Okay . . ."

It's clear he's struggling to put his thoughts into words. Something is still weighing him down. "Is there something else? Something you want to tell me?"

When he finally speaks, his voice is barely there. "It was supposed to be a game . . ."

I don't say anything right away, letting his words sink in. "What do you mean?"

"It's all my fault. I told Sandy I was really mad at Mom for marrying you . . . I didn't want a new dad. Then Sandy said her mom had a game we could play. To get back at you. Sandy's mom told me to do all these things around the house. Little things. She told me to say stuff she knew would scare you. She said if I did it, you'd go away and it'd just be me and Mom again."

I think back to all those moments in the house, the inexplicable things that kept happening. Eli. The whole time. "You knew?"

"I didn't think it would end like that . . . I didn't know Sandy's mom would . . . would . . ."

Just a game.

"The bruises," I say. "Your mother told me she found bruises on your arm . . ."

"I did it—" he swallows "—to myself."

I realize my fingernails are digging into my palm. "Have you told your mother?"

Eli shakes his head, *no*. "Nobody was supposed to get hurt. Honest."

He thinks I'm mad at him. He's afraid of what I might say, that I'll give him up to his mother—but what I can't admit, not to Eli, is that I've been feeling the exact same way. This boy has held my fate in his hands for months now. We've stalemated each other.

"What do we do now?" I ask.

Eli leans over and fishes through his backpack next to the bed. He pulls out a crumpled envelope. He's held on to it for a long time, from the looks of it. The paper appears like it was wet, then dried. The ink has blurred a bit across the front, but I can still read the name:

SEAN.

"I found it in my backpack," Eli says. "After the accident."

I take the envelope. It's not sealed. "Did you read it?"

Eli doesn't answer. Of course he has. *Curiosity killed the* . . . but I stop myself. He's six now. Whatever it says, I have to imagine—I hope—most of the words go right over his head.

This must be Jenna Woodhouse's final word against me. Her punishment. Did she know this would end with her death? How could she?

I push the thought out of my mind. Whatever's written in here, I'm sure it has the specific intent of poisoning my relationship with Eli. With Tamara.

They're lies, I hear myself—hear Sean—whisper. *Nothing but lies.*

I rip up the envelope.

Eli's eyes widen as I send a flurry of torn paper into the air. I don't need her words in my head. I will not let her have the final word over my life.

"It's okay." I almost say *water under the bridge.* "I love you, Eli, no matter what."

He nods.

"We just have to—"

watch out for

"—trust each other. I'm willing to do that, if you are. What do you say?"

"I love you . . . Dad."

"I love you, too."

"Will you stay with me?" he asks. "Just until I fall asleep?"

"I'll stay as long as you want."

I take in the room as Eli slowly drifts off to sleep. The stillness of the space is palpable. The dull glow of the building's utility light just outside his window seeps into the room.

Something catches my eye through the open curtains. I sit up, my feet finding the floor.

Someone is out there.

I spot a glimpse of their silhouette from the other side of the window. Their ashen features linger in my reflection, like two faces superimposed on the glass.

A drab man hides inside me, the reflection of his face nestled within my own.

The gray boy stares back.

I walk to the window. Glancing out to the shadowed street, I search but can't see him anymore. Just the halogen lamp, casting a coffee-colored patina over the patch of grass below.

There's a car parked down the block but no one's in it. There's a tree kids climb and play in during the day, but its branches are empty now, buckling in the breeze.

I hold my breath, waiting for the brick. For the glass to shatter. I sense it coming for me.

Any second now.

Any second . . .

"Who is it?" Elijah asks. He's hoisted himself up on one elbow, trying to see what I see.

I close the curtains, sealing us in. I turn away from the window, my back to the glass. I smile back at him.

"No one."

Dear Sean,

The first time I found you was outside your bedroom window. I don't know how long we stood on your lawn, watching you and your mother as she read you a story. It felt like hours to me, but I was only five at the time. I couldn't stop shivering in my pajamas. You looked so warm inside.

"Look, Jenna," my mother said. "Just look at them."

I remember wishing I was at home, in my own bed with my own mother reading a story to me, instead of hiding outside yours, freezing in the dark. All I could hear was my teeth chattering. I didn't want to be here, peering into your life.

"These are the people who ruined your father," my mother said. "They ruined our family. Look how happy they are."

She had brought a brick with her. I'm not sure if she had been carrying it the whole time, but I remember watching her throw it. The arc of her arm. The sudden, ear-splitting shatter of glass. The sound was so loud, it echoed throughout the neighborhood.

I remember hearing you scream.

Before I knew it, my mother yanked me away from your house. We ran down the street. My feet couldn't keep up, but she wouldn't let me go. She didn't slow down until we reached our car blocks away. "Don't tell anyone," she said. "This will be our little secret."

I felt giddy at first, sharing this moment with my mother. We did something mischievous together and nobody else knew. Just between us. Our own little secret.

It's the last fond memory of my mother that I have.

Even though she would say otherwise, eventually laying the blame at my father's feet like everyone else, I knew my mother never believed it. Your lies. She said what everyone else was saying to save her own skin. She knew that if she didn't play along, people would start blaming her for what happened, too. She would be sucked into the same sinkhole that was swallowing up my father. I hated her for it.

Hated you.

I've known you my whole life. My earliest memories are of you. You were always there. On the six o'clock news. The front page of the newspaper. I'd turn on the television and there you'd be, talking about how my father was this monster, even though we both know that isn't true. My father was so gentle. He loved me and cared deeply for all of his students, every last one of them. Even you.

How many people did you hurt, Sean? Have you ever tried to put a number to it? You know . . . just done the math? I have. You can easily tally up the teachers and administration who were put on trial and served time in jail . . . but your lies extended into the lives of our community. Across the country, making so many people afraid. The power of your voice, your lies, was malignant. It spread everywhere . . .

Growing up, it felt like I couldn't get away from you.

And then, just like that . . . you disappeared. Sean Crenshaw ceased to exist.

I thought you were so lucky.

You got to vanish.

Nobody would let me forget who I was. Who my father was. Moving didn't fix anything. My mother and I changed our names but that didn't stop the stigma from following us. The stories always found us, somehow. Mom forced me into therapy because everybody assumed I'd been molested, too. By my own fucking father. I wonder if you know what it feels like to tell people the truth and not be believed.

I moved out the second I could. I tried to get as far away from my past as possible, cutting out every last little bit of who I was until nobody knew. If I could go one day, just one day, without being reminded of my dad, it would've been progress. Healing.

Or forgetting. Whatever you want to call it.

I was making good progress when I was living in Richmond. I had my own apartment. People who passed as friends. I even had a job at a coffee shop down the block.

When my manager told me we were going to host an art show, he asked me to close up the night of the opening. Why not? Free wine and cheese. I figured there'd be a few bottles of Two Buck Chuck left behind.

That's when I saw the sketches in the back. Simple charcoal drawings of boys and girls dancing in a circle, hand in hand. In the center was a boy. He was barely there, like a ghost.

There was something familiar about the picture. Something I remembered.

You probably don't remember this—do you?—but you came up to me, pretty tipsy from the boxed wine, pleased that someone, anyone, was checking out your work.

"I can get you a good deal on this," you said, flirting. "I know the artist."

I recognized you almost immediately, even though it had been decades at that point. But you didn't recognize me.

"Hey," you said. "I'm Richard."

Richard.

I wanted to punch you right in the face for that, but you did me a favor that night.

You gave me an opportunity to get to know you.

We moved to the bar after the show was over. Every time I thought you recognized me, you'd simply shake your head. I was scared but at the same time I didn't want any of this to stop.

You talked about your foster family. Your hopes and dreams as an artist.

I kept waiting, hoping you'd catch on. That you'd recognize me. I was right there, right there in front of you. Inches away from your face. And still—still—you couldn't see me for who I was. But I could see you. I could see right through your bullshit.

At one point, I called you Sean. It slipped out, but you must not have heard me. Or maybe you did? How wasted were you, really? Blackout drunk? Or are you just a black hole? If I reached into your head, would I get sucked in? Would I disappear, too, just like Sean had? Sometimes that's all I ever wanted.

Going back to your apartment was a gamble. It felt like we were playing chicken. Who would flinch first? Just another minute longer, I'd say to myself, one more . . .

Just when I thought you'd remember . . .

Just when I thought you'd call me out . . .

Just when I thought I couldn't go any further . . .

I left before you woke up. I was almost positive you'd forget me. I had given you a fake name anyway, just like you had, so it didn't matter if you remembered or not. If I stood in a lineup of one-night stands, I highly doubt you'd be able to pick me out.

That's the trick about denial, isn't it? Once you start lying to yourself, there's no one else to stop you from believing your own bullshit. No one to call you out on your lies.

I never wanted to bring anyone else into this life. It seemed wrong. Who wants to bring a child into a world like this?

I kept telling myself I'd get rid of it, but I found myself stalling. And the longer I waited, the more I realized what a gift you'd given me.

That's when everything changed. Now I had a daily reminder of you in my life. The more I watched Sandy grow, the more I saw you in her.

I love Sandy with all my heart, but I've had to restrain myself from taking my anger for you out on her. I've always known how fucked up this all was, but it was too late. I'd made a choice to keep her and I never regretted it for a second. But I had to find a way to free us of you.

I read everything I could find on public record about you. Every last court document, every transcript. Your words were out there for anyone who was willing to look. But now it was my turn to tell your story. This time, I would tell it the way it was meant to be told.

I told Sandy we were working on a secret art project. She never questioned our collaboration. It was fun. Something to bond over. I couldn't have done this without her. To be my eyes and ears at school. To leave behind little reminders of your old life for you to find. To befriend your son. In your own way, you brought Sandy and me closer together. Thank you.

She still doesn't know. The one thing I haven't been able to bring myself to do is tell her who you are. I never wanted to lie to her, but I had to protect her from the truth. Protect her from you.

I wondered if you'd recognize me, almost seven years later. Would a new hairstyle and different clothes be all that it takes to hide from you? Would you really not remember me? Then I realized you never saw me in the first place. Never truly looked.

Open your eyes, Sean. It's time to see. Look at me. Look at what you've done.

By the time you find this letter in Eli's backpack, you'll be back where it all started. In Greenfield. I always found it surprising that they never did anything with the property after the school burned down. You'd think they would've built condos or a shopping mall or something.

The police will find you and Eli in quite the compromising position, and then you'll have to explain everything to them. Meanwhile, Sandy and I will be on the road, heading far away from here. From you. Finally free.

I'm breaking the circle, Sean. You'll never find us now.

You're such a good storyteller. I'm assuming you'll come up with something spectacular to crawl out from under your heap of lies. You can even use this letter as proof of your innocence, which is why I'm giving it to you. I've even included a copy of Sandy's birth certificate, just in case. Your own get-out-of-jail-free card.

But first, you'll have to admit to the world who you really are. Can you finally do that? What's better? Living with your own lies, or living with the world knowing your truth?

I want to set you free, Sean. I'm giving you a chance to come clean.

A fresh start.

Jenna

ACKNOWLEDGMENTS

The following books proved invaluable when researching this work of fiction:

We Believe the Children: A Moral Panic in the 1980s by Richard Beck (PublicAffairs, 2015).

Satanic Panic: The Creation of a Contemporary Legend by Jeffrey S. Victor (Open Court, 1993).

Remembering Satan: A Tragic Case of Recovered Memory by Lawrence Wright (Vintage, 1994).

Satanic Panic: Pop-Cultural Paranoia in the 1980s edited by Kier-La Janisse and Paul Corupe, Spectacular Optical, 2015.

Michelle Remembers by Michelle Smith and Lawrence Pazder, M.D. (Pocket Books, 1980).

Humblest apologies to William Peter Blatty, Dan Chaon, Roland Topor, and Ira Levin for their inspirational masterworks. Please forgive me my satanic panic fan fic.

To Chris Steib for being my first-responder read. To Andrew Shaffer for giving me *that idea*.

To my high priestess, Jhanteigh Kupihea, and the team at Quirk Books: Nicole De Jackmo, Christina Tatulli, Katherine McGuire, Rebecca Gyllenhaal, Jaime-Lee Nardone, Jane Morley, Kate Brown, Jen Murphy, Mandy Dunn Sampson, Megan DiPasquale, Kate McGuire, Molly Rose Murphy, Shaquona Crews, Brett Cohen, David Borgenicht, and everyone else (you too, Ivy) . . . thank you for your trust, your faith, to tell the stories that I want to tell and believing in me, even when I didn't believe in myself.

To Dillon Asher and Nick McCabe and everyone at the Gotham Group, thank you for always fighting to find a home for my stories. You too, Eddie Gamarra, wherever you roam.

To Judith Karfiol for being the pit bull of my heart, always standing up for me and protecting me.

To Indrani Sen for the most loving of all papercuts.

To my sons, who I pray never read this. Ever.

To Sue. To Joe. To Henry. To Donny.

To my family and my friends.

To you. Thank you for reading.

READING GROUP GUIDE

1. *Whisper Down the Lane* is based on a true-crime event known as the McMartin preschool trial, which kicked off the Satanic Panic era of the 1980s. If you're familiar with the event, how did you see it reflected in this novel?

2. Storytelling and memory are two important themes in *Whisper Down the Lane*. What do you think the book is ultimately trying to convey about the act of storytelling and recounting history?

3. There are many parallels between Richard's and Sean's storylines. Which ones stood out to you, and why?

4. Chapman connects the anxiety parents felt during the Satanic Panic to the anxiety parents feel today. How did you respond to this comparison? Do you agree or disagree with it?

5. There are many Easter egg references to classic horror novels and movies sprinkled throughout the book. Which ones did you catch? What do you think Chapman is trying to convey with these references?

6. Richard's storyline is told from the first-person point of view, and Sean's is told from the third-person point of view. Why do you think Chapman made this choice? How did this impact your perception of each character?

7. Sean tells his initial lie because he thinks it's what his mother wants to hear. What did you think about this explanation? Did your opinion change once it became clear Richard was narrating Sean's story?

8. At times, Richard wonders if he was responsible for the incidents at the Danvers School. Why do you think he suspected himself? Did it make you reconsider Richard's version of his own story?

9. The letter at the end of the novel gives an explanation for the events we've witnessed in Richard's storyline. Do you sympathize with this explanation? Do you question it?

10. Discuss this novel in the context of other novels, movies, and TV shows about mass hysteria and large-scale conspiracies. How is Chapman's depiction of this phenomenon similar or different to other pop culture depictions? Do you think it was successful in conveying how and why people get swept up in conspiracy theories?

DON'T PANIC!

Your Friendly Satanic Panic Reading and Viewing List,
Annotated by Clay McLeod Chapman

NONFICTION

We Believe the Children: A Moral Panic in the 1980s
by **Richard Beck (PublicAffairs, 2015)**
The most humane exploration of paranoia I've ever read. Beck's book
is an absolute must.

Satanic Panic: The Creation of a Contemporary Legend
by **Jeffrey S. Victor (Open Court, 1993)**
An expansive, near exhaustive look at the ripple effect of paranoia
throughout the United States.

Michelle Remembers
by **Michelle Smith and Lawrence Pazder, M.D.**
(Pocket Books, 1980)
The controversial best seller that kick-started it all . . . Is it fact?
Fiction? Only the devil knows.

FICTION

The Exorcist
by **William Peter Blatty (Harper & Row, 1971)**
The gold standard of good versus evil.

The Tenant (Le Locataire chimérique)
by **Roland Topor (Buchet/Castel, 1964)**
Not particularly satanic in its panic per se, but this novel's look at
paranoia makes it a must-read.

Rosemary's Baby
by Ira Levin (Random House, 1967)
The slow-burn suffocation of poor Rosemary wandering into the clutches of Satan can't be beat.

FILM

Paradise Lost: The Child Murders at Robin Hood Hills
directed by Joe Berlinger and Bruce Sinofsky (1996)
Vexing and heartbreaking, Berlinger and Sinofsky's film sets the template for true crime docs to come.

Devil Worship: Exposing Satan's Underground
hosted by Geraldo Rivera (1988)
Just when you think it can't be true, that none of this Satanic Panic malarky really happened . . .

Rosemary's Baby (1968) and *The Tenant* (1976)
directed by Roman Polanski
Read the novels first, then see how Polanski perverted the paranoia even further with his fish-eye lens. Throw in his 1965 film *Repulsion* for safe measure and make it the holy trinity of cinematic depravity.